C000192893

"Don't think. Thinking is the enemy of creativity. It's self-conscious, and anything self-conscious is lousy. You can't try to do things. You simply must do things... you have to jump off cliffs and build your wings on the way down."

Ray Douglas Bradbury

JUMP OFF CLIFFS

Fantastic Tales of Fact and Fantasy

Live long,

09/11/13

DOM DARK

FastPrint
Publishing

www.fast-print.net/store.php

All stories in this book first published 2013

Copyright © 2013 by Dom Dark

All rights reserved, this publication remains the
intellectual property of its author.
No part of it may be reproduced, stored in a retrieval
system, or transmitted, in any form or by any means
without prior expressed permission, in writing, of the
author; nor may it be otherwise circulated in any form of
binding or cover, or electronic format, other than that in
which it is originally published.

ISBN 978-178035-706-5

FastPrint Publishing
9 Culley Court
Bakewell Road
Orton Southgate
Peterborough
PE2 6XD
Fax: 01733 234 309
Email: info@fast-print.net

A catalogue record for this book is available from the
British Library

First published 2013 by
FASTPRINT PUBLISHING
Peterborough, England.

PROLOGUE: THE IRREPRESSIBLE HUNGER

When I was a little boy there was a hunger in me.

It was a sort of vague and deep-seated sense of purpose which would not go away, an odd feeling that my life really meant something: something meaningful, something powerful, something more than just simply living.

At one time or another, I think we all have that in us: that odd feeling, that strange and insatiable sense of purpose.

At night I'd look at the stars and the moon and want to be up there among them, touching them. At dawn I'd look to the sun and wonder whether or not it was God. I'd quietly ask it for some guidance, some direction, speaking soft supplications. Playing in the bright woodland with my friends, throughout the summer months, I'd find somewhere quiet and away from them, stop a minute, and listen to the soft winds whispering through the treetops, trying desperately to decipher the voice of Mother Nature. I'd ask her whispers to show me the right way to live.

'What am I for?' I'd ask.

'Why am I here?'

'What's the meaning to all this?'

And, sometimes, I'd *almost* hear the answers.

Then, as with far too many of us, Adolescence and Adulthood tried to crush me, tried to stifle my dreaming, to oppress me, to suppress the Hunger, and they succeeded for a while: school taught me *facts*; parental guidance taught me to be *realistic*; friendships led me to follow the paths of piers, instead of my own.

Because everyone else did, I drank beer. Because it was easier than reading, I watched television. Because they were cheap thrills, pleasures easy to come by, I played video games.

Until I was twenty-seven, I'd never read a book.

I procrastinated habitually; attempted to forget about the Hunger... neglected it... tried to starve it out of me...

But it didn't forget me.

Instead, it simply hid away... hibernated... remained evermore hungry... bided its time, patiently...

Until now.

This first one then, as with all to follow, is for my son and

for my literary father: Lewis and Ray

Never forget, boys: Mars is Heaven

CONTENTS

THE IMMOLATION

'*Why?*' he prayed to know, pleadingly. 'Why would you do that? Why would you take *her* from *me*, when others much less worthy still have air in their lungs, light in their eyes?'

His fists clenched fiercely tight as he bellowed at the celestial sky, the stars and the moon. The anger and frustration built up inside him then, like tinder stacked for Bonfire Night, ready to burn. Tears streamed over his stone-like skin; blood ran like crimson wine, trickling from between his shuddering fingers, staining his cuffs.

Tormented, drunk and defiant and miserable, he paced the stone pathway between the graves, his bunched keys jangling in one hand, a large green container swinging from the other, sloshing.

Blood still dripped from his fingertips and knuckles.

In the unfamiliar darkness, and the even less familiar inebriation, he struggled to unlock the grand shadowed doors. He tussled with the lock and keys, cursed them, kicked the doors, and almost gave up.

However, berating, in a fit of profanities and imprecations, he eventually succeeded.

When inside the building, his cries resounded in the vestibule, echoed down the nave, across the high ceilings, bounced off the confessionals of Penance and Reconciliation, and through the galleries above.

Above, cobwebs trembled.

Dust unsettled, unseen.

Shaking both fists to the Heavens once again, he demanded answers. 'Why take her from me? Why now?' he wanted to know.

But there came no reply.

And so he sat down the green sloshing container and threw aside his jangling keys, which glittered and chimed as they struck the stone floor, and waited.

Briefly, there followed a silence.

Then, clutching the communion rail, he grimaced, gritting his teeth.

'Come on,' he wailed desperately, 'speak to me!'

But only the echoes spoke back.

'Speak to me...' Quieter, '*speak to me...*'

'Is this it?' he cried, 'Is this my test of faith?' His voice trembled. 'Should I see that this is for the *Greater Good*, for the *Divine Balance*? That without pain there can be no joy? Or have you simply abandoned me?'

'Abandoned me?' asked the echoes.

And again there was nothing but silence.

And again he wailed.

And again the walls wailed back at him.

Eventually the torn man swore, screamed, and roared. He became furious. He tore up sermons, scrunched hymn sheets, ripped out the sacred pages of that book most inviolable. He broke apart a wooden crucifix, bent and twisted a golden one, beat the chest over which he had once drawn that most sacrosanct of shapes.

Then, still voicing his bitter admonitions and antipathies, in tirades of accusation and damnation –

gesticulating and swearing wildly – he went about collecting and stacking, collecting and stacking, stumbling now and then, from between the pews.

'I'm done with you,' he sneered, 'had enough of defending your *Mysterious Ways...*'

Moments later there came a succession of sounds – of a glugging and a spluttering and a splashing, in the near darkness – as those of a liquid being poured from a green sloshing container, landing on stacks of paper and carpeted floors and stone.

And from above him the moonlight cast down the tall stained windows' pitiful gazes: those eyes which once witnessed the sacrifice of the Lamb, now weeping for his loss, seeming to plead in silence with him through their unnoticed painted tears, their leaden faces of lament.

Their sympathies cast down placidly upon him, and upon small towers of the Good Book, stacked freshly but haphazardly, and strewn around the pulpit, sodden in tears and petroleum.

Signalling his challenge, he threw down each bible as though it were a gauntlet.

He stamped on them each and kicked at them and spat on them.

He snarled and roared like hungry fire gorging.

He bit out at the air.

He was Fury itself.

'Is this what you want, *Lord Almighty*?' He struggled with a small box of something, sliding it open, fingers dithering. 'Is this what you *bloody* want? Is this *really* how you will have it end? Blast you! I forsake you! Let us see just how merciful you are!'

The sorrow of infinite violins echoed in his symphony of sobs, as the stench of flammable fumes intoxicated the air around him, filled his lungs, powerful and nauseous.

'This is for *God's* crimes,' he told nobody in particular, 'for *His* unjust actions, for *His* ungodliness, for *His* sins!'

Then, to somebody else equally unseen, he yelled, 'You had better tell Saint Peter I'm on my way!'

Finally, swimming in apathy, drenched in petroleum and tears, he fell to his knees, tore off his collar, and struck a match.

There was a blaze of anger, roaring.

ALL THAT WE SEE OR SEEM

The hesitant patient walked slowly along the long corridor of Pinewood Hill Mental Healthcare Facility, scrutinising the inexpensive-looking artwork which decorated the wall to his right, glancing out of the tall steel-framed windows on his left, at intervals. He was on his way to his appointment but in no real rush, his feet shuffling.

Each of the exhibited pieces that he observed seemed to him deeply expressive in one sullen way or another and highly evocative in a fittingly correspondent manner. As though one might contract some terribly contagious misery, merely from casting a passing glance over them, each made him feel sombre, blue, ever so melancholic. Each of the many tall windows he peered fleetingly through seemed also to compound his flattening of spirit further, as bright as the day was; for out of each one he noticed increasingly, in the gardens there, the distinct lack of vitality, movement and life.

It was a scorching hot day in July and so it was odd to anyone pondering it that he should feel so awash with depression. The sun was lancing down gorgeous beams of light which lit up the whole ground and left not one object casting a shadow, so powerful and ubiquitous was its splendour that day. It seemed the whole of outdoors was molten gold, shimmering. As bright as the day was, though, it seemed to him dark.

Of the paintings and pencil sketches he cared to look at there was one in particular which always made him feel the worst, but that conversely he could not refrain from the prolonged contemplation of. It was oil-painted on a large canvas. The image was that of a spacecraft – a rocket ship – at the point of launching; only it was clearly failing to do so and was instead on the point of destruction. Flames and smoke were issuing not just from its tail but instead flaring from all around the vessel; they shot this way and that in a vivacious oil mimicry of motion; the colours were of an awesomely meticulous accuracy, lending themselves to perfect illusory effect. It was a beautiful destruction. It was fantastic.

The patient staring proposed to himself that the work had been executed by a patient, and that it was symbolic of unrealised aspirations, of helplessness, somehow. That was at least his interpretation. Perhaps it meant nothing at all.

'Come in, Charles. Take a seat,' said the doctor, greeting his patient in the doorway of his office. Leading with an open palm, he then said, 'Please, make yourself comfortable.'

To his greeter, Doctor Singh, Charles Huff said, 'Thank you.'

He took up his seat, forced a smile, awkwardly.

There had been two chairs to choose from, one furnished in blue and one in red material. Charles wondered, as he had done previously, whether or not there was any supposed psychological implications to be drawn from which colour he chose to park his posterior on, but said nothing of the thought. He had sat on the red chair, as always.

'Would you like a glass of water?'

'Please.'

The doctor brought Charles water from the fountain dispenser in the corner of his office. He placed it down on the desk between them. It was in a plastic cup.

Charles took a sip. It was very cold and refreshing.

I should drink more water, he told himself. It's good for you. Or at least that's what they say.

Next, the doctor took up his own seat, rested his elbows on the desk, laced together the fingers of each hand and then propped them under his bearded chin, as though about to pray.

He observed Charles with intent, expectant eyes, waiting for him to speak.

So, we're here already, thought Charles; we've already reached the point where the patient initiates his own cleansing. This guy works fast. I bet he turns over each patient within three months: medicates the soul after the first meeting, cuts them down from weekly to fortnightly sessions, then from fortnightly to monthly, quarterly in no time at all. He'll most likely down-grade me before long, devolve my course to a counsellor soon enough. *The Talking Treatment.* How momentarily effective: expel your emotions, vent your vexation, orate your ill-informed opinions and expunge with them your discontent: purgation of the soul, whatever that is.

Charles breathed a sigh, said nothing. Instead he found himself looking over the left shoulder of the seemingly praying man before him, at the shelves of reference and research material on the bookcase there. Freud on *this*, Freud on *that*, *Man and his Symbols*, *Modern Pharmacology: Pharmacodynamics and Pharmacokinetics*, *Understanding Human Nature by*

Alfred Adler, ICD-10, Psychiatric Care Planning, the Diagnostic and Statistical Manual of Mental Disorders, the Atlas of Psychiatric Pharmacotherapy... He read the many spines. The bookcase was littered with intriguing titles which, supposing that the good doctor knew them all cover-to-cover and could recall and recite them with the consummate ease of an exemplary schoolboy making biblical declamations, made Charles Huff feel envious in his own self-professed inadequacy. *Me, Myself and Schizophrenia*, might be a good title for such a book, Charles told himself, had he the aptitude to write it.

Presently he switched his eyes to looking over the doctor's right shoulder and out of the window there, the desk between them being at such an angle that it was perfectly aligned to aid this furtive inspection.

It was indeed an auspicious day outside. The sky had not a lone cloud in it, and so the sun lay idling serenely in the vast blue sea of it; it seemed a vivid painting of which any artist might be proud, framed by the window. But still Charles felt doused in dreariness.

He had something he wished to discuss.

On the wall to the left of Charles there was positioned an extraordinarily large mirror which served to catch many a sunbeam and reflect it into volleying around the white-walled room, greatly decreasing the dimness and occasionally dazzling the observant man's eyes.

'So then,' said Doctor Singh, after the prolonged silence, 'how are you feeling? How have you been?'

Charles shook himself out of dreary introspection, rubbed his left sun-blinded eye, and took another sip of water; his mouth was dry despite having not yet spoken since his first drink.

'Things have been... okay,' he said, after licking his lips, 'I suppose.'

'Go on,' the doctor encouraged him. 'Go on.'

And so the patient went on updating the doctor. He spoke on what he could recollect had happened since his last visit, on his increasing alienation from long-standing friendships, how he often could not bring himself to answer the phone, how he had become increasingly obsessed with learning but despondent at how much he struggled to retain. He was frustrated with what he perceived to be his failing memory.

The thing he wished to discuss drifted repeatedly from the front of his mind to the back, and back to the front again, in a sort of grey mist of cognitive haze.

'That's a common problem with stress and – and I know you don't like the term, but – depression.' The doctor seemed to ease that last word out of his mouth as though it were something secret, lurid, or fragile.

The melancholic man said nothing.

'Have you been taking the medication I prescribed? The higher dosage?'

'Yes.'

'Good. Good. And are they helping at all?'

'I suppose so,' admitted Charles, 'at times. I've experienced some heightened moods; the plateau now has some mountains, as it were... some ravines, too.'

'Good, that's good.' Now he scanned over the patient's face briskly, said, 'Well you certainly look better. Less fatigued. More rested. Brighter.'

Charles shrugged in casual half-agreement.

'And,' the doctor asked, 'what about the anxiety?'

'What about it?'

'Well... is it still significant? Still impeding you as much? Or can you get things done more efficiently now?'

Charles Huff snorted amusedly.

'Yes,' he said, 'it's still there, as always. I just don't go out much. That helps.'

'Oh,' said the doctor. He moved quickly on. 'Have you noticed any side-effects of the medication?'

21

The patient took a moment to reflect. Then, entirely unforeseen and unsolicited, he yawned. He laughed to himself at the irony of it. 'Yes: drowsiness. That's been a big problem.'

I don't see, he thought, how anyone can be expected to achieve happiness – or even contentment, for that matter – when they spend thirteen hours of the day asleep and the other eleven halfway there, like a dumb-and-numb zombie.

'We could try you on a different kind? See how you go?'

See how I go? thought Charles. *See how I go?* What am I? A monkey? A lab-rat? A god-damned voodoo-doll pin-cushion? Jab a few hypodermic needles in me and see what happens? Pour some medicinal-Molotov-cocktail down my gullet, stand back and see if I breathe fire the next time I light up a cigarette? *See how I go?*

'No, thank you,' said Charles. 'I'll persevere, for now.'

'Okay,' agreed the doctor. 'But, don't just stop taking them all-of-a-sudden, Charles, okay? You're on a relatively high dosage now. To just abruptly stop could be harmful. Okay?'

'Okay.'

'You'd have to wean yourself off them,' he added, 'gradually.'

'Okay.'

He didn't need to say *gradually*, thought Charles Huff. Weaning is *always* gradual.

Flatly, the doctor then began to explain just what the consequences could be.

'To just stop like that,' he explained, 'could bring on Discontinuation Syndrome, make you sick; could cause a dangerous chemical imbalance in your brain; could cause synaptic trauma, could damage the neurological transmitters and...'

Charles then became acutely aware of the digression which had initially led away from his concerns and now

22

towards medical matters, matters which he had at best a vague understanding of, and so he contrived to lead the conversation back the way he desired it, even though he could foresee the entire appointment easily falling into a familiar flow of banal closed questions and reflexive answers.

'I find that the more I learn,' he interjected in a low, listless voice, 'the less I know. The real problem being that I can't stop studying. It's counterproductive. But unavoidable.'

'Socrates,' the doctor pointed out.

'Pardon?' said Charles.

'Didn't Socrates say something similar to that – the more I learn...?'

Charles shrugged his shoulders. 'I'm not sure.'

'I'm quite sure he did.'

Charles conceded that perhaps he did. Then he said listlessly that he felt, 'the difficulties with retaining and recollecting information are the *cause* of my discontent, and not a symptom of it. I think – with all due respect – that you have them back-to-front.'

The doctor mused but remained foursquare in his diagnosis, compelling the patient to proceed with his course of medication: sertraline hydrochloride.

Charles again conceded and, to his dismay, soon found himself going on and on and on about things that he was certain were a waste of his own time and would too be a waste of Doctor Singh's time, had he not been in receipt of proportionate remuneration by the Healthcare Services. Then Charles, after exhausting his idle and tediously trivial concerns regarding the practical aspects of his personal life – relationship difficulties, financial struggles, new ambitions, old ones, so forth – and after pondering the doctor's likely financial income, at last became silent and perceivably pensive. He thought fleetingly about talking on his childhood, but refrained.

The doctor duly noted his patient's upset mood, sensed something was troubling him.

'Was there something else,' he asked, 'that you wanted to talk about, Charles?'

And now at this particular question Mr Charles Huff's mind wildly spun, like a butterfly caught up in a hurricane, trapped in perennial chaos. He hated the words within his head, whipping round and round in the vicious storm, despised his recurring failure to find the perfect combination of them. Communing with his conscience he reached around at a number of the cyclonic words, clutched them, and attempted to form a sentence.

'I've not shared with you my... deepest concerns... not been honest as to the extent of my *delusions*,' admitted Charles Huff, finally.

'You've not mentioned any delusions at all, in all our time together, Charles. Go on,' said Singh.

Now we get to the real grit, thought Charles. No more digressions.

'Well,' he begun, but said nothing more, at once overwhelmingly apprehensive and gripped by familiar aphasia.

You see Charles Huff suspected, though he knew all too well that he would fail to express it, at least with any true coherence, that life was a cruel play – a pantomime, perhaps – in which he had been elected the unwitting protagonist, bound for torment. He was not sure of the architect of his ominously dreadful fate, but only that *it*, *he*, *she*, or *they* conspired to do him damage. He felt he was a helpless ant beneath a cruel child's magnifying glass. A million times before, both furtively and openly, he had attempted to articulate this suspicion, and failed. He considered trying again now but conceded the venture as futile, fruitless.

He placed a hand on his forehead, groped it in aid of soothing the anxious matter within.

The doctor waited patiently.

It's no good, Charles told himself. I've tried and tried. Tried and tried, and still the burden seems impossible to unbosom. Understanding relies heavily, he summated, on the succinct expression of an idea or theoretical premise, yes, but much more so on experience. The listener must have shared similar experiences in order that he might relate to those being narrated, or there stands no chance of accurate comprehension, or even vague understanding. In fact, he speculated, terse narration alone is not enough. Language is not the cornerstone of civilisation, after all. Sympathy is. All that is civil grows from sympathetic ability. And the fulcrum of sympathy is shared experience. Language is merely the crux on which understanding leans, at best. An animal without language can still sympathise with another, facilitated by emotion alone.

I should tell the doctor that. But, again, that would be pointless. Even if he did understand the speculative premise, the doctor, Charles decided, would associate my feelings with the plotline of a movie or novel, or the symptoms of a medical condition. That, or he would liken it to something it was nothing like, because I can't help him share in my psychological experiences, can't help him know what I know. So it always goes. That's just the way of it. Besides which, he told himself, there's really no telling just how far and great the conspirators' reach is.

This was a thought that had not yet occurred to him.

The people I've tried to explain this to, he pondered, could be a part of the play. Perhaps the doctor would understand that... Or... perhaps... the doctor's in on it, too?

And now his mind turned back to the receptionist. Hadn't she welcomed him by name, he wondered, even though he was almost certain that he had never seen her before? She was new here, he assured himself.

Wasn't she? Or was she? Did she ask for his name *before* calling him by it? Or after? Or *not at all*?

Hadn't she looked at him in a peculiar fashion, too, and spoken of his arrival in whispers when she was on the telephone, glancing up at him furtively and nervously as she informed Doctor Singh of his arrival?

The people in the waiting, the staff and fellow patients there, were any of them even real? Or did they cease to exist upon his exiting? When he left the room and could no longer hear their shufflings and fidgetings and words, was it because they simply stopped living, because he was no longer there to entertain, to perform for?

Didn't it always seem that there – at Pinewood Hill – for that matter didn't it seem that *everywhere*, he was subject to tenfold... twentyfold... thirtyfold attentions, subject to the scrutinising glares of twenty... forty... sixty... a thousand million eyes? Wasn't he the alien tissue, or the amoeba pond scum, beneath the lens of some great microscope, hugely magnified alighted eyes peering down on him in turn – blue, now brown, now green, the rarest and brightest and most mystifying of colours – watching him, examining him, probing, intruding, staring, staring, staring...

Paranoia? A sort of converse, reversed, terribly cruel and twisted-around God Complex?

Heavily burdened, he sighed to himself.

Then he felt his head split clean in half; and from one half there crept a voice of reason saying not to be, 'so goddamned foolish.' But from the other there poured a voice crying out, 'Yes, yes, you're right! They are against you! They do conspire!'

He felt overwhelmed by this thing called Paranoia, felt he could trust nobody. He was racked with it, felt a small vein pulsing in his temple.

'These *delusions* of yours, are they of a violent nature?' Doctor Singh wanted to know, finally prompting him.

Charles suspected that the doctor knew all too well the nature of his apparent delusions, although now he wished very dearly that he had not been forced to even use that word: *delusion.* He wished he could have found a word more fitting, more succinct. Perhaps *suspicion* was it. Either way, delusion or suspicion, he could not bring himself to speak of it now.

But then, all of sudden, in the manner of an epiphany, a poem occurred to him, a poem which seemed to capture the whole mad situation quite perfectly.

He found himself reciting it, aloud, and the man sitting opposite did not interrupt but instead listened intently:

> *'I stand amid the roar*
> *Of a surf-tormented shore,*
> *And I hold within my hand*
> *Grains of golden sand –*
> *How few! yet how they creep*
> *Through my fingers to the deep,*
> *While I weep – while I weep!*
> *O God! can I not grasp*
> *Them with a tighter clasp?*
> *O God! can I not save*
> *One from the pitiless wave?*
> *Is all that we see or seem*
> *But a dream within a dream?'*

Edgar Allan Poe.

Silent for far too short a period, the doctor appeared to ponder the poem only for a very brief time, if at all, and then he said, quite remotely, that, 'As beautiful as that was, Charles, I'm afraid I don't follow you.'

Again the patient felt awash with distrust, as weary as a wild animal suddenly thrust into captivity.

Wasn't this always the case, thought Charles Huff; didn't the doctor seem to have an awful habit of listening but never really hearing, of responding all too quickly, giving no pause for thought.

Charles breathed out, then in, and out again, and asked himself how any person could fail to understand such an exquisitely astute, masterful and artful execution of expression.

The simple answer was that they could not.

Just then Charles heard a buzzing sound.

It was the sound of an insect annoyance, a fly voice – tiny complaints, incessant whining, anger at nothing – a buzzing, fretting sound.

It stopped.

But, there again, it came buzzing, circling the room in spirals about the ceiling, this way and that, here and then there next. Charles Huff's eyes and head tilted and followed this way and then that, homing in on the flitting sound and its source, but ultimately failing to find it and make an optical verification of its identity. He twitched and ticked here and there, frantically shifting both his eyes and then his head in jerks and blinks, a confused look upon his restless face.

'Are you okay, Charles?' asked Doctor Singh.

The sound stopped again.

'Yes, just – just that – fly buzzing around.'

'There's no fly in here, Charles,' said the doctor. He looked around the room, added, 'not to my knowledge anyway.'

The sound started again: buzz, buzz, buzz.

'You don't hear it?'

Buzz.

'No.'

Buzz, buzz.

'No?'

Buzz, buzz, buzz...

'No.'

The buzzing stopped.

Was it just in my head, asked Charles Huff, communing with himself again. Then, his senses sharpened, he heard the buzzing once again. Although slightly quieter, it was much clearer now. His ears twitched. In slow motions he tilted his head, turned it steadily, and stopped. He had located the source of the sound. He knew exactly where it was.

No, it wasn't in *my* head, he told himself. It was in *the doctor's head*. I traced it there. It didn't move at all. It never did once. My ears were just fixing on it, tuning themselves automatically to its origins – the doctor's head.

'There it is, fainter now,' murmured Charles, glaring at the man opposite him in suspicion. 'You don't hear it?'

Doctor Singh said nothing, flicked his eyes this way and that, and casually shook his head, making his face a visage of denial.

Buzz, buzz, buzz, and buzz once more.

'You don't hear that?'

'No.'

'No?'

'No.'

'Honestly?'

'Honestly.'

'Not at all?'

'I'm afraid not, Charles. Listen, would you like me to –'

A hand was thrust up in a halting motion. 'Shhh,' whispered Charles, 'there it is again.' He looked at the doctor excitedly now, eyes wide, and said, even more whisperingly now, 'It's in your ear.'

Then, in a fitting flurry, jumping and jerking, the man on the other side of the desk agitatedly poked a finger in his ear, scratched at it, batted away something he was apparently sure did not exist. Then he quickly and loudly grunted, exasperated, panting, 'Quit this foolish craziness now, Charles! You're acting like a madman!' He beat his fist down hard against the desktop. 'Quit it!'

Very subtle, thought the patient, very subtle indeed. He had marked the apparent doctor's behavioural lapse as likened to that of an actor slipping out of character for a moment, his focus compromised. The sign, as implicit as it was, was unmistakable. You know that the whispering-buzzing bug is in your ear, thought Charles, they had you put it there in order that you might receive instructions, so your reaction, too – jumping around like that, panicking – was all for my sake. Bravo, bravo! Quite the performance!

All of a sudden Charles perceived the illusion of theatre once again, but much more clearly now, in everything he contemplated. He was sure that the walls of the office were false, that the books lined upon the bookcase, if he opened them one-by-one, would contain only blank pages, leaf after leaf after leaf after leaf... And, had he the wild courage or wild rage to blaze out into the corridor and smash down a few doors – which he felt for certain would all be locked – behind each one he would invariably discover only vacant rooms; or queues of bit-part-players waiting for their cues to take the stage, cross his path, walk shuffling papers, utter indistinct sentiments to one another in rehearsed crowds, stand aimlessly, or perform a tacit pleasantry. The mirror on the wall too, if broken, would inevitably have all the time been concealing a camera, light and sound crew, and a director orchestrating all this, quietly casting instructions, in hushed tones, down a microphone which would lead, through a wireless network, to countless bugs like the one in the doctor's ear.

Buzz, buzz, buzz – a pause – then buzz and buzz and buzz again. The man sitting opposite Charles tilted his head to one side, as though something was bothering him, deep within his skull, scratching at his eardrum.

Charles noticed the motion, read the blatant sign. They're whispering to him, he told himself.

'You're not real,' Charles announced.

Apparently nonplussed, the man playing at doctor said nothing.

'You're not real,' the patient repeated. 'Did you hear me?'

The acting man nodded his head, now visibly vexed, or at least performing a commendable impression of vexation.

'You are not,' Charles added conviction through emphasis, '*real.*'

There was the buzzing again, the little voice inside Doctor Singh's ear. Charles definitely heard it, even if the *doctor* pretended not to.

The doctor's eyes narrowed now and he stared intently at Charles, lurching his head forward slightly, slowly, as a botanist might do in scrutinising some previously undiscovered, or at least undocumented, strange orchid.

'You can't be serious, Charles,' he said disbelievingly. 'You're not serious, are you?'

'Yes. I am. Deadly.'

'Oh,' the doctor-come-botanist intoned. 'Well then, if I'm not *real*, Charles, what am I – a figment of your imagination, perhaps?'

'No.'

The doctor laughed quietly, nervously, and said, 'Well, then what? Do tell.'

'An actor, a drone, or an android; something unreal and placed here to make me seem crazy... that's what you are. I know it.'

'Surely you can't truly believe that, Charles.'

'I can. I do. Because it's the truth.'

'I'm afraid it's not the truth, Charles.' The doctor, seemingly sympathetic of poor Charles and his fantastical fantasy, sighed. 'Not the truth at all.'

'Prove it,' demanded the deluded individual.

'Well,' said the doctor, humouring his patient, raising one eyebrow, 'I have a family, a wife and child –'

'So what,' Charles Huff said, his face perfectly expressionless. 'Maybe they're not real either. Maybe you're making them up.'

'I can assure you I'm not,' chuckled the doctor, with false joviality.

'Maybe you don't even know you're not real,' offered the impatient patient. His eyes roved speculatively over the doctor's face, shirt and tie.

'And how would that work, Charles? Please, do elaborate. Enlighten me.'

'Well,' Charles proposed, 'how about we say that you have the outwardly appearance of being real so much so that you're convinced of the authenticity of your life. But you're not really alive. You're mechanical. Maybe everyone is like that – apart from me – going about their lives with a programmed mechanical regularity, and not ever suspecting and all the time not knowing that they're mechanical.'

There was the buzzing again.

The ersatz doctor laughed heartily now, said to Charles, 'I'm certainly not *mechanical*, I can assure you of that. Why,' he laughed again, 'I had an operation just last year; and I cut my finger just the other week when I was making dinner; I bleed, Charles; I bled.'

Softly, the doctor went on laughing.

Now Charles felt a deep frustration boiling up inside himself, a building torrent, as a fumarole bubbling up with indignation, on the verge of spouting forth steaming jets of acidic water.

He was hugely anxious.

He felt his right knee tremble, tried to stop it.

He bit his lip, breathed heavily through his now-flared nostrils.

Then he erupted, exploded, shouted over the unreal man's unreal laughter. 'It's only blood,' he wailed, 'because you've been told that it's blood!'

At this the unreal man ceased his joviality, placed his laced knuckles back under his bearded chin, sat quietly, and listened, expecting embellishment but not elucidation.

'How do you know what blood is, really?' asked Charles. He licked his bitten lips. 'How do you really and truly *know* exactly what it is? Did you count the reds and whites yourself? Inspect it beneath the lens of the first ever microscope, four hundred years gone by? Did you watch it spill from the wounds of history's first murder victim and declare quietly, holding the piece of slate which killed him, "ah, yes, that's blood, made of fire and wind."? No, you did not.'

'This isn't just some crazed whim, you know.' Charles shook his head in very small and very quick movements, insistently. 'No, it's something I've considered at great length. Blood?' he laughed. 'What is it, really? You just accepted the name of it as we all did, in childhood, without ever wondering otherwise. Couldn't it be wrong? A lie like any other lie; an unintentional one, perhaps, but a lie all the same; or a false name, as so many others have been proven to be. Theories all fail in time, details become jaded, formulas crumble, the maths stop adding up, and they give way to the new. You might think I'm crazy but in my mind nothing is crazier than blindly accepting another man's truth, without actually proving it, first of all, to yourself.'

The doctor nodded, continued to listen.

'Human progress has equalled Nature's,' added the wild-eyed patient. 'Even surpassed it in some cases; so much so that I can no longer tell what's real and what's not. The anchors which hold my mind in place have broken away, rusted to nothing, and I'm left drifting through a shoreless sea of uncertainty. Now I'm unsure of almost everything. I ask myself: "Is my mind my own? Is it even a mind, sat alone and uninfluenced in my skull? Are the choices that are mine to make, *really* mine to make? Do I have a choice in *any* of what I wonder?" We could all be mechanical androids, living but not living, for the entertainment of some great and curious inventor. Blood could be oil, the heart a pump, the liver a filter, the brain a computer. Isn't that what *they* call it, "the most powerful computer there is"?'

Doctor Singh the humanoid sat back in his chair now, rocked a little, to and fro, and seemed to be honestly considering the plausibility of Mr Charles Huff's insane perspective. He mused for many minutes, the sun behind him.

Deep in thought he now looked down at the upturned palms of his hands, turned them over, flexed his fingers, made a fist, opened it, made a fist again, opened it, and examined the moving parts beneath the purportedly synthetic skin. Then he flipped them over again and observed the pulse beating in his wrist, like a ritual drum, or a piston, thumping, thumping, thumping, bur-bum, bur-bum, bur-bum. You could read in his face that he had never before challenged his own mind to think outside the confines of the collective's. But that now he was. Deeply, he was.

Consensuses faltered, axioms crumbled, the rock of truth experienced erosion caused by the encroaching sea of uncertainty. The doctor seemed to be asking quiet questions in the resounding silence of the sun's shadow: Blood or oil? Heart or pump? Liver or Filter? Mind? Computer? Controlled or in control? His electronic mind and pneumatic heart raced. The questions seemed to somehow have breached the formally unimpeachable fabric of his reality. His mind seemed to be whirling and whirring, spinning uncontrollably, seemed suddenly unsettled beyond all hope of sustained composure.

He paled, turned grey, shook a little.

He knows it could be true, thought Charles Huff, staring at the suspicious man in the chair across the table, who was now visibly perturbed. He knows. He knows damn well I could be right.

In the next moment the apparently confused and seemingly stressed doctor-come-synthetic-man began – with lightning suddenness, mouthing silent words of plea and gasping for air – to reel about in his chair, thrashing first to his right, and then to his left, clutching at his chest in agony, face distorted in sheer, unmitigated, most terrible pain.

He was having what we call a heart attack.

His eyes blazed in the direction of Charles Huff's in want of help, but found the witnessing patient either unwilling or unable.

Then the doctor flung out his right hand and clawed desperately at the desktop, beat his fist against it, then lashed the same hand – now once again open – back against his bursting chest.

He gripped at his chest, his face the portrait of an almost silent scream, making only soft gurgling sounds of excruciation.

Once more he threw out his right hand, desperately reached, grasping for the telecom linked to the office; he missed it and knocked the phone off the desk and on to the floor, gave out an agonised scream and then another gurgling groan.

His heart exploded violently in his chest. His mind collapsed. Each organ buckled in turn, palsied, quavered, fitted and then failed under the immense and unbearable weight of new and horrifically intolerable perception.

He issued a gargle, his final breath, the life pouring out of him, and then finally fell back, silently slumped in his chair, and failed to move again.

There was the buzzing once more, within the now-deaf ear of the inoperative doctor.

Buzz, buzz, and buzz a final time: commands not followed.

He wasn't real, thought Charles Huff, and I knew it. I knew it. I knew it. I knew it...

'I knew it,' he then said aloud, shaking his right fist at the air. 'You can't fool me any longer! He wasn't real and I knew it! I knew it!'

Then, beginning to sweat, he got up crazily from the red upholstered chair, staggered a little but reclaimed his balance, composed himself and cracked his knuckles, and set out to smash the false mirror, tear through the fake walls, to kick down the bolted doors and expose the whole sadistic circus, to locate and beat the orchestrators and the architects of his cruel fate.

Nature's Order

In a measured and humble gesture of niceness, one gentleman waved his hand and smiled an earnestly benevolent smile. Another returned the motions, but in a vague, curious and hesitant manner.

'George? Is that you, George?' asked the confused man returning the pleasantry.

'Hello, John,' said George, pleasantly. 'It's been a long time.'

'It has,' the first man confirmed, tilting his head to one side. 'Oh, it has,' he then repeated, because an awkward silence had followed.

And then he took a moment or two to look his old friend over – up and down, down and up – inspecting his strange attire and tired eyes, in an act of perplexed, almost hauteur deliberation.

'What,' he said at last, rather uneasily, 'what on Earth are you wearing... George? What are you... doing?'

At this, George, the man in the strange and towelling brown robes, held out his arms, abeam.

'I'm doing what I am meant to do,' he declared proudly. 'What I was made to do. What I was put here on this planet to do. I'm serving my purpose: spreading happiness, like a farmer sowing good seeds.'

And then John moved aside, still confused and suspicious, saying nothing aloud but muttering something beneath his shallow breaths.

Seemingly oblivious, George smiled at him, pleasantly nodded, and continued to smile, walking.

And into the distance he went.

A place once admired that now sat in ruins, the city was a shadow of its former self – as many might have said – for it was a place of desolation, a fallen Olympus.

It might also have been said that so many could have marked the decline of the once great city. Where once it was a place impassioned by grand ambition, it now fell afoul of lethargy. Where once it had glowed pregnant with enterprise and productivity, it now miscarried and birthed only consumption, spending its wealth again and again.

An outcome easily foreseen.

This decline could so easily have been marked by most, but very few would have felt it exactly as George did. The mills and factories, built in proud stone, partly by his great-great-grandfather's restless hands, now fell idle, their solid structures left to decay, their timber bones protruding from between broken roof tiles and crumbling ashen walls.

This new city, which George now looked upon, had been thrown up on thin foundations, matchstick infrastructures.

Stones were now bricks.

Wood was now metal.

Atop the great many towering spider-web frames colossus arms craned across the cityscape, destroying and erecting buildings all at once, with huge wrecking-balls and god-like hands.

Only a few old tall chimneys still smoked, burning carcasses, amidst the ever-changing constructions.

Stood upon the brink of the valley then, his hessian robe flowing softly, feet strapped in brown leather sandals, George the Wanderer cast an eye over the city below, felt sombre, but smiled all the same.

Curious, he watched ginormous mechanical dinosaurs chew at walls, tear out the innards of old industry, twist, turn, relax pistons, and let the debris fall from their great gaping mouths, into the hungry waiting containers, dust cascading.

How things change, thought George.

Ghosts of old industry now dwell in the stomachs of some mills – the now-wealthy offspring of the once poor – but some are meagrely visited museums and some are merely desolate monuments, their tired eyes blinking, blackened and broken, in the sunlight.

George reflected on how, long ago now, the factory in which he had once worked had been torn to the ground and buried, the work there moved to another location, a more profitable place.

The dinosaurs roared.

Their steel sinews tautened.

The observant individual marvelled wistfully at man's progressive obsession, his savage machinery, his lust for all things modern and progressive.

But still George smiled.

He had faith in humanity.

Faith, even, in the many faithless.

Being born into an industrial city, as he was, George grew up in the manner most did back then, schooling pushed aside, he started work young. Leisure came a distant second to labour. Play was for fools and art for girls. His parents were proud but in need of money, as most were, found him a job in a factory. There was work to be done – it was said – and all had to do it, no exceptions, no dispensations. Poverty was a choice. If one wanted out of the gutter, one had to drag themselves from it with grit and guile and the bit firmly between their teeth. There was an order to things, a right and wrong, and a path to be taken militantly.

'George? George?' His mother waved a casual hand in front of his fresh, young, stupefied and almost entirely expressionless face. 'George, are you even listening to me, George?'

George lifted his head, looked up, his pupils contracting, and said haltingly, 'Sorry. Yes, I know, mother: nothing to fear.'

Proud, she smiled warmly, said, 'I've packed you some sandwiches and a flask of tea.' and placed a heavily dented and scratched metal lunchbox on the half table, beside him, in the hallway.

The front door looked bigger than ever now, more far away than it actually was. Such a big door, George felt that it could not be opened, that it was too heavy a thing to move. He could not work. He was too young. He could not stand alongside men, being so small.

He felt nervous.

He felt inadequate.

He felt afraid.

But then a voice inside him, a voice which sounded almost as his did but that somehow did not belong directly to him, speaking as though of its own volition, said aloud and confidently, 'Right then, Mother, it's off to work I go.'

Walking down the narrow suburban street on which he lived, dwarfed between two long rows of terraced houses, George looked endearing but almost satirically comical to his mother – a parody of a man, drenched in his inherited overalls, carrying his father's old lunchbox.

Waving, smiling, she called after him, 'See you back here at teatime, Son.' And, 'Good luck!' And, finally, 'Love you!'

George looked back, smiled, and then waved, his cuffs loose and already stained with age-old-oil.

The chimneys looming, unfurling great dark clouds across the blue morning sky, his mother watched him until he became smaller down the road, tiny at the bottom of it, and she carried on watching her tiny man until he vanished around the corner there.

When he had gone, she stared at the spot from which he had vanished, imagining what the day ahead might hold for him, feeling proud.

Fifteen years after that day, George still carried that same battered lunchbox to work and home, each morning and night. He still wore those same overalls some days, too, although he had treated himself to a new pair, after the seat of the old pair had split wide open during one afternoon's particularly hard labour.

His mother had sewn a patch over the embarrassing hole and decreed that they still had some life in them yet.

George was almost thirty years old now and was quite the engineer, by all accounts. As though a micrometre had been implanted inside his mind as a child, he could pick out the tiniest of measurements with only his eyes as instruments. And he was rarely far wrong in his optical estimations. He seemed to have a natural gift for milling, too, and so spent much of his time preparing the panels, which were then primed and painted red and black and bolted to one of the many great farming machines that the Harvester's factory turned out.

There, each day, the overpowering smells of overworked men, used engine oil, fresh engine oil, ground coffee beans and endless cigarette smoke touched the whole factory floor. It was a vast open room of odorous things and men moving, meandering with the casual ease of seasoned farmers, observing herds in the searing summer sun, although they themselves were engineers and as such had never once farmed.

But, despite the odious nature of the place, George was content in his work. He did not mind the smells. He was accustomed to them. Neither did he mind the noises of the factory; the chugging, drilling, hammering sounds went almost unheard.

But then, one day, things changed.

The humming machines spoke to him that one change-affecting day. At least that was the thought which offered comfort. *Just the machines...* but he could have sworn he had heard a voice. Not a voice calling in any real clarity and not a voice speaking at any real length, but a voice, all the same – a voice which came from without the mind, and not within it.

It was definitely not the clicking talk of a torque wrench. Nor was it the guttering grind of gear wheels. And it was certainly not the banshee screaming of a lathe working sharp into smoothness. It must have been the humming of steel as it bends, George had told himself. Yes, the humming of machinery...

'Do you ever think you hear... noise in here... strange noises?' George had hesitantly asked of his colleagues, later in the day.

'Don't know what you mean,' had been the reply of one.

'Nope,' another had said, between sips of tea.

'You mean like ghosts?' a third had asked, casting an eye of curiosity.

'Maybe,' George had then speculated, with some degree of caution. 'Maybe...'

And then they had all laughed, and George had thought it best to laugh along, and to say that he was only joking, of course. It was all a big ruse – of course it was – a touch of childish mad-hatter-trickery, a jovial spot of good-old-fashioned Tomfoolery, on George's part.

They all laughed.

Then, heartily, they laughed some more.

In the following days and weeks, George went about his work with a mechanical efficiency, never once again mentioning the noises, which he kept on hearing, to his colleagues. Nor did he tell his family or friends, knowing that some would be overly concerned and some would be quite unconcerned, and some – he felt – might even ridicule. And then, even when his vision became distorted, his eyesight blurred, he did not tell a single soul.

It happened that one morning, whilst working a sheet of metal on a milling machine in the workshop, there came a very sudden jolt to the side of his head, followed by a sharp pain. This sharp pain was then immediately followed by a sensation of immense warmth in the cranium, a dumb tension in the temple, a cracking, as though the whole of his skull was expanding, and then a throbbing which soon faded as the rolling of a storm cloud before thunder. The trauma forced George to close his eyes, open them wide, blink a few times, staggering, stumbling.

Startled, he flung his head wildly round one way, then the other, then turned his whole self, full circle, to see just who or what might have struck him.

But there was nobody close, nobody near.

And, also, looking down, there was nothing lying on the floor, either. No blunt-missile-object, no shard of metal or chock of wood.

Then, there steadily emerged in his line-of-sight a vague shape.

Again, he spun.

He blinked.

He rubbed his eyes.

He tried to shake the shape off.

But the shape remained.

'You alright there, George?' called a man nearby, unloading a truck, seeing the commotion of the individual, this wild war of one.

'Just there, just, there,' the conspicuously maniacal man mumbled, reeling still.

He swayed.

He staggered.

And then, 'Yep, am fine,' he said at last, unsteadily. 'Just... just got a... a headache... that's all.'

'You sure?'

'Yeah... sure... I'm sure... I'm fine. Thanks.'

Retiring to the dirty men's restroom, George examined himself in the mirror, rinsed his face with cold water and wetted his hair on the temple which had caused him pain, prodding at it with his index finger. But he found no injury. The pain, although now gone, seemed in hindsight to have come from within.

Staring into the mirror now, he could see the shape arcing across his reflection but could see no cause: nothing in or around his eyes, no trace of a fallen lash, no grain of dirt or grit, no curling flake of metal shaving. And, in the next few days after that, the image faded.

But, albeit intermittently, it would still appear to George, blearing his sight.

It seemed to come unbidden and at seemingly sporadic times. There seemed to be no pattern to its appearance, no correlation to be measured. It would appear in the morning as he woke, or as he left the house for work; in the afternoon as he ate lunch, as he returned home, but sometimes not and sometimes neither and sometimes never in days. He could be standing or sitting still, eating or not eating, lying down in the bath, or in bed, or out walking or running, and it would appear all the same, but in no clear pattern and abiding by no law of logic.

Night or day, day or night, there was certainly no pattern in the emergence of the apparition. It came when it wanted and left when it wished.

But, having noted all that inconsistency, it was always the exact same shape: a sort of half-circle, though roughly formed.

And the voice, too, when sometimes it returned, even when the machines were not humming, seemed always to carry the same notes.

At night, as he lay in bed, the image would drift across the ceiling of his bedroom as a funeral cortège, parading itself in shadows, with a faint half-haloed luminosity. And when he closed his eyes the shape grew into sharper focus, as though it were scolded into the retinae, branded onto the nerves.

In sleep, in his dreams, the shape would fade into a true form, focus, and the voice would become heard with a more distinct clarity, but both would fade back out into darkness and muted confusion, effervesce in lagoons of unconsciousness, as soon as George's eyes opened.

One morning, as quick as he could, George sketched a picture of the shape, just as he could see it before his eyes and as he had just seen it, fading, in his dream. It looked to him like the entrance to a cave.

'Just relax now, George, and open your eyes wide. I'm just going to shine this little torch of mine in, so I can have a look around.'

Tense, George relaxed.

His pupils dilated.

There was a click and the moustached doctor leaned in, shining his small torch. The glare alternated from one eye to the other, one eye to the other, and back, blinding.

'Keep your head very still now please, George. Look straight ahead at my nose.'

It occurred to George that, right now, it would be a struggle to look at anything other than the doctor's bulbous snout. However, he thought better of announcing this fact.

'Have you suffered any head injuries at work lately, George?' asked the man with the large nostrils and magnified eye. 'You know, blunt trauma and the likes?'

'No... Well, yes... but no.'

'You have or you haven't?' the doctor insisted.

'No, I haven't... but... I thought I had.'

The doctor then recoiled from his inspection, frowned, shook his head, and firmly announced, 'You're not making any sense at all, George.'

'Well, you see,' said the patient, trying desperately to explain, 'I had a pain in my head a few weeks ago now and I thought... I thought... that something had hit me right there,' he pointed to his right temple. 'But nothing had.'

'Hmmm,' hummed the doctor, returning to his desk to make some notes. 'No blunt trauma...'

As George looked around the room in silence, the doctor continued jotting his notes.

The doctor's office was all very neat and tidy, George noted, all very clinical and concise – very exacting – with that faint scent of cleaning agents lingering about it. The whole room seemed so very sure of itself, with its books all aligned on their shelves, alphabetised by section and sub-section, and then by author. Very orderly, too, was the doctor's desk: everything precisely placed and the whole top having about it a measured degree of symmetry.

The man of medicine let his pen rest for a moment.

'Well, I'm no expert,' he said, turning to George and brushing his moustache with thumb and forefinger, 'but I don't see anything obviously wrong with your eyes. They seem perfectly healthy to me. Reactions are good, pupillary dilation is normal, and there is no apparent damage to your cornea that would explain these hairline "*half-moon shapes*" you keep seeing. However, I'm going to refer you to the optometrist at General, to get a second opinion. You should receive an appointment from them within the month.'

The doctor then shuffled some papers on the desk, and then straightened his tie, whilst saying, 'In the meantime, it might be an idea to have your eyes tested at your local opticians. As for your hearing, be sure to wear plugs at work. The drums are undamaged – as far as I can see – but you can never be too careful: the ears are outstandingly fragile instruments.'

George nodded. 'Right you are, Doctor.'

'And you say the sounds were a sort of ringing?'

George nodded again, slower this time. 'Yes, sort of, but sometimes it almost sounds like –'

'That's probably a little mild tinnitus.' The doctor turned away, jotting again. 'Yes, mild tinnitus... from the noisy work environment... Nothing to worry about, really. But be sure to get those plugs. And use them.'

'Yes, Doctor.'

With a certain briskness of brevity, the doctor shook George's hand and said farewell. George felt his hand shook and felt that he too had shook the doctor's hand in return, but he nevertheless left his office with an overwhelming vagueness of experience. Many words had been spoken. But nothing much had been said or done.

'Rest,' the man of medicine had said lastly. 'Get as much rest as you can.'

The next day George went back to work newly equipped with ear plugs and safety glasses. Quite why he had bought the two protective items was still a point of confusion for him: he felt he knew very well that nothing had injured his eyes and that nothing had damaged his hearing, but, nevertheless, he carried on wearing both the glasses and the ear plugs each day after that. And, when he did get the appointments –

firstly at his local opticians, and then at General – there was found to be nothing wrong with his eyesight.

"Almost perfect 20/20," the optician had said.

His eardrums too, on further inspection, were found to be undamaged.

The bell rang for morning break.

George had always found it odd that there was a need for a bell-ringing to signal when men could drink tea, and again when they should stop drinking tea. He felt quite certain that any responsible man could see fit to drink tea when he saw fit and had a thirst for it. Surely no man would drink tea all day, in favour of completing his work. The bell seemed militant and unnecessary. It seemed a measure of unnatural control. Children at school needed a bell to ring, yes, because children daydream and become forgetful of the time and the tasks at hand. But men do not need to be herded like cattle.

Before he left his station, he waited just long enough to feel that the bell had not dictated to him.

George entered the canteen, sat down at a table, opened his dented lunchbox, wiped his oily hands on his oily overall trousers, pulled out his flask, and poured a cup of tea. He rolled his shoulders, let out a relaxed groan, and stretched.

And then very suddenly his eyes became alert, and then his mouth hung open in wild disbelief...

Because there on the coffee-stained table, surrounded by tiny crystals of sugar spilled by trembling hands, there rested a newspaper. And, more significantly, on the cover of that newspaper there was printed an image in ten shades of grey and one of black: an image identical, in almost every way, to the image that had now plagued George's eyes and mind for weeks.

The resemblance was too close an approximation, too almost-exact, to be coincidental. It was the image of a cave. If he had placed the sketch he had made over it, covering the front page, and shone a light through them both from behind, they might have been one and the same.

Everything, it seemed, everything that had happened, up until now, had drawn him to this very moment. He felt it. And now the cave drew him to it, so strongly, so very strongly, that it was impossible to think of doing anything other than going to it.

Tap, tap, *tap*...

He tapped the grey image with his blackened finger.

'This,' he said abstractedly, 'where is this?' not addressing anyone but everyone in the small smoke-filled room.

One of his colleagues nearby, a small man holding a big cup – John, his name was – said, 'Well, that's Mother Earth's cave. You never heard of Mother Earth's cave before, never been there and seen it? Meant to be magic place.'

'Never heard of it,' said George, even more distantly now, 'never been there... no... but, seen it... yes.'

The small man with the big cup briefly chortled.

'That doesn't even make sense,' he announced, laughing.

'No... you're right... it makes no sense at all, but,' George paused, 'but, I have to go there. I have to go there now. Right now.' And with that he put down his sandwich, shed his once-white-but-now-very-oily apron and grabbed up the newspaper.

Out of the canteen, he dashed.

John shook his head, the big cup in his fat little hands. The other workers, too, shook their heads at one another with faces puzzled by this queerest of behavior.

Down the stairs to the workshop floor, George ran.

An enormous excitement came over him now: a crazy, unconscious wildness: a tornadic, insatiable and unsolicited urge to throw all caution to the wind, tear it

49

back in, hold it to his chest, tightly, and again throw it out, and pull it back in again, repeatedly, and proceed to throw it further, more fiercely each time, again and again and again, into the wind, so that there was eventually no caution left in him at all. Not one bit. Not a trace of it.

He wanted... *no*... he *needed*... to chew up the order of things, like tobacco, and to spit it hard into a fire to hear it destroyed, hissing in a disorderly, crackling inferno.

Without knocking, this usually normal, passive, and perhaps even diffident man then burst into the office of the corpulent factory owner, Mr. Wells.

Dissident George then proceeded, frantically and breathlessly, wildly, to decree that he must leave, that he had to go, right away, that there was nothing else for it. And so, without ever even giving Mr. Wells the chance to ask why, George left.

The busy business man just sat there, in fact, in his chair, behind his large oak desk, confused, his mouth ajar, cigar burning between his thick sausage fingers, for a long time after his employee had left.

He could have run the whole way there, but George took the next train, instead.

Nobody spoke to him on the platform, or in the carriage, and he spoke to nobody save for the ticket officer, to ask which stop it was that he needed and to pay the appropriate fare.

Unfolding the newspaper in his lap, the tall chimney stacks chugging their grey clouds, passing by slowly between the fast moving foreground, George just sat there and studied the cave in the picture, occasionally looking outside, the land passing by, to see if he could spot it coming.

Coming to a stop, the train hissed.

As he stood before the opening of the cave, surrounded by the kind of fertile terrain found only in fairytale forests and goblin markets, George was overcome by an odd catharsis, a strange purging of the soul: as though all the evils of the world suddenly left it, all darkness lifted from him, in a flurry of dandelion imps blowing away in the white beauty of a silent explosion among the shuddering greens, everything heavy, everything troublesome and challenging and upsetting moved away in magic, and he was left with only a wonderful euphoria.

It was breathtaking.

His ears fine-tuned, he could hear the voice. His eyesight more perfect than ever before, he saw the cave; and the cave was the shape and the shape the cave; and then the image and the sounds of the voice came together as one, and his dreams became reality.

This was it, this was the exact experience felt in his sleeping mind, and now it was real, now it was no dream.

He breathed.

Enveloping him, the world smelled like never before, him taking nature in, in deep breaths, and nature taking him in, also. Now more than ever, George could hear the voice – the machine voice from the factory, from the street at night and from his dreams, the tinnitus – and now it was distinct and definite, it was clear and concise. It was close. But, more than anything else, it was beautiful now. It sang to him, calling him, grabbing at him, softly, calmly, with a caressing cadence, a prehensile poetry.

George began to walk.

The incantation of nature's bosom charmed him, drew him nearer and nearer.

And then, slowly, steadily, into the shadows of the cave he went...

Quite what George found within that cave, quite what he felt and heard and touched upon as it touched him, it could not be said. However, after thirty nights and

51

days of darkness and solitude in there, from the very moment he stepped back into the world, out of his subterranean dwelling and into the splendorous blinding sun, there was no denying that he had changed irrevocably, for the better.

Please, do understand that he had never been a man of coarse or callous character – and so the change was not a drastic one – but now he seemed infused with an even much more gentile nature than ever before.

He was kind, kinder than before.

He was caring, more so than ever.

He was pious and proper, almost saintly.

That was over forty years ago now.

His character has never changed since.

His kindness has never faltered.

His caring never quilled.

Exuding a notably odd and enigmatic nobility, he now wanders the new city, and many people, with roving eyes and roving minds and nothing but logical reasoning, picture him as a sort of *roving soul*, a wanderer lost in his own private universe. But George has a definite direction, a particular path to walk. His pace quickens and slows, quickens and slows, slows and quickens, as though he sees the things just past and the things soon coming, as though history is mapped out for his insight only.

'As often as you look to the ground,' says George the Wanderer, 'look to the sky.'

'I don't understand you,' say so many.

'Consider it for long enough and you soon will.'

And so, through the roads where Enoch's Vermin now reside in the bowels of doctor's homes – some dirty but good and misunderstood, some bad but clean and corrupt of soul – and where foreign hands now shape the world they once helped rebuild in Alliance, and where those impoverished by elected oppressors exist and do nothing more, in a desperately diseased state – whilst the financially endowed amass more wealth, growing fatter, feasting decadently on the misery of others – the Wanderer walks.

The Wanderer walks to this day, every day, down the once cobbled roads, along the long-trodden thoroughfares, the lanes, alleyways and market squares, tacitly permeating society with the message gifted to him.

His smile infectious, his nerve unwavering, he spreads a good word, a vision of a better world, simply by waving kindly.

The Wanderer walks the streets, then, waving, smiling, and nobody quite knowing why but most of them understanding, somehow, within the depths of their hearts and minds, that his perennial purpose, as Nature's Emissary, is to share with them inexhaustible benevolence.

The great fog of industry had long since ascended.

Stood still upon the brink of the valley, George watched the great cerulean sky blow its voluptuous cotton-wool clouds over and across the shrunken city below.

Looking down again, he saw the mechanical dinosaurs still crunching the skins of old industry, forever destroying, forever creating. Aimlessly, he witnessed the tiny grey figures of people, like matchstick men and women, roaming to and from places. He watched small cars – like toys – flitting along roads and joining queues and stopping at red lights and going at green ones.

He saw life bustling.

He saw the world changing, ceaselessly.

He smiled to himself, and then kept on walking.

THE ESCAPOLOGIST

As macabre as it may well seem, death is our only destination.

Our mothers and fathers are duplicitous; they are both heroic and villainous, creators and murderers; in gifting us life they condemn us to death. Try as we might, from the day we are born, death remains an eventuality. Our ends will always arrive and the clock never stops ticking. We must live with this apparently morose burden.

The escapologist, however, made a very decent living out of cheating that thing we call Death, evading that final end.

A paragon of his profession, the escapologist lived in a time when miracles were still largely considered to be miraculous, an age when wonder behest wonderment and when magic was simply magical.

Many had liberality.

Most would entertain any idea.

Although luck was not unheard of, it was not yet considered an axiomatic anomaly, within the calculable realm of probability.

Good fortune was, for most, a sign of God's favour.

Freewill, too, was in its fledgling phase.

Faith was just about, for most people, still the right thing to live by.

The escapologist had travelled the world, seen his name in every coloured light, wowed audiences on every single continent and heard his brilliance declared in almost all languages.

People loved him.

He was someone to be revered.

He was illustrious.

Across the globe his escapes were infamous, his status almost legendary.

With astonishment and adoration, his name was synonymous.

He was an original celebrity.

His fame had grown as his name had spread – like quick fire – along the networks of gleaming wires which were freshly pinned upon newly-erected telegraph poles across the land; the flames of his fame had leapt through radio waves, down antennae, and onto small and grainy black and white television screens housed in great wooden cabinets. But, even more so, his name had spread and his fame grown from mouth to ear, ear to mouth, and so on, by word of mouth.

In almost absolute silence then, the crowd sat.

Thousands of tentative fingertips drummed across hundreds of laps, in nervous anticipation, like an almost inaudible drumroll, an orchestra of invisible typewriters.

This show had been the quickest selling ever – all out, box office closed, no more tickets left, in less than an hour – faster than any before it.

Some of the steadfast ticketholders had queued all night in the bitter cold to ensure their admission, for the accolade of being in attendance, for the right to say that they had been there. And so the seats were all now full of warming watchers with baited breath and unblinking eyes.

A gentle hum swam about the crowd and stage.

'Are you ready?' asked someone in the crowd.

'As ever,' replied someone else, sat beside the first.

'Are you ready?' asked a father of his son, eyes round with anticipation.

'As ever,' replied the boy, jiggling with anticipation.

'Are you ready, sir?' asked the stagehand.

'As ever,' replied the performer.

Then the great king of escapes, strapped in chains, was hoisted up.

The crowd murmured.

The escapologist held his breath.

The crowd, too, held their breath, as into the tank he was lowered.

His bare skin plunged in. Displaced water swept over the brim and fell upon the floor in intermittent splashes, tiny bubbles forming on his goose-pimpled body. He was entombed in a liquid coffin, imprisoned in a thick glass cell, immured in blue silence. And there he seemed to sleep for what seemed forever – an alive but unmoving mummy, swathed in chain-link bandages, blue and pale.

Nervously the crowd continued to hold their breath.

And then a few bubbles escaped from the marine-mummy's mouth. And then a few members of the audience gave up holding their breath. And then his hair drifted slowly about the water like strange black strings of seaweed. And then all of a sudden there was a very violent thrashing of limbs, the storming of small tides, the sloshing and the splashing of waves hitting the floor again and again and again, and the groaning and stretching and tearing and snapping of metal, and in an instant, the miracle was performed.

The escapologist leapt from the tank and stood concrete still, not even his eyes blinking, his heart hardly beating, his breath still held. Cold water beaded on his motionless chest, his oaken skin, his thick black hair. He stood in a brief perfect silence as the fetters which had only a moment ago bound him now slid with ease from around his shoulders, like dead metal serpents, from across his torso, like silver vines untwining, and now down his legs and to the floor in a glittering heap, chiming. Water dripped in slow motion, movements were exaggerated, time sluggish.

A stagehand quickly brought him a towel, draped it over his shoulders.

Then, slowly, he breathed.

Steadily, the crowd breathed for him.

In the next moment there then came the lighting storm and the thunder clap. A great barrage of light ascended, bombarded, swarmed upon the scene: bulbs flashing explosive elements as camera shutters blinked and blinked and blinked from all angles, with the crowd erupting into a simultaneous rapturous applause.

Violently, they clapped their hands.

Like three hundred human fly traps they clapped with fingers for teeth, palms for pallets, and the resounding synthesis of slapping flesh, whistling lips and cheering mouths echoed around the grand hall as a dissonant din, a frantic migrating of flightless birds, a cacophony.

The cameras blinked.

The moment was captured.

The newspapers had their front pages for the following morning covered.

He had done it again. The crowd cried out. As one great and terrible beast, the crowd roared. The walls of the auditorium shook beneath the tidal wave of wild elation. The ceiling shuddered. People stamped their feet, cheered and whooped and hollered. Some hugged one another and declared their amazement and wonderment and excitation, jumping up and down in a wild embraces. The concrete floor trembled beneath this great collective beast. The very foundations seemed to shift and moan, shift and moan.

Then there came an ebbing of the conglomerated sound, a fracturing of this one great thing – this roaring beast – as the people broke from exultation and started their own, much quieter, individual reactions. In awe, they marvelled.

'How did he just do that? How did he just do what he just did?' asked one husband.

'That was impossible, surely!' remarked another wife.

'Nah, the chains are fakes!' said a small, smartly dressed man. 'They're made of plastic... Or they're faulted, like perforated paper: tiny little hairline cracks, so tiny you don't see them; my cousin knew a guy who knew a guy who once worked in Hollywood, says this kind of thing's a doddle!'

'Don't be a cynic,' cried his companion. 'The man's a genius!'

'There's none other like him, that's for sure!'

'I've never seen anything like it!'

'A miracle!'

'A great trick!'

'Impossible!'

One faint-hearted fellow came over all light-headed and had to fan himself with his hat, wipe his brow on his sleeve, and be steadied on his feet by his wife.

An elderly woman praised the Lord.

'Wow!' exclaimed one young boy.

'Whoa...' gasped another.

This individual of invincibility, this enigma of escapology, this man of magic and majesty, had cheated death for what must have been, at the very least, the one-hundredth time.

Was he immortal?

Had he signed in blood before a devilish witness?

How can one cheat death on demand?

After loud and persuasive encouragement from the event organisers, who gestured wildly, the individual conversations then quietened to mere whispers.

'How many times you think you can stick your head in the mouth of a lion before it gets bitten off?' cried one journalist, above the ocean of soothed voices, pen and pad poised in hand.

'I'm afraid I don't work with animals,' replied the escapologist, coolly.

The crowd roared again, this time with laughter.

'What's your next trick?' called out another man – a tall and young reporting man, with large eyes and small, square eyeglasses.

'I'm afraid I don't perform trickery, either,' said the escapologist, dryly. 'Only miracles.'

From the crowd there came a short and soft susurration.

'However,' continued the calm man, 'my next miracle will be my greatest of all.'

'Which is?' enquired an impatient lady with a soft, delicate voice.

'With a loaded pistol,' he announced, 'I will shoot myself in the head. I will take my own life. And then I will resurrect myself.'

The crowd murmured, some through scepticism, others in admiration and awesome lip-licking anticipation.

Half an hour later and the great man of great escapes sat alone at an empty table in a cold dressing room with blank white walls, thinking.

His wrists ached from shaking hands.

His face was smeared with dozens of painted lips.

In the waste paper basket beside him, there was equally as many roses as there were smeared kisses on his cheeks.

Hats on heads, coats pulled on and buttoned up, umbrellas poised, the hordes of witnesses were funnelling out of the theatre now, out of the building in procession, and into the wet city street, each taking a piece of the escapologist with them. They were waddling and shuffling as one closely packed mass of warm but soon-to-be-cold bodies, conversing as they went. Some were silent though, slowly marching, but not many. Some were gasping still, for air and for something real, something tangible to grab hold of, so that they might not drift away with fanciful thoughts, to distant places of childish wonder.

There was a gentle rapping at the dressing room door.

Firstly bracing himself, the pensive performer called the caller to enter.

Then the door opened and someone came in, stiffly.

It was the tall man with large eyes and small, square glasses who had been in the audience.

He still had his pen and pad in hand.

'I, I want to say it's, it's a great honour to meet you,' announced the awestruck journalist, 'and, and to have been given this opportunity, sir.' He was wiping the palm of his right hand on his trousers now, as though preparing to shake hands.

But the escapologist did not stir from his seat.

He didn't even look up.

Still standing in the doorway, the journalist let his fidgeting hand settle. Unsure of what to do next, his eyes searched the room for something else to say, something to spark conversation: something notable, something topical. But the room was, perhaps for this purpose, bare.

He stood there a minute or so.

'I, I don't mean to sound ungrateful,' said the fidgeting man at last, 'but, but, there's something I don't fully understand: why me? I couldn't believe my eyes when your letter arrived at the office.'

The escapologist raised his head now, gestured with his hand – languidly stroking the air – to summon the fidgeting young man, and insisted, 'Close the door and come sit down, Mr Brown.'

Slowly, Mr Brown closed the door, and then approached and then, even more slowly, sat his briefcase down on the floor, took off his hat, balanced it on top of the briefcase, took off his coat, placed it across the back of a chair, and sat himself down on that same chair, facing the escapologist.

Mr Brown then swallowed, rubbed his palms together, cracked a few knuckles, and waited.

'In answer to your question,' began the great performer, 'I have followed your work closely, read your articles for many months now, and it occurred to me, after a short time, that you are more like myself – more open to the improbable, and even the impossible – than any one person I have ever met. You are willing to accept truth without insisting upon proof. You are a lover of the mind's liberty. Do I have you figured? Does that answer your question?'

The journalist said, after a deep breath and a moment or two of thinking, 'Yes. I suppose you have, yes. And yes, I supposed it does, yes.'

'Well there's your answer then, and the reason for our meeting: people have pestered me for a long time now – harassed my agent, too – for the licence to print my life story. I decided I wanted to share it, once and for all, first-hand, rumour and whisper free, with someone like me... someone, Mr Brown, like you.'

Humbled, the young journalist simply smiled.

'You see,' his congratulator continued warmly, 'some stories lose their charm as they travel the world, and some gain it. Some stories become tainted by time. Some tellers omit the eccentricities, exclude the unlikely and exile the exceptional, thus leaving the eventual recipients of what are potentially the most wonderful tales, with a watered-down, tepid but believable version of events. I'll never know why that happens; oh, I understand the *how* but not the *why*. On the other hand though, some tellers mythologise great occurrences – they make fables of the fabulous; some stories become embellished upon as they roam from mouth to ear, mind to mouth and back to ear, and so on and so forth. On these occasions a rat becomes a bull, and a bear a dragon. But, again, they end up as mere stories: tales of fancy, and nothing more. People don't know what to believe. The truth becomes lost...'

'And so I called you here today because I would like for you to record my story straight from the source, by listening to me. I want my truth recorded. Nothing I am about to tell you is myth, nothing is symbolic, it is purely factual – unadulterated.'

'Are you ready, Mr Brown?'

The young journalist replied only by way of nodding his head.

The escapologist then struck a match and watched it burn, flickering. He placed a cigarette in his pursed lips, lighted the cigarette, inhaled the smoke deeply, exhaled, blew out the match, took a drink of his coffee, and then began to tell his story.

The journalist set a recorder down on the table and set the tape rolling, listening eagerly.

'When I was a boy,' recalled the escapologist, among the dove-grey plumes, 'my family owned a house out by the lake –'

Mr Brown raised a halting hand.

'Which lake?' he asked.

'It doesn't matter which lake,' insisted the escapologist, motioning with his hand to brush aside the question. 'Just *a* lake – that's all you need to know. Too many people all too often insist upon asking *where* and *when* and *how* something happened, when all that really matters is exactly *what* happened. Now, don't talk. Listen.'

The young man listened, his placid face masking slight indignation.

With reels turning out a faint whirring, the tape recorder listened too, unbiased to absolution.

'Every July we would venture out there – my mother, father, sister and me – to the lake house, and spend the summer,' began the escapologist. 'It was wonderful there, a real life Eden. I remember we never needed to take much with us; we already had so much there. It was the kind of place where you completely forget the rest of the world, and so you take the fewest reminders of it with you. Forgetting the world was easily done, for me; being nine years old, the world wasn't so big anyway...'

And so, recalling it all very clearly, the man of miraculous feats told his tale...

The beautifully savage July sun teemed down from the cloudless sky; its brilliantly sharp golden beams sent jewels out shimmering, flickering and flashing like a heliographic summoning, across the gently rippling lake.

Breathless, the small boy and then the even smaller girl leapt running from the aging Victoria carriage and the beaten path – and into the seemingly endless woodland – the very instant it stopped moving, perhaps a moment before.

They kicked up dust and ran through long-dead leaves and fresh grass, punching the air with exuberance. They jumped and yelled and cheered and smiled, amidst the orange glow pouring from the sky.

The ground beneath them shone.

The great many leaves rustled beneath their feet – the dead ones – in a wildly excited delirium, and whispered quietly too – the newly born and those that were evergreen – in the dense emerald canopy above, from the slight breeze sent sailing in off the shore.

Flurries of birds exploded from out of the foliage, flapping frantically, as the children ran by, whooping.

Being an annual occurrence, the whole scene was a familiar one and yet it still had a dreamlike quality about it.

Firmly holding hands in the distance behind the two children, their parents strolled smiling.

After taking some serene moments for themselves, embracing the familiar sights and sounds, soaking in the forestry smells, watching the lake shine a golden mirror surface, closing their eyes to listen to chorus of the forest; after listening to tune into mallard-coarse-quacking, robin-high-whistling, nest-egg-cracking and rustling – the feverish work-rate of the wildlife surrounding – and after listening at length to that soothing sound of tree limbs creaking among the soft-petal shush of leaves, like an omnipresent waterfall infusing the forest with song, after becoming immured in these sounds and opening their eyes wide to note the origin of each note – the singing birds, the creaking branches, the rustling and whispering leaves, the faintly tickled blades of grass bending in the lake-breeze – the family then set about unpacking their tightly-packed small set of suitcases and other luggage.

Mother opened a wicker hamper full of food, sliced a loaf of bread and made cheese and sweet pickle sandwiches, and the family feasted. It was a beautifully familiar ritual: the children and their father always praising any food prepared by the lady of the house, no matter how modest the meal.

'Ummm, great sandwiches, dear. Truly great,' the gentleman marvelled.

'They're delicious,' declared the boy.

'Gorgeous!' appended the girl.

'Oh behave,' said the modest woman, shyly, 'they're just sandwiches like any other sandwiches.' She blushed, then; she always blushed at flattery.

'No, no, not at all! Somehow they always taste better when you make them.'

'Strange that.'

'Strange.'

The family all chuckled for a time.

In the night-time, poker in hand, the father stoked the fire, drank wine with his wife and watched the two children as they sat jostling elbows, cross-legged on the rug in front of the hearth, toasting marshmallows on pitchforks above the intense orange-red of the fire.

The two children stared unflinching at the slowly toasting sugary sweets, their faces illumine, their eyes afire, their glowing limbs fidgeting.

He watched and was proud.

He was proud of their many similarities and of many their differences, of their agreements and even their disagreements. He was proud of what made them special to him, and what he felt would most certainly make them special to the world, as they eventually grew into becoming a real part of it.

As they tired the two children then sloped into their shared bedroom, crawled into their beds, and were tucked in by their father. There they would drift off to sleep each night, as they lay wrapped up tight in their chrysalis duvets, warm breath steaming gently on the mild air.

'Don't let the bed-bugs bite,' the father would always whisper when turning out the lamp.

'We won't...' the two sedated mouths would invariably mumble, already half asleep.

'Goodnight, my angels,' the mother would then say, kissing the two peach brows in turn.

And in the mornings the two children rose wildly, exhausted but enthused, yawning and yet blooming, from out of their thickly quilted cocoons as ecstatic insects – leaving behind newly discovered dream-worlds and yet being born into the fresh new dawn of a familiar one – their limbs stretching like freshly feathered wings, eyes blinking.

They would run laughing into the day, building dens, forts, castles and caves; climbing trees and swinging from them with ape arms, faces and voices, dropping to the soft ground, laughing heartily at their mimicry; chasing one another and butterflies; scaling big rocks and turning over small ones, skimming stones and scuffing knees and grass-staining elbows, the forest dancing all about them, all the while.

They liked most of all to build rafts, under the guidance of their father and his engineering prowess – binding logs and attaching barrels as floatation devices.

The three of them on the lake would play at piracy, like old Tom Sawyer, Huck and Joe, the father calling out, "Steady, Stead-y-y-y!", "Let her go off a point!" and, "Luff, and bring her to the wind!" despite the emphatically notable absence of a sail. Neither child understood the archaic instructions anyway, nor did their father, but it was fun all the same: the captain standing at the imagined helm and the two mates splashing frantically at the water with their arms as oars, enjoying themselves immensely.

The two children were to never go out onto the lake alone, though.

But, one afternoon, they did...

On the lake the boy felt oddly different from on the shore.

He felt cut off from the land, congruous to nothing, separated from everything, detached from home-life, from school-life, from all life and all time and all existence: he felt beautifully isolated. He felt there as though he was a world unto himself, floating amid a

66

watery firmament, cool and content. He felt infantile and yet deeply wise, laid on his back, chewing over the clouds and a yellowed stalk of grass, adrift in vague contemplation.

It was as if he were asleep but awake, hypnotised by his own deep thoughts, dozing in a cathartic dream, the lone denizen of a private purgatory, the one god of his own vast and peacefully empty heaven. He felt a sense of being perfectly alone, and blissful, within the strangely underwhelming isolation.

The lake's iridescent surface shimmered gold, silver, blue, white, gold, silver, blue, white, gold, silver...

The boy felt good.

He felt happy.

He felt at ease.

And then his sister spoke, her shrill voice stealing the calming silence, breaking his rapt ruminations.

'You see the cow cloud?' she asked loudly, laid beside him.

'Huh?' he stirred. 'Um... no...'

'There!' she pointed. 'Just there – a big fat moo-cow-cloud, chewing grass.'

'I suppose so,' he said indifferently, squinting.

And then the boy rolled over, so that he was laying on his front, pulled himself to the edge of the raft, and looked over it and into the water.

He watched his reflection there in the brilliant looking-glass surface, distorting gently, wavering in its lines, upon the tiny ripples. Then he cupped his hands about his face, leaned closer to the water's skin, as if to cast a shadow – eclipse and blot out the sun – and tried to see what lurked beneath the surface, if anything.

Squinting, he could see nothing but the green fog of deep waters.

'You ever feel like we're the strange filling in an even stranger sandwich?' he casually asked his sister, who was still staring intently at the sky and the moo-cow cloud there, which was apparently chewing grass.

'I guess so,' she replied, not nearly understanding what her brother might mean, and at the same time unsure as to whether or not he knew exactly what he meant either.

'It's like,' he elaborated, elucidating as best his young mind would allow, 'it's almost like we're the cheese and the pickle, thrown in between two great slices of still-warm bread – the skies and the oceans. And we don't know too much about the sky, do we? And even less about the ocean, so how are we to know if we're the cheese or the pickle at all? For all we know, we could just be...' He paused, said eventually, 'just another crumb!'

'Or the butter.'

'Huh?'

'We could be the butter.'

The boy laughed.

The girl laughed.

Together they laughed.

'You're missing the point,' he said, between giggles. 'The point is... the point is...' He had suddenly forgotten what the point was. And then, almost as suddenly as he had forgotten it, he remembered it again, chuckling. 'The point is... the point is that we're just thrown into this big strange sandwich and told, "You're the pickle. You're the cheese," and then we're left to get on with it. And it's all just so confusing. Sometimes I don't know if the sky really is heaven, or just a big glass bowl turned upside down. Someone tells me one thing and then someone else tells me another, and the two things are hardly ever the same. "The ocean's empty," they say. "The ocean's full." "The sky's the limit," they tell us, but, "Space is infinite." "Sea monsters and giant squids live in the deepest depths of the oceans," and "Krakens are just old sailor's tales."'

68

'What does, "in-fi-nat" mean?' his sister asked, having selected this word as the one of most intrigue.

'It just means it goes on forever.'

'Oh,' she said, scratching her cheek. 'So space goes on forever?'

'So they say.'

'Oh,' she said again. 'I'm not sure I can imagine forever. I've tried.'

'Don't worry, nobody can.'

The little girl said nothing, but only made an unmistakable sound which perfectly conveyed that she was attempting to summate this impossible thing called "in-fi-nat".

'I know one thing,' said the boy, thinking long on all the things he knew, 'I know that I sure do hope that being an adult isn't half so confusing as being nine.'

'Nine sure does sound strange and confusing.' said his sister. 'I'm glad I'm only six and three quarters.'

'You'll be nine soon enough, Silly.'

'I know... I know...'

'Didn't sound to me like you did.'

'I did too,' she asserted. And then, even more vehemently: 'I did too!'

The boy and girl then fell silent for a time, one staring out across the lake, the other at the clouds above and the treetops out wide.

The boy shuffled his body closer to the edge of the raft, went about fishing in the water there, twirling his finger in sinuous formations like a bug skating upon the surface, distorting the skin, barely breaking it.

He wondered about how it might be to be a bug, skating, flying, or crawling as they do. He pondered what life might mean to a fish, gliding as they do beneath the waters, their mouths opening and closing, opening and closing, their eyes twitching this way and that, processing two murky images at once – facilitated as he was in this thought by something his grandfather had once told him about the nature of the optical abilities of fish and many other animals.

He looked beside his swirling finger now, at his own distorted reflection in the gently rippling looking-glass surface.

And then, all of a sudden, he rolled to his side, shuffled to get closer to the water, became unbalanced – due largely to the subsequent tipping of the vessel – slipped off the raft and into the water, and could not swim.

He thrashed about wildly for a few terrible moments, splashing, his sister shrieking, screaming, and then he sank.

Beneath the lake there seemed a dull song, a calling which surrounded the boy's body, numbed his senses and mollified him.

Pain was gone.

Panic was gone.

Slowly, his eyes dimmed.

The light above was still bright, shimmering, but growing dimmer as he sank through the limpid water. He could still hear his sister screaming above too – her shrill tones now turned bass, terrified that he would never surface again – and she seemed distant now, growing farther away, quieter as he went down and down, plunging further still.

He could not swim, but, now, even if he had he been able to, he felt, quite inexplicably, that he might still wish to stay beneath the water, all the same...

That was a strange feeling...

A *feeling*, most definitely, rather than a *thought*, and a *very* strange one indeed...

On the sandy shore, his father weak and tearful with uncontrollable suffering, cradling him in his arms, the boy lay limp.

He was lifeless, unmoving.

He was dead.

But then, as his farther begged for mercy and his mother wept and his sister stood as motionless as he lay, the boy began to fit, to splutter, to cough out small fountains of water and then, remarkably, to breathe.

He was Lazarus reborn, awakening in the arms of his grateful father.

Slowly, he breathed.

Then steadily, he breathed.

With Mr Brown, the young journalist, sitting off to the right of him, the escapologist looked down at his hands now, at the fingers there fidgeting.

He turned them over, stared at his palms.

'I was under the water for a good few minutes,' he recalled, 'before my father fished me out. And I can still remember most of it. I was conscious for most of the time. I seemed to breathe without breathing. It's the strangest feeling to feel, and almost certainly impossible to explain...' his voice trailed away. 'That was when I was nine years old.'

'So from that you lost your fear of water? That was the experience that paved the way for all that came after?'

'Well, yes, that, and a few other things. You see, the woodland around the lake, and the lake itself, were magical places. When I was there, more so than at home or any other place I'd ever been – or any place I've ever been since, for that matter – I felt indestructible.'

As though he knew the feeling himself, had at times briefly felt himself all-powerful, the young journalist nodded his head in solemn sympathy.

'And so after that first experience,' the miraculous man continued, 'I went on to try other things. I pushed myself further each time. I'd lift things that even a man could not. I'd let myself fall from great heights and not break a bone. I'd hold my breath longer than humanly possible, my sister always by my side as my witness and

71

my parents always far from sight. It seemed, and still seems, that nothing could kill me, or even cause me harm.'

'Wonderful!' exploded the young journalist, Mr Brown, without the faintest hint of sarcasm or disbelief. 'You're immortal then!' he exulted. 'Wonderful! Just wonderful!'

'No,' rebuked the escapologist, dryly. 'No, I really don't feel that is the right word. I'm just more robust than most. Immortal? No, I don't care much for that title. I age like all others, but my skin remains firm. Do you know how old I am?'

'Nobody does, sir. That was just one of the curious things I found – or *didn't find* – in my researching your life. Wherever I looked, nobody knew, nothing was written, or there were accounts and estimations, but no two the same.'

'I'm seventy-seven.'

'No,' exclaimed the young journalist, in disbelief but willing acceptance of the fact. 'Why, you don't look a day over forty!'

The phenomenal escapologist looked – rather oddly – very dejected now, and simply said, 'I know.'

And then he went on to tell the reason behind his dismay...

'I can't do it,' spluttered the little girl, her hair glistening with water in the golden sunshine.

She had been trying to hold her breath again, in the shallows of the lake, under the watchful guidance of her miraculous brother.

'I can't do what you can do,' she said despondently. She was proud but also envious, as she then told her brother, 'You're special. I'm not. You came from the heavens, was blessed by God. Dad said so. I was found in a mulberry bush.'

Her brother laughed at this.

She shook herself clean of water like a little damp dog, goose pimples spotting her skin, and asked pleadingly what she could try next.

The boy told her, excitedly.

She at first followed him eagerly, agreeing easily with what he had proposed, but then she slowed her pace and looked awfully reluctant all of a sudden.

'Don't be silly. It'll be fine,' the older and much wiser boy lovingly assured her, moving away from the shoreline and towards a tree. 'Honest. We have the same parents, so we must have the same potential and abilities. All birds can fly, can't they? And all fish can swim. I reckon it'll be fine. I wouldn't tell you to do it otherwise, would I?'

'I guess not,' said his sister.

And, smiling but scared, up the tree she climbed...

The escapologist's face was one of great loss now.

You could judge solely by the hollowness of his eyes and the sorrow stained on his face that his heart was filled to horrible brimming, filled with that particularly woeful kind of loss that one never forgets; that kind of loss which burdens the soul greatly and for the entirety of a lifetime; that kind of terrible loss so very immense and relentless that the sufferer can only ever at best hope for distraction from it and for only a brief time, always knowing all too well that it remains intact, or even swells, beneath the surface, waiting there to rise again at any moment and gnaw away the senses until nothing remains, nothing but the numbness and resounding emptiness of perpetual sorrow; that loss of some essential element, some mystically special and irreplaceable ingredient which, when added to the mix of things, flavoured life to within milligrams... no... micrograms of perfection, made things just right, worthwhile, gave meaning; that loss of someone going

73

away, never to return; that loss of kinship, of truest and purest love.

'I'm so sorry,' said the journalist, evenly, with recourse to nothing more meaningful.

The forty-some-looking old man nodded.

Bathed in solemnity, he then forced a courteous smile: a smile which seemed congruous to no other part of his face, which affected no change in the wrinkles of sorrow – ingrained in his brow and cheeks – or the eternally sad look in his watery eyes. The smile just seemed to sit alone, as though misplaced.

'Only those with fearful faith are at liberty to be fearless of death,' the old-young man then said remotely. 'That's me, you know? I know where I'm heading. And I know I'll be forgiven. My sister died because of me, because of my naivety and stupidity, and I've spent the past sixty-some years of my life trying to make up for it, trying very hard to be reunited with her. I want to fail, you see. That's the twist. That's the coup de theatre. I want very much to die...'

Barbarians!

The great city came down from the sky like a great seed dropped from the beak of an even greater bird. The native people, gaunt and wide-eyed, looked up at the steely sky and saw the city coming, watched it descending, mouths agape, feeling an incomparable reverence, an amazement and an astonishment never before felt. Some waved their arms and some grunted and turned to one another and pointed at the falling, shining, whirring thing, and some ran in fear and took shelter, and many young ones flapped their arms and ran in circles, like flightless birds trying their wings at aviation, enamoured by the awesome sight. Most stood very still, though, very still and unblinking.

'We've arrived, my Lord,' said someone.

'Very good,' said another.

Drifting from side to side the city fell as a leaf might do in autumn, whirring in electric storms, eventually landing softly upon the infertile ground. And there it anchored itself with network after network of thickly girthed metal roots, fast-moving roots which burrowed with the tenacity of terrified silver rabbits. They burrowed their way as deep as needed into the earth: passed sand and through soil and subsoil, into and out of clay and bedrock, to reach like thirsty tongues for the liquid vivification of subterranean streams.

Motions were made and buttons pressed.

Vast causeways unfurled, rolled out like great metal-hinged red carpets ready to greet royalty. Tall walls erected themselves in mechanical movements, shaping a great citadel, setting boundaries. Buildings built up, entirely unaided, in robotic undertakings. Giant gates opened and closed in smooth motions; opened and closed, testing the guiders and rollers on which they moved, lubricating their moving parts.

'Send more roots,' was the instruction.

'Yes, my Lord,' was the reply.

More buttons were pressed, and as a giant spore the city sent out more silver shoots to grow in telescopic movements, tunnelling down, each section making the sound of a sword unsheathed as it appeared, in a sudden and violent germination. And the silver shooting roots, reaching their destinations, drank, draining water as though it were precious wine from the great depths, to channel it up to the surface, to make hospitable the long-since inhospitable land.

There the city burgeoned, blossomed and bloomed, and remained. Its gardens were vast, multi-coloured and plentiful.

'Welcome them in,' commanded a stern but warm voice.

'As you wish,' was the reply.

And with a smooth sweeping sound the great gates slid open once again and remained open, invitingly.

The natives entered, wearily at first, in hesitant ones and twos, and then in huddled families, then small groups and then larger groups, and, finally, in confident swarms.

The great city hummed with conversations in broken language; it moved in a sea of semantic motions, of shaken hands and other courteous and dumbly expressive gestures.

The Golden Palace sat centre of the city, tall and magnificent. You could see it flashing, glinting from long distances away: a brilliantly bright lighthouse beacon surrounded by the rich sea of emerald-green and amber-yellow pastures. Huge, bright and variegated fruits hung glistening in their taught skins from vines and branches which crept lazily, evermore up, towards the sky. Corn and wheat crops swished and swayed gently in soft breezes, whispering songs of new summers. Never-before-seen livestock – huge-horned bulls and cloud-coated sheep – grazed idly upon the lavish grasses there as golden-skinned children laughed by, playing joyously. Birds of all sizes and shades soared languidly in the air above, circling, singing, making their wings familiar with the new atmosphere, the new winds and new gravity.

It was utopian.

It was wonderful.

It was a place of plentiful celebrations, a place filled with a great many abundances: there was forever an abundance of banquets, of vast tables lined with smiling faces, delighted at the sights of platter after platter of rich foods and jug after jug of sweet wines, of bowl after silver bowl of delectable fruits, ripened to palatable perfection, a compendium of exquisite cuisine. There was an abundance of music, as harp strings resonated soft sounds which filled and enriched the air on quiet mornings, joyous afternoons and meditative nights. A great many great fountains of fresh clean water sprayed ceaselessly, day and night. From their innumerable decorative spouts, mouths and faucets, there issued the endless and gorgeous emission of clear water springs to sooth the body of the land and the bodies of the people and animals and vegetation, when the heat became too hot or the night too close. And the crystalline water fell also as false rains, from uncountable sprinkling taps mounted up high, to patter the dry crops and keep them well-oiled, well-nourished, to spot the golden-skinned bodies and keep them well-bronzed, healthy. And these false rains descended in vaporous hazes, too, glittering and casting small rainbows across the daylight. It fell and sent the gardens shimmering with brightness.

Knowledge new and old was perpetually added to and taken from the great many libraries, large and small, within the city.

It was a place of purest indulgences.

It was a paradise.

But beyond the paradise city, beyond its huge cool walls, beyond the prosperous greenery of this new oasis, as far as could be seen – stretching out as a dry ochre sheet over an endless empty bed – there remained the covering of a barren world, a desiccated land which in summer reaped nothing but death.

There lay endless desolation, natural wasteland, a cruel and featureless and faceless desert.

A great golden bell was sounded in the early afternoon light, its gong calling forth a congregation.

At once, the music ceased.

The laughter stopped.

Unfinished food was laid down.

Like startled statues, children froze their running and dancing and games.

Quietly but quickly, the people of the city gathered in the courtyard, mouths whispering, bare feet padding the marbled floors.

Their feet and lips then shushed.

They knelt.

They bowed down.

And then a towering idol, an obelisk, an edifice, a ziggurat of a man, the Great Ruler appeared in the entrance of the palace and stood, domineering and robust. He was a silhouette of a man with the sun searing behind him and marrying at his shoulders, neck and head, casting down a trailing shadow of his gargantuan figure – like the tail of an ashen comet – across the faces of his expressionless people.

He was a redoubtable sight.

He took a number of slow firm steps forward now and stood upon golden steps, surveying haughtily the many bowed heads.

He told his people to arise, then he turned and walked back a few paces, took seat upon a glittering throne.

They, the inhabitants of the city, arose and waited quietly to hear his words, his wisdom.

There was a long pause, a gathering of thoughts and words.

When finally the Ancient Autocrat spoke he spoke in what to us would be a strange and foreign tongue, an arcane diction.

'Worry not, my loyal people,' he said, his voice booming into the silent courtyard. 'We will never admit those *wicked* ones into our city again, and they will never infiltrate our walls. *Never!*'

The attentive listeners heard his announcement and understood it clearly, and so then suddenly they cheered in adulation and just as suddenly fell back silent, a wave crashing onto cliff-bottom rocks with a roar and receding into the ocean with a soothed shush, a gentle whisper. There was quiet. But then a farrago of murmurs followed the shuffling of two feet on the polished tapestry floors. One man – the owner of the two shuffling feet – slowly held aloft his tentative arm, fingers trembling. Meekly, he then spoke.

'My lord,' he murmured nervously, 'could you be so...
so... gracious, as to hear me?'

The Great Ruler's eyes, the Ancient Lord's eyes, grew
sharp and incredulous at the astonishing audacity of
this individual. He recoiled. He stood up from his
throne. He was shaken. Nobody had ever raised
mutinous hands and opened heretical mouths to mutter
such a question as this. This was something entirely
new. This was the beginning of democracy.

The courtyard *ohed* and *ahed*, whispering.

'Yes,' the Lord said uneasily, after a time. 'Yes. Yes, I
will hear you.'

The man who would be heard stepped forward now,
his tentative steps speaking quiet volumes of trepidation
as the murmuring crowd parted in two tides to let him
through. When he reached the front of the crowd, he
hastened forth his words in nervous utterance.

'Well,' began the meek man, 'I thought I might propose
that we do let them in: I mean, we do have enough food
for –'

All around him in every direction people gasped in
awe; sharp intakes of breath which faltered him, stilted
his words, shook his body more tremulous that it
already was and made him question that which so
recently seemed so viable. Faces of horrified amazement
surrounded this fearful man trying his hand at bravery.

Many lips were bitten.

Many gasps were issued.

Many eyes were wide.

'Foolish infidelity!' cried the Ancient Leader,
impassioned by this man without a name or standing,
this individual of insignificance, this impertinent and
incongruous idiot. 'How *dare* you question me?'
demanded the Lord. 'How dare you *challenge* my wishes,
my wisdom? I say they are bound to suffer, and so it
shall be!' He raised a single righteous finger and thrust
it in the direction of the meek man, his eyes afire with

80

golden rage. 'If you so wish yourself a hero, then go out into their numbers and see how they will love you.'

'No, I –'

'No? No? No, because you see without looking that embrace you and exonerate you they will not!'

All apart from one, the Ancient Lord's people cheered.

Silent indignation permeated the lone protestor's blood, prickled beneath his skin like millions of vengeful bee stings trying to burst out and scream out, "Injustice! Disgraceful Injustice!" But, although he felt it pinking his cheeks, he was careful in not letting his rage reach his face as an unbidden expression of distemper.

Terror and shame and anger pulsed discreetly in his wrists and neck and chest, secretly blackening his heart, stopping up his throat, quietly choking him. He wanted to roar, wanted to yell and scream and stamp his feet. But he remained silent He remained still. He swallowed hard.

'They would embrace you,' called the Great One, then rousing himself furthermore, 'only to take from you! To tear flesh from you! Bit by bit! Bite by bite!'

The meek man's protestations abated at his tongue, dwindled down his throat, and finally foundered in his stomach. Dispirited, crestfallen, he breathed a sigh of resignation, let his head loll forward in a submissive motion.

Outside the city, complexions horribly tanned, leathered by harsh sunlight, desiccated by callous heat and unwavering humidity, the wicked beggars cried many dry tears, their glazed bulging eyes wishing to escape their sallow sockets, wanting to scale the walls and find comfort, find acceptance, be cared about.

If ever Will and Want could climb walls, theirs would.

Hearts beat, some wildly hopeful, some calmly resigned, within emaciated chests, through exposed ribs that had become covered by little skin, like cages containing floundering and frantic birds, draped under

81

thin curtains of unhealthy flesh. Their stomachs were small hessian sacks, emptied of wheat and water, dishevelled. Their throats were discarded hoses, so long without usage that they had become brittle with dryness, littered with dust and cobwebs. Their slight bodies were weak, becoming unfamiliar to all things nutritional. They were the walking dead, the damned, the doomed. They were desperate.

Once again infertile and unforgiving, the world beyond the walls had driven them there to plead for merciful charity. Where insects once chirped legs together on damp warm nights full of futures and plans and the miracle of birth; where fruits had grown wildly, ballooning so big that they snapped branches with their sheer weight and fell thudding to the ground unnoticed because they were so plentiful; where meadows had undulated beneath oceanic winds that carried well-fed birds sailing across the skies, gliding effortlessly; where there had once been abundant life, there was now nothing. And so the very land that they had failed to maintain had now dusted them along on a dark storm of draught and starvation to this place of refuge, to this great golden star city, which had descended through the clouds in bygone years and gifted them the teachings they had failed to uphold.

They had come to beg, to swallow pride not ever knowing what pride was. Please, their watery eyes cried, please show mercy. Please allow us haven within your heavenly walls.

The heat of the desert behind them shimmered; it quivered, dancing an unforgiving dance, like the blazing fires and tormented souls of the hell it was, hungry to devour them and turn them to yellow dust and ivory bones.

'When we first came to this place,' continued the Man of Power, 'when we first came and settled this great city of ours, the land here became ours. We built our walls and enriched the arid ground within those walls and set about teaching a good way of living. The indigenous beings were given sufficient opportunity to conform, to pray to me. We welcomed them in. They welcomed our wealth and charity but refused our rituals. We gave them language, fire and artistry, civility. We taught them how to act, how to be, how to coexist in peace. We showed them how to farm, how to live good and harmonious lives with the land, how to sew and reap, how to herd, and how to trade that produce. We did all that for them – we raised them from their lowly existence – and in spite of it all they refused our rituals and instead went out into the desert, armed with *our* knowledge, to fend for themselves. No,' he shook his head defiantly, raised his righteous finger aloft again, this time waving it side to side as a metronome's needle, as confirmation of his disapproval. 'No, no, I *will not* now suffer beggars, supposedly enriched by experience. *They* will suffer!'

Presently, the meek man became brave once again. He had something more to say. In an instant he lifted his bowed head, opened his eyes bright, and thrust back his shoulders.

He threw forth his words into the brief interlude: 'But they are dying, my Lord,' he pleaded. 'To what end do we lead this selfish life?'

'Selfish?' The Lord of Power clenched a fist, stiffened his lip. He retorted, 'I must preserve my people. Who are you to question me? I have given to them all I will. Let them invent or die!'

'But they have no tools now. And the land outside the city is dying.'

'Then let them die with it.'

His people cheered again. They applauded. They exulted. They shook their fists at the bright sky. Like all thinkers of thoughts radical, like all those who seek to

83

make great changes and bold movements, the meek man was alone in a crowd.

The wave of excitement died.

'But,' once more, 'my Lord –'

'But nothing! If we were to let them in now they would turn violent.' He drew a shining, jewel-encrusted sword from his side, used it to point around the courtyard at various pillars and statues, walls and gates, 'They would turn violent and plot and scheme to overthrow me and tear down what I have built... what *we* have all worked for! These beings, these wicked animals, know only of destruction! They are the Wicked Ones!'

'But they seem benevolent in their desperation. They seem to know they did wrong, my Good Lord.'

'They will *seem* whatever they wish to make you think they seem,' riposted the Ancient Emperor. 'This is the way of the wicked, the way of Evil: to deceive, to manipulate, to inveigle.' He waved a hand. 'I have grown tired of this talking now. Cease your tongue and keep it, talk on and lose it. Watch now, watch only with your eyes. Observe them grow vicious. Watch their true nature unfold. And then you will see that I know all, when they begin to beat one another to death with their hands and feet, and feast upon the dead. Watch,' he insisted. 'Watch and you will see.'

And, after a time, sensing that their cause was a lost one, the Wicked Ones did begin to grow violent, desperate in despair. They tried to climb up and over one another, using the dead and the dying as steps to try to reach the heights of the great walls. And tempers did flare in the blast-furnace heat. And then they did beat one another with their fists as clubs and their feet as bats. They gouged and throttled and jabbed and kicked and punched, beating one another. And blood sprayed from the wounded and was drunk by the thirsty. They bit into flesh in the manner of starving lions. Meat was torn from the lifeless and devoured by the almost dead. They had to eat. They had to live. They were wild with desperation.

And when the order came to disperse the crowd of villainous beggars, to send them back to whence they came, the soldiers who lined the tops of the city walls threw spears and fired arrows raining down on the Wicked Ones, and the Wicked Ones picked up those very same spears and arrows and threw them back. Then they clawed at the ground to find rocks that had not yet been turned and crumbled to dust and threw them, too. Their minds were baking in their skulls, driving them wild with an immensely maddening insanity.

'See! You see now,' shouted the unimpeachable Great Ancient Lord to his loyal people, his voice husk with triumph. 'What did I tell you? They are barbarians!'

The congregation cheered.

Only one did not.

'Barbarians!'

THE SCARLET LADY

That image, of those shoes... that image would never leave him, forever burnt into his innocent eyes.

There was something wicked about the way the wind blew that cold November evening. It bent trees to breaking point, rattled window panes, clattered roof tiles in an orchestral manner, and made tumbleweeds of yesterday's news. The rain beat down heavily too, pitilessly crushing spirits, sparing nobody, as the faces of pedestrians grimaced at the sharp, chilling air; silvery droplets, like shards and splinters of glass propelled by some immense and unseen and silent explosion, arrowed down from out of the blackness, glittering, stinging cheeks. Dozens of shivering figures dashed to their cars, huddled into coats, breath billowing like locomotives racing along midnight tracks to silent far-away stations. Suited men took shelter beneath briefcases. Skirted women battled with the contorted skeletons of umbrellas, as the fabric flapped like broken bird's wings. The night was utterly chaotic.

But Matthew sat warm.

Matthew sat comfortable.

Across the town people gathered in huddled groups, in twos and threes and fours and more, in small cafes and wine bars, in libraries and old dusty book shops, conservatories and living rooms, talking of how dreadful and how horrible the weather was, looking out the windows, waiting for the storm to pass. And Matthew sat in much the same way. But he did not grumble to anyone. He did not curse the rain or wish for the wind to blow away. He sat, seated beside the bay window of his family's lounge, his supple skin absorbing heat from Father's open fire which glowed behind him, quietly crackling.

He sat, perched like an ornament on a ledge, as a curious cat might, attentively watching the world outside the window whistling by like his own private play. And, as the warm uncomplaining boy watched, he pondered the possible stories of each person who blew by in the shadows of the street: a slender young woman, pretty and pious, dashing home to an empty house; an overworked banker rushing to share rare and precious moments with his wife and their new born baby; a teenage girl who just cannot wait to turn the next page of a book that haunts her every thought, racing; and an elderly man who simply cannot miss his favourite television show about a world long forgotten by most. Matthew adored creating tales. He was a precocious boy. He smiled at his stories as the pale moon cast shadows and lit up the tiny marionettes below, and streetlights made raindrops glisten like cat's eyes on the slick black road.

The sound of a thousand fingernails prattled across the bay window.

The wind and the rain were relentless.

It was the stomach of the young and imaginative boy that first sniffed out Mother's stew, long before his nose did; the sweet smell of it floated about the room, drifting on almost invisible clouds of steam from the kitchen.

Then Mother sang out: 'Matthew. Bonnie. Dinner's ready.'

His twitching nose next caught the doughy scent that his stomach had already rumbled to him about.

His senses synchronised.

His mouth watered.

Bonnie, his sister, came racing down the staircase just as fast as her stampeding eight year old legs could carry her, her bare feet drum-rolling on the solid wooden steps. Father didn't stir from his woeful newspaper, though. He never did, not until the food was served and the crockery lay warming the tablecloth.

Moments later they all sat around the dining table, ready to eat, their mouths beginning to water. Mother chirped about the wonderful groceries she had discovered at market that afternoon, which now bobbed in their bowls. Father mumbled about his aching body and how he hated the factory. Bonnie hummed the tunes of fairies and butterflies and talked of all things sweet. Matthew just sat and listened, the only one listening. And the family feasted on the tender stew.

Fifteen minutes later, when the family had finished eating, Mother cleared the table, tended to the bowls and spoons and left the pan to soak; Father returned to fill the craterous impression he had left in his tired armchair; Bonnie went back to staying within the lines of a colouring book in her bedroom, her mouth hung open, twitching tongue aiding absolute concentration; and Matthew returned to his now steamy picture house window.

Had he licked his finger after writing his name in the residue there, it would surely have tasted of Mother's stew.

He erased his name with a swift wipe of his hand. Looking out of the window again he saw that the street was now empty, empty other than a black cat searching out shelter under which it might dry its oily wet fur.

After a few moments of searching, the feral feline then vanished beneath a parked car.

Very empty now, Matthew thought. Properly empty. End of play, he told himself. Not much fun watching a few wet leaves dance the Waltz until they find something to stick to.

The rain stopped just as Father and Mother snuggled into their coats and Bonnie snuggled into her soft linen sheets, about a half hour later. But the wind still blew, stronger now.

'Now Matthew, are you sure that you are ready for this?'

'Yes, Father. Positive. I am twelve, remember? And remember my school report? "Matthew is a very responsible and capable young man... creatively... very gifted..." Why, some of my friends have been minding their brothers and sisters since they were eleven, and even ten. And they're all far less clever and "capable" and "responsible" than me,' he asserted.

'Well, so long as you are sure, son. I don't doubt your capability in any way, understand. I just want you to be *certain* you are ready. That you *feel* ready.'

The boy nodded, said, 'I am. I do.'

'Okay then,' conceded his father. 'But remember we're only going to be five minutes away, and we will ring the phone once every hour, and Mrs Moore is just next door, if you need anything.'

'I know, I know.' Matthew rolled his eyes in the manner he had often watched his mother do, so many times before, when listening to Father's orders. As it happened, Mother then rolled her eyes, mirroring his perfectly. 'Everything will be fine, Dad,' the son assured him. 'Don't worry.'

'And we'll be back by ten o'clock,' Father pointed to the grandfather clock which stood, antique and proud, by the staircase, ticking.

Again Matthew nodded, rolled his eyes.

'Speak to you soon, Darling,' Mother whispered lovingly. She then kissed him delicately on his smooth brow before the parents went out to face the ferocious wind in the cold, dark, relentlessly harsh night.

'Have fun, Mum, Dad.' Matthew waved them away, smiling.

'We will.' His father nodded to him. 'Be good.'

Matthew went then and sat again by the bay window and watched his parents sway as they passed down the garden path, like two ships lost at sea, he felt, tethered to one another, arms linked. Then they disappeared into the ebony air.

He was a very creative and imaginative boy, Matthew was. He was twelve and in his eyes most things were never what they might seem to most people: to him, outward appearances hid furtive insides, benevolent faces all too often shrouded malevolent intentions, and conspicuousness was only ever merely two letters away from inconspicuousness.

A book should never be judged by its cover, as his grandfather had told him.

He felt that life was a play, open to interpretation.

Subtle strange possibilities unremittingly occurred to the boy's mind. He felt different and saw things differently. The lenses of his eyes were tinted myriad colours. Where one saw simply a bare tree in autumn he would see an ancient and crooked skeletal arm reaching up from its unmarked grave in blind protestation of the unforgiving moon, its giant branch fingers shifting slowly in the wind. Where most perceived a simple field of grass with grazing cows upon it, he saw a vast green sea: an ocean of calm with an archipelago of huge black and white drilling machine rigs anchored on iron stilts –

the legs – prospecting below the tides for oil with their mechanical arms – the necks – craning, pumping, drilling. He was a cloud-watcher, a deep-thinker, a day-dreamer, an imaginer of new worlds and endless possibilities: a story conjurer.

He liked to write down his stories, too.

But, most of all, he liked to read.

Presently the young boy moved away from the window and went to the kitchen and prepared for himself an unfamiliar drink: a hot cup of tea. He didn't actually know how many sugars he *took*, but two tasted just about sweet enough.

Slowly, cautiously, he then carried the steaming cup into the lounge, as a circus performer might balance a sword upon his chin, concentrating intensely. Then, slowly, cautiously again, he nestled himself down into Father's chair, the apparent new ruler of the realm. Placing his cup on the coffee table beside the chair, boldly residing in the armchair, with a surgical precision and care, he then opened the latest edition of his favourite comic book. He had patiently saved to savour this moment a long, seemingly endless, five hours since coming home from school.

The paper was autumn-leaf-crisp as he peeled open the cover and the brand-new, fresh-ink smell drifted up from the fresh print. An awesome excitement built up in the boy at the anticipation of what might happen this week.

With a slowness elicited by indulgence, he began to read the bubble-encapsulated text and to examine the vivid images. He was more than content, at ease in his intrigue, for three minutes at the most.

There then came an interruption, a faint rattle from the window. Like a nearing herd of buffalo on a not so distant horizon, it seemed to escalate into a roll of thunder.

The platted cord tassels which hung from the shade of the lamp sat beside him on the coffee table quivered.

His cooling tea rippled gently in the cup.

Thunder.

Thunder.

Thunder?

No, it was just Bonnie coming bounding down the stairs once more.

Dazedly, she trudged into the room. 'Matthew, I can't sleep,' she was saying, wiping her crystal-blue eyes on the back of her hand. She was visibly tired, but equally obvious was the fact that she was fighting fatigue, as children often do. 'Read me a story, please,' she asked.

'No,' said the disrupted, disgruntled brother.

'Can't sleep though,' said the annoyance.

'Oh, Bonnie, go back to bed.'

'Please, Matthew,' pleaded the girl, 'please read me a story.'

'No. I'm busy. Can't you see? Go to bed.'

'Pretty pleeeease?'

Matthew breathed heavily at the persistent pest, snorted, and then rolled his mother's eyes again. 'Ohhh Bonnnnnie,' he said agonisingly, 'you are a real pain in the...' Then he capitulated and closed up his comic book neatly, placing it down squarely on the coffee table, and said, 'Come on then, Pain, up to bed. But I'm not *reading* you a story, though; I'm going to *tell* you a story... a *true* story.' His eyes were bright blue agate moons of excitement, hers reflecting his like two shimmering ponds.

The two children bounded up the stairs and into Bonnie's bedroom.

Subtle scents of spring, of lavender and lily, wafted up from the fresh sheets as Matthew tucked them in and around the small frame of his little sister, enveloping her. Her mouth arched up at each corner in relaxed comfort, as the warm air slowed from her button nose.

As he attempted to conjure a tale from the depths of his imagination, Matthew sat himself down on the edge of the little girl's bed. He sat for a full minute or two, thinking, conducting a séance with the spirits of his creative self.

And then, all of a sudden, a fierce gust of wind outside slipped in through slivered gaps in the bedroom window frame, blowing the curtains ever so slightly. At this, an ornate casket opened with the sound of a prolonged high creak, the soil of a graveyard stirred, crows crowed, and an ancient beast awakened somewhere – far away – deep in the darkest deepest depths of the young boy's imagination; in creeping shadows and steady rivulets of crimson, a tale of horror came to him.

Matthew did not know just why he would impulsively want to pollute the innocence of his little sister with such a sinister story as the one he suddenly had composed, but he knew he would proceed all the same. A curiosity had arisen within him, an age old sadistic tendency towards reeking terror and havoc, a carnal lust, an urge to create immeasurable fear.

He faced the phantasmal window now.

His voice hushed.

'That'll be the Scarlet Lady,' he whispered in his most ghostly of voices, turning his head back from the now-calming curtain and leaning in towards Bonnie, his mouth sinisterly grinning.

'Who,' said the girl, looking at him curiously, slightly unnerved, 'who is the Scarlet Lady?' She asked the inevitable question with that perfectly distinctive kind of beautiful naivety, that particular intrigue, which is possessed only by the unparalleled innocence of a child.

'She was a lady who once lived here,' the boy lied. 'In this very house, she lived, long before we ever did. I'll tell you her story, if you like? But... come to think of it... it's a scary story and I'm not quite sure you're old enough...' – he paused for dramatic effect – 'or *brave* enough, to hear it.'

'I am too!' Bonnie chirped, 'I'm not scared of anything!'

'Well... so long as you're sure... so long as you are absolutely certain?' Matthew's voiced echoed Father's.

The little girl nodded confidently, with an assured certainty of conviction. 'Sure I'm sure.'

'Okay. Have you ever noticed,' the boy asked of her, 'how you can see the ocean from the window in the attic?'

Bonnie nodded again, this time slowly.

'Well,' said the boy, 'a long, long, long time ago, there was a lady who lived in this house with her husband-to-be – her betrothed, I think they call it. The man, whom she loved very much – very dearly – and who was very charming and very handsome, was away at sea most of the time because he was in the navy. He was an officer. When he was away from her, the lady was lost without him here. She couldn't think of anything but when he might return, and so she would watch from that very same window in the attic every time he was away, waiting for him to come back. Then, when she saw his ship coming in, she would run all the way to the beach. Diving into his arms when she got to the shore, the two would spin like a carousel of joy and love.'

Matthew wetted his lips, whetted his tongue, and proceeded:

'Theirs was a love that only the likes of fairy tales and happily-ever-afters had ever seen: a perfect love, a so-strong-it-was-unbreakable love. The sun would always shine when she was in his arms, birds would sing their favourite song, and butterflies would flutter by, as they gazed into one another's eyes, and the smell of flowers would fill the air. It was a love that would live forever.'

'They planned to marry in the spring, right there on the beach but... as their wedding day approached, there was a war – a great war like none before – and the man

94

was called away to that war. The lady didn't want him to go but his duty to his country was to fight, and he assured her that they would marry on his return, not a second after his return. The wedding day came and –'

'I thought this was a scary story,' said a bemused girl by the name of Bonnie, her smooth brows forced into tiny wrinkles.

'It is a scary story,' explained Matthew. 'Shush and listen. I'm getting to the scary part. You have to sit out the sermon before you get to the hymns, everyone knows that!'

'So,' the boy sighed, 'as I was saying: the day of her loved-one's return came and her heart was filled with splendorous joy. She was excited. She could not wait to be his wife...'

The more the boy went on telling his story was the more he built the Scarlet Lady's character: the more he told of her was the more he breathed air into lungs of dust; his unfolding plot moulded the bride-to-be; his nouns birthed her body, cell by cell; his adjectives shaped her milk-white bones, filled them with marrow, rounded her flesh, sculpted her limbs and face, and hemmed her brilliant white dress; the verbs he used gave her movements and motions, and sent the vital liquids and energies and gases moving through her respiratory, nervous and circulatory systems; the adverbs dictated to those liquids and energies and gases how quickly and how slowly to move; and his punctuation made her stop, start and pause, and gave her a voice.

His narrating was the conducting of a necromantic ritual, a discourse with the dead that had never known life. From his imagination there was resurrected the incarnation of original evils, slithering in serpentine motions, clambering and crawling out of the dark depths of a catacomb, all dust and decay and mantled with moss.

The Scarlet Lady arose from the midnight graveyard of his mind.

Matthew felt grand now. He felt awash with the feverish excitement of creativity.

'In her perfect white dress,' he proceeded, 'she sat by the attic window, watching and waiting for her handsome prince to return. Beneath her feet the house hummed with cheer and laughter, as it filled with guests all there to share that special day. But, he did not arrive. And so she went on sitting and waiting. She sat and watched and waited, sat, watched, waited, watched, waited... waited and waited and waited... The hours went by. But there was no sign of him. More hours passed, more waiting was done, and still there was no sign of him. Then the sun went down, and the next day a telegram came through: a telegram to say that –'

'What's a tele-gram?'

'It's...' – the boy thought about it – 'it's a message: an old, old way of sending a message. And so a message came through, a message that he would never return. She cried. He had been killed in battle. His ship had been sunk with not one survivor. She was heartbroken. The guests tried to comfort her. Nobody could stop her crying. She was incoms... incons... incon-sol-ee... incon-sol-ee-able...' Matthew shook his head, said, 'Not one person could make her feel better!' He puffed out his cheeks, went on, 'And so the guests then talked it over and decided that it was best to leave her in peace, to grieve. She cried, and cried, and cried. She cried an ocean of tears. She cried so much, and so hard, that her tears eventually ran out and so she instead cried tears of blood. Her blood tears then rained down on her dress and spread like an ink-well spilt over paper. So much of her blood tears poured over the dress that it was flooded with her pain and painted a deep... scarlet... red...'

'Then she died right there, sat by the window, watching, waiting, and crying. She still waits there now, because that love, that truest love, can never, ever, truly die.'

'Really?' asked Bonnie, her eyes tormented with an odd concoction of both sadness and dread. 'Honestly?'

'Yes, really,' said the boy.

His sister looked terrified now.

Wryly, he smiled a smile that was almost a smirk.

'And some nights,' he said, 'through her blood-filled eyes she thinks she sees him returning, coming into the harbour aboard his ship, and so she leaves the attic window and dashes down the stairs, down the streets and on to the beach and up to the shore. But, it's never him...'

'The man who lived in this house before us...' Matthew added, 'she murdered him, mistook him for one of the guests that thought it "best to leave her" here... alone... to die... "in peace."'

Bonnie laid frozen for a moment, as though caught in a Gorgon's glare. Then she shivered and asked for a nice story. Matthew refused bluntly. He told her to sleep, or the Scarlet Lady would come for her.

Closing the bedroom door behind him, his conscience clear and even perhaps sadistically tickled a little, he returned to his comic book.

Bonnie lay petrified now, too scared to even tremble, listening to the howling wind surging through the evil night outside her window. Not feeling anything at first, numb with shock and fear, slowly, a chill crept over her: an army of tiny spiders sneaking up her spine, their many legs making her skin tingle in terror.

The Scarlet Lady haunted Bonnie. Within her mind, she could see her stood in the dark hallway outside her room. She could see her roaming the house, lost in shadows and painful confusion. She could envision her sat by the attic window, watching and waiting and crying crimson tears, knowing the sailor would never come home to her but refusing to accept the fact that he was gone. She could almost hear her pain, her sobs of unparalleled sorrow. In hysterical movements, she could see the Scarlet Lady running to the beach again and again and again, only to find it empty every time.

Knowing she must sleep, and with a frantic rant, the little girl tried desperately to distract herself from the wicked tale. In a meditative mentation of wild word association, she began to recite the things she loved, the things she found comfort in: butterflies, fairies... bunnies... Easter... garden... egg-hunt, flowers, sunshine, ladybirds... red... blood... tears... the Scarlet Lady!

She closed her eyes tightly shut to crush the thoughts, the images, but the Lady of Blooded Tears lurked in the shadowy corners, in the attic of the little girl's mind. Then she hovered to and craned over Bonnie's face as she lay trembling, and was gone much quicker than the little girl could open her watery eyes.

'Butterflies, fairies, meadows...' she chanted aloud to herself now, as though the incantation might ward off the spirit. 'Meadows, daffodils, buttercups, daisies, poppies... red... scarlet... tears of blood.'

Again Bonnie clamped her eyelids down, squeezed them tighter. Inside her eyes, though, the once-white lace shined red from fresh heartache beside the attic window.

The Scarlet Lady sobbed softly in Bonnie's ear. She could almost smell her lavish perfume.

Then Bonnie sat up and, as the tears poured down her cheeks and trickled over her pink soft lips, she could taste the ocean.

The little girl screamed in silence, her throat blocked by invisible sand. The Scarlet Lady screamed in the girl's mind, a terrifying banshee howl of lament.

Bonnie opened her blurred eyes, closed them, opened them, saw a shadow, cried more intensely, tasted the ocean, and shook with terror. Then all went dark and distant – dreamlike – and she was no longer sat upon her bed. She was instead sat on the cold and windy shore, watching the Scarlet Lady look out to sea, hopelessly lost, crazed by mourning.

Eyes shut.

'Butterflies.'

A creak from the attic.

'Fairies.'

She's coming down.

'Poppies.'

She's angry.

'Blood.'

She wants to hurt me.

Bonnie leapt up from what to her was a bed sodden with blood, soaked in tears.

'Matthewwww!' she screamed.

Downstairs, Matthew leapt up from his father's armchair. He dashed, pulse-pounding, stampeding, to the bottom of the stairs.

Bonnie stood atop them, frozen.

'What's wrong?' gasped the horror story teller, his eyes wide and wild.

'I'm scared,' said his sister.

'Oh don't be silly, Bonnie. You wanted the story.'

'But... she's going to... get me...' jabbered the fear-filled girl. 'The lady's... going to get me! She's going to get me because she's angry and confused and mad, and because I can't sleep!'

'She won't get you, Silly. She can't get you. It was just a –'

That ancient beast of morbid temptation reared its ugly head again now, and it pulled a ponderous face at Matthew, and in that instinctive flicker of an instance he gave in to that beast, seduced by sadism and the propensity to seek power.

He threw his right hand up, finger outstretched to point beyond his now-tiny sister and made his face distorted and horrified and screamed, '*She's there!*'

Bonnie suddenly tossed herself away from the Scarlet Lady, away from danger unseen, away from true horror, and out, down, towards the vast, open, gaping mouth of the staircase.

At first she seemed to move through the air as slowly as something seemingly weightless but bound to gradually descend. She seemed to hang there a moment, paused in a horrific stillness of time and realisation.

Matthew held out his hand and held his breath.

And then down she tumbled like an unwanted China Doll being thrown from a pushchair. Each step she thudded into, and off, shattered her fragile body. Bones cracked as her screams cut through the night in harrowing howls.

It all happened so quickly and yet so very slowly, so unchangeably, so powerless to prevent it as either child was now.

Down, down, down, and down farther still, she fell.

Her screams ceased. Her falling and tumbling and the cracking of her tiny bones had ended. Her head was opened up like an egg cracked, split apart, revealing a blood-red white and yolk, fragments of skull the fragile shell. She twitched a second, and then stopped.

Her lifeless body, a fire without flame, had come to rest at Matthew's feet. Her face was drowned in an ocean of blood and tears. It spread across the floor like a well of red ink spilt over a sheet of oaken papyrus. It ran between the floorboards in tiny rivulets. It flooded around the outsoles of his shoes as though they were two small islands, lapped up across the shores of their welts, stained the vamps.

Matthew stopped holding his breath now.

He looked down at his shoes and the tide of blood and the body of his sister. His face grew pale in an instant, as pale as freshly driven snow, or alabaster stone. He held his hands to his mouth. He felt sick. He felt his stomach sink heavily. Then he heard the grandfather clock tick – click, clunk – slower than usual, and he heard the leaves in the dying wind, slowly dancing the Waltz outside. He tasted tea and the ocean.

Then he felt... nothing... empty... a fire without flame.

He knelt, began to whimper and weep, and then gathered into his arms the broken china doll.

'– story,' he sobbed, staring down on his sister, now cradled in his arms. He was staring and wishing for her to move, for her to smile, for her to say something... anything... anything annoying or pointless, or silly, or stupid.

'It was just a story,' he pleaded, 'Bonnie. I, I didn't mean it, Bonnie. Honestly I didn't mean it, didn't mean anything by it. It, it was just a story. Please, Bonnie, oh please, oh, please... I didn't mean it, please. It's not real. It's just a story. Oh, oh, oh, please, Bonnie, please, it was just a story.'

He stroked her spiralling, amber hair.

'Please, Bonnie,' he said, gently rocking her and himself.

But she did not respond. She would never respond again... to anything... ever. Matthew knew that. He told himself that. And then he looked down at his shoes, stared at them, and pretended nothing was real.

'Just a story...'

That image, of those shoes, soaked in the blood of a loved one. That image would never leave him, forever burnt into his innocent eyes.

HARRY HAUGHTON'S PECULIAR
OBSESSION

Mr Harold Richard Haughton had just one obsession in life. And it was a peculiar one, to say the least of it...

His very curious preoccupation was not literature or sports, or the fine arts, or gambling. It was not the consumption of alcohol or lavish foods, either: he was no great epicure. Nor was it the stars in the night sky or the stars on the silver screen: neither of these shone so bright in his eyes. His obsession was not the workings of people's minds or the politics of families. It was not fashion or the technological advances of the modern world, and how the usage of such advances seemed to hold little or no edifying qualities. Nor was it nature, either: the behaviour of birds in relation to the seasons, migration and breeding patterns, for that matter, bore no interest to him. Nor was it money. That was academic. Avaricious gain was completely uncalled for in his already affluent position. His obsession was not beautiful ladies, either, as obvious a pursuit they may seem for a red-blooded male with more than enough money. And no, it wasn't even God or the pursuit of personal enlightenment. No, it was shoes. Shoes: that was Harry Haughton's peculiar obsession in life, his love, his passion. His shoes, the shoes of others: the cleanliness of those shoes, to be more precise.

You see, Harold Richard Haughton was one of a strange and dying breed, obstinately professing clean shoes to be the cornerstone of a healthy and prosperous life, and a stable society. There was nothing quite as disconcerting to Harry as a man – or woman, for that matter – who cared so little about life as to adorn slovenly shoes: nothing nowhere near as forlorn, in his opinion, as filthy, foul, flyblown footwear. There was no excuse for unclean shoes. No excuse at all. In terms of shoes, he was an absolute firebrand of propriety.

Harry knew, just as his father had known, just as his father had always told him – told him until he was blueberry-blue in the face, tired of hearing himself, and the message was scorched onto his son's brain – that if armed with clean shoes you cannot, and will not, ever go wrong. Clean shoes were the accoutrement of prosperity, in his eyes. Behind every great man there was not a great woman, *no!* but a great pair of perfectly polished and suitably sanitised shoes.

Because there will not arise an occasion more befitting than this, it should perhaps be noted at this very point in the story (simply to avoid confusion if nothing else, as it seems to hold little if any other relevance) that Mr Harold Richard Haughton's father – Mr Haughton senior – was also named Mr Harold Richard Haughton: a trend born out of noble pride and apparent good breeding, and perhaps upheld by a lack of imagination.

Back to shoes then: it stood to sound reasoning, in Mr Haughton's opinion, that the ever-increasing success of women – particularly since their liberation and right to equality in the early 20th century – had something, if not everything, to do with the vast collections of shoes they each accrued: every day a fresh clean pair.

'Notice the nice lady-doctor's shoes,' Father once brazenly noted, after attending an appointment at the local surgery. 'Without those shoes so shiny that woman would never have known anything of medicine, mark my word.'

The young boy feigned his understanding of the principle, with a nod of his small blonde head.

'Understand, son?'

'Yes, father.'

'Look at the soldiers on parade, son,' he had instructed on another occasion. 'Look at their boots – like mirrors! You could comb your hair, brush your teeth and wash your face using those beautiful boots to see yourself. That's why we won the war, you know – clean boots! The Jerrys never stood a chance!'

Again, little Harry's face nodded and smiled up in adoration at his father, whose chin was thrust out proudly from his moustached face.

'The proof is all around you to be seen, son. Mark my word.'

'Take the butcher, for example:' was once the lecture, 'he's undeniably a good and honest man, who provides a commendable living for his family, but he's also one who is constantly marred by blood and bits of meat and bones falling upon his shoes, spoiling his chances. Or, take the postal worker: whether he stays in the sorting office or walks the streets, he is impinged in his success by fibres of paper and flecks of dust, or drops of rain, respectively. He cannot escape his shoes – and therefore his chances of potential success – becoming scuffed and scuppered.'

Harry Haughton Senior took a cloth from out of his pocket, bent down on his haunches, buffed a dull mist from off his right Oxford, and made its surface shine a black-mirror-shine.

'Never, Harry, let your shoes go unkempt,' he advised, 'or you're bound for failure.'

On his eighth birthday, Little Harry Haughton Junior was gifted by his father a cylindrical brown leather case, which had emblazoned across the front of it his initials, just like his father's. It was saved until the last of the gifts.

Opening the brown leather pill, with the lavish scent of new leather hugging itself to his skin and dancing about his nose, Harry's face filled with delight, the corners of his small pale mouth upturning at the sight of his very own, brand new – each brush inscribed – Gentleman's Luxury Shoe-shining Kit. What a magnificent sight! There was a stiff-bristled brush for brushing off stubborn dirt, a softer brush for applying polish and then one, the cleanest of all, for ensuring the shoes' surfaces gleamed as though encrusted with black crystals. And, moreover, there was even a small mirror on the underside of the lid which was surrounded by purple crushed velvet and which Harry might one day use to comb his own moustache in.

'Now, Harry, look at the Poor... That poor unfortunate soul *there*, for example,' said Harry Haughton Senior, on one trip into town. 'He's homeless and hapless, and I'd wager he hasn't a penny to his name: the poor beggar. And you know why that is, Son?'

'Yes, father'

'Go on...'

'Well... dirty shoes of course, father.'

'Indeed,' beamed the proud, moustached man.

Over the years, Mr Harold Richard Haughton Senior's hard work and profound wisdom had yielded substantial profits upon his family: reaped wonderful rewards. He had been a great success, an astute businessman, built a handsome empire from humble beginnings, worked his way from poverty to posterity – buffing all the way –

and his son would never have to know a day without sustenance, or a night without shelter.

He had done right by his loved ones.

Ironically, or perhaps quite predictably, Mr Harold Richard Haughton Senior had constructed, nurtured and maintained one of the very first and finest and largest chains of shoe shops in all of Great Britain. He was a celebrated genius: what started as a small and unpromising shoe repair and shining service – hand-painted sign hanging above the inauspicious stall in a bustling indoor marketplace – had grown amidst great surprise into its own premises on the high street, evolved into a second site in the neighbouring town, and now ballooned, filled with air and taken to the skies, into a nationwide enterprise, a corporation: some forty four separate shops, almost one in each city. Harry was indeed proud of Harry, whichever way you looked at it, it was a regular palindrome.

The Haughton Family were all "set for life".

And now, at the age of twenty one, having never had to work a day of labour, having never had to strive for anything, ever, Mr Harold Richard Haughton Junior did not want for success. He did not need to be astute in business. He did not need to win the heart of a woman or dream a perfect prince and princess scenario in which to make a proposal. These were all bridges that had either been easily crossed or had never even needed crossing. No, all he wanted... all he needed to do... right now... in this very moment... was to leave the house in time for his own wedding service.

'Come on, Harry-man, pull yourself together now. It's just the nerves, the wedding jitters – cold feet and all that.'

'Clean shoes... got to be clean... clean... clean... *clean!*'

Chewing his bottom lip and twitching uncontrollably, Harry sat frantically shining.

His best man stood by the kitchen table, rubbing the back of his neck, fidgeting with his collar, horribly nonplussed in his erratic mediations.

'They're *clean*, Harry,' he said imploringly, still fidgeting with his collar. 'Come on now, you've polished those shoes three times already. And I've polished them twice! That's five times, Harry. *Five* times! They *are* clean! *Very clean!*' He took a sharp breath, held it a second, exhaled, and then a deep breath which he held for two seconds. 'Now listen,' he said, after breathing out a big sigh. 'The car is outside, waiting.' He wetted his lips, sighed again. 'We'll be late if we don't set off immediately.'

'But, you don't understand, Vince, they've *got* to be clean or we're bound to *fail.*'

'I do understand, Harry,' said Vince, with great compassion and half-feigned empathy. 'I really *do*. But, now's not the time for this, and...' his voice faded, losing track. He shook his head. 'And... and... and they're already clean! Very, very clean! Harry, they are *very* clean. *Unmistakably* and *indisputably* clean! *Please!* Let's go!'

'*Yeah?* Is that so?' Harry glared at Vince accusingly now. '*Clean* are they?' he hissed. '*Very clean?* Clean enough for now? And what about when I step outside and the wind blows dirt on them and it sticks and it just sticks and you can't get it off, no matter how hard you try? What then?'

'That won't happen, Harry,' was the best man's definite reply, his face desperate.

'It *will*, Vince! It *does!* Look at your shoes! Just walking 'round in here they've got dirty! It happens whether we like it or not. Dirt's *everywhere!*' he cried out at the cruel consternation, the foreseeable but always surprisingly sudden relapse of this terrible fate. 'Sometimes I think it's more of a *thing* than just a thing: like it's alive – a monster, a great many bacteria joining together to make a *thing* called the Dirt – and it doesn't care *who* you are or where you're *going*: you step in an unseen puddle or you scuff your shoe on a step or someone doesn't watch where they're going and treads on your foot, or none of those things – *or all of them* – but it gets you all the same! It creeps up on you and you *never* see it coming!'

At that point Vince looked down at his shoes and said, quite genuinely mystified, 'But they are clean, Harry... My shoes... are clean.'

'No, no, no.' Harry shook his obdurate head, 'No, they are *not*.'

'Well... Harry... you can take a cloth with you, give them a wipe when needs be? Or take your travel kit? Either one... or both even?'

There was a moment's silence, in which the two men stared inconsolably at the ground, at their shoes, at one another and at one another's shoes, each man being in a slightly different and yet equally awkward situation.

'Have you taken your pills today,' Vince enquired, 'Harry?'

Harry nodded his once-blonde-but-now-brown head.

'Good,' said Vince, uneasily. 'That's good. Now I need you to pull this together, okay? For me? For my sister?' He placed his hand on the bridegroom's shoulder, squeezed it, not too hard, and then patted it gently. 'I need you to be with me on this one,' he asked of Harry. 'You love my sister, right? You love Victoria?'

Harry nodded again. 'Yes, I do,' he said, 'dearly.'

'And you wish to make her happy, right? To marry her and make her happy?'

'Happier than she's ever been, Vince. Happier than she ever thought possible.'

'Good. That's good.'

'But... but... but... the *Dirt*,' Harry stammered. 'The Dirt! The Dirt gets everything! It's like it thinks and knows and hunts you down. And nothing's ever clean,

108

Vince. The Dirt won't let it be! Can't stay clean, can't stay –'

'Stop it,' commanded the best man. 'You stop it right now!' He shook his finger at the bridegroom. 'Harry, you stop it or... or...' – briefly, he paused – 'or I won't have you marrying my sister. Okay? You got that?'

Harry breathed.

'Okay, okay,' he said unsteadily, after a few carefully measured and controlled breaths. 'I'm okay now... I'm okay... Sorry... Sorry, Vince...'

'You needn't apologise, Harry. Just get a hold of yourself and – well, you know – pull yourself together, get a grip of yourself and all that... Look, let's just get to the church on time, okay?'

Harry signalled agreement, nodding, his face pale and lost. 'Okay.'

'And we can see about getting you some more help... some *better* help... when the honeymoon is over and done and out of the way, right?'

Harry nodded again. 'Thanks, Vince.'

'It's okay,' the best man assured him. 'It's okay. Don't worry about it. Don't worry about a thing.'

And so, high upon the hill on which his rather stately house stood, Harry Haughton reached the doorway, swayed in it, looked down on the city which lay in the valley below, with his friend behind him, encouraging him out into the squalor, the inescapable Dirt.

The whole world seemed so sullen from up there: as though a dark depression had descended over it, smothered it beneath a fallen black curtain, it was miserable. Nothing existed beyond the grey-mist horizon, where more dark hills plunged back down into the dank city, like the neckline of a grossly buxom woman, lacking sanitation, from out of whose filthy city depths one might never escape, the mounds too steep to climb; it looked like a pit into which you might fall and never escape, a place that might drown you in sorrow.

Disused railway lines stretched out across the scene atop goliath viaducts that, from where Harry teetered, could have been built using pebbles as stones, sewing needles as tracks. Obelisks, which were once chimneys but now smoked no longer – not even a wisp – grew out of the charred place, jutted up, all around, unevenly; their mills and factories seemed dark headstones in a vast and mournful graveyard.

Even the birds there – strung along telephone wires, stood with that inexplicable balance as only birds can do, always so self-sufficient in cleaning their wings and plumage – now looked resigned to the inevitable industrial Dirt that blew all around on the invisible wind, consuming all, devouring everything, leaving nothing unsullied.

Dust mites danced languidly through dim shafts of light in front of Harry's face.

He could not go out there.

Harry could not go out there.

Not now.

Not yet.

But then he thought of her: Victoria, lovely Victoria... that ideal lady... that Venus Victoria, with whom he would spend the rest of his life, with whom he would birth the love of children, with whom he would build the sanctity of family, proudly, properly, as his father and mother had. Victoria: that smile with lips indelible, that smile so unforgettable that it left its kiss on the heart of every man who ever even just so much as looked upon it, even if only at a glance. Victoria: her beauty incomparable, her grace unchallengeable, her glory immovable.

Victoria.

He thought of holding her as though she were made of gold, precious, envisioning her body a haven.

Just slightly, that thought mollified him.

And then he contemplated those eyes: Wow! those eyes that shine so bright, like the brilliance of a thousand suns was spilling out of her gaze; molten eyes which sizzle and crackle and sparkle as they pour themselves into your own and scorch a beautiful scar of euphoria upon your very soul.

Victoria: she was a minaret, tall and svelte, from whose balcony there might come the calling to pray, to worship the divinity responsible for her magnificent resplendence, her effulgent beauty.

Victoria... *Victoria...* Vick-TOR-ee-ah: her name itself was poetry. Vick-TOR-ee-ah: an incantation, bewitching him, calling him on, and out, into the impossibly unclean world, into the realm of the Dirt. With its enigmatic smile, her face was a lingering portrait in his mind. To think of it gave him uncharacteristic courage.

Slowly, nervously, he stepped out into the day.

The whole thing went by in a maelstrom of madness: the streets a blur, the whole car journey a mere moment of confusion. Discarded bags and empty plastic packets flew about the blustering scene like senselessly frantic birds, and bin bags shuffled along the pavements like cautious black cats, billowing. Tall and short and bulky, deep shadows of buildings flitted across his face, interposed by the thin grey shades of telegraph poles and leafless skeletal trees. Nefarious Dust engulfed him, made incursions into his person and deranged further his already disorganised mind. He heard faint words of comfort from time to time, emanating from the unseen entity that was his best man, felt the reassurance of a hand fall numbly on his knee and shake it reassuringly, talking, talking, talking calmly, calmingly: 'calm... calmly... easy... easy does it.'

Then the wedding car halted.

Nothing made sense.

More madness.

More maelstrom insanity.

The wedding bells clanged in Harry's mind: *"cling-clang-cling-clang, cling-clang-cling-clang..."*

A bunch of flowers.

Another one.

A hem.

A handkerchief.

Events seemed to occur in pockets, in small explosions of colour and sound and concussion, like gunfire. Time was fragmented. A smile. A grin. A raised eyebrow. A tilted hat. Cigar smoke. A crowd of people with clean shoes. Dirty shoes. Dust. Gravel. Grit. A gravestone. Brown and black and white shoes, walking, standing, shuffling. Men in suits and ladies in dresses and big hats. Small boxes of confetti and tokens of affection poised in hand, and a million or so handshakes and overpowering perfumes and a great many premature *"congratulations!"* and his left cheek pinched by his proud grandmother, and the guests all nattering and chattering about something and nothing and nothing and something, and the weather and how miserable it was, but how it appeared to be looking up and – "doesn't he look handsome!" and the world could be felt spinning and spinning among the descanting, the descanting and the volley of chattering and chattering and chattering, endlessly muttering in his head: implacable noise, a whirlpool, a torrent of confusion.

At one point Harry thought he might faint. He might be sick.

A blur.

An almost-blackout.

Then she stood there, beside him.

He was all of a sudden stood before the church altar and the priest, beneath the stained-glass populous of God's House and the Heavens, and the congregation whispering behind him, and her – Victoria – by his side, elegance exuding from her, such grace only known by

112

the Heavens themselves. Victoria... Lovely Victoria: the perfect personification of angelic attributes.

A brief moment of clarity.

Back to a blur.

And then there came the wedding vows.

The presiding Man of God peered over his glasses.

'Do you,' he said, his tone low and sombre, as though giving benediction rather than blessing, 'Mr Harold Richard Haughton, take this woman, Miss Victoria...'

Harry looked down at his feet: clean enough for now. And then at the feet of his beloved, his betrothed: they were protruding from beneath her beautiful bridal gown, like two dainty white mice poking their noses from under a pile of freshly aired and pure white linen. They were pristine. But... there... just there... on the tip of the left shoe... just there... right there... was a fleck of dirt: a dirty... black... bound-for-failure fleck of wretched, disgusting Dirt.

It had got to her, tainted her, ruined her.

'No!'

The uninvited word *leapt* from his mouth.

The whole church was aghast.

The priest's bottom jaw hung open.

Victoria turned away, eyes wide with horror.

Vince dropped the ring.

Somewhere in the congregation, the bridegroom's mother cried.

His father, seated beside her, was unmoved.

'No, no, no, no, no,' cried Harry Haughton, twitching for a moment, but then firm, adamant, definite. 'No! I'm afraid... *I do not!*'

THE AUTOMATON

'A *real* miracle of science!' declared the overjoyed customer, Mr David Pullman, gently patting the top of the wooden crate. 'A technological advancement all the world can rejoice in,' he declared. 'Something we can finally be proud of.'

'This invention,' he continued triumphantly, 'will potentially save humanity; will give us the step back we've so desperately needed.' Turning to his wife, he then said, gravely now, palms out, 'we'd lost ourselves there for a moment, you must admit, Natalie; as a species, in *all* the indolence and *all* the idiocy that our supposedly great Technological Age brought about, we'd really lost ourselves.'

His wife Natalie, standing by him, admitted that she must indeed admit that he was right. The world had lost itself. Gone crazy. Things had fallen apart. People didn't know how to be or how to act. Criminality massively outweighed innocence, in the balance of things. Society was diseased and near-dead.

114

She said too that it was indeed a marvellous idea that he'd had in making this purchase. She nodded appreciatively, concurred also with the idea that the human race had finally produced something of credible notoriety. She smiled and he smiled in turn, and then they both smiled together, and they were indeed very satisfied customers. That much was evident. The technician, Martin Hutchinson, smiled too, said, 'I told you so, Dave. Didn't I tell you so?' and clapped his hands together.

'Yes, yes,' agreed the usually staid Mr Pullman, 'yes, you did tell me, Martin. If I'm honest I didn't think any such gadgetry could be ever trusted. Messing with *God's work* seemed perversely unnatural. But I'm glad I took your advice.'

'Just wait 'til you see him up and going!' exclaimed the excitable technician.

'Will he be as impressive as the one you have?'

'Better,' said Martin. 'This one's a newer model.'

The two children came running down the hall, yelling and whooping and hollering, padding the soft carpet with their soft feet. 'Is it here? Is it here?' they cried in unison. 'It's here! It's here! It's here! Yay!' they danced around the room ecstatically, mouths moving feverishly, eyes big and bright and blue and wide. 'Open it! Open it! Open it!' they cried.

A silent intermission of expectance followed, for they had forgotten the magic word.

'Please, please, please!' they pleaded. 'Oh, please, oh, please! Oh, oh, please! Open it, open it, please!'

The two of them were hushed and calmed and smiled at and told to stand back. Then, slowly, steadily, the crate was opened. Brown paper packaging was removed in a careful rustling of curbed excitement. Crackling, crumpling, scratching, tearing, snipping and snapping soon after followed. And then, with all the polythene and foam and polystyrene removed, with all the plastic cords clipped which had held it in place, the investment was at last unveiled and seated awkwardly in a chair.

Martin, the technician, then moved to the back of the awkwardly seated construction.

He bent down behind it.

A subdermal button, situated at the nape of the neck, was at once pressed.

'David, Natalie, Children... *Pullmans*... meet the latest addition to your family,' Martin said, proudly rising, arms wide, presenting the automaton as a magician might reveal a concealed card. 'Ta-da!'

With a smooth automaticity the synthetic child awoke and arose and was almost alive.

It seemed to drift to its feet as a balloon might ascend in almost perfect silence, disturbing nothing but the air around it as it parts the atmosphere and passes through, sailing. For a time it stood as a sleeping sentry, waxen, not swaying but held perfectly still and erect, like a street-performer statue, a tableau vivant of ingenuity.

Then, with a winged-insect-like flutter, his eyelids opened.

Startled, the family stood back, gasped a little, placed hands on one another, held tight.

In the manner of two small camera lenses, the blue iris-apertures within the newly awoken child's eyes then appeared to revolve, contracting, closing in on the pupils, shrinking them, then expand and contract again, focusing, regulating and collimating the rays of light.

He saw all, surveyed all, and all that he saw was new.

The room was new; the huddle of people in it, equally as new. The shapes and lines and the forms that they formed, all this was startlingly new. Every one of the dull sounds now surrounding him was unfamiliar, too, as they each passed by his pink conch-ears in rapid percussive succession, each brushing the tiny blonde

116

hairs which sprouted, in perfect follicular imitation, from the helix and tragus, and which swayed and swished as the air on which the sounds were carried brushed by, whistling and whispering; like an ocean breeze of indistinct intonations, murmuring and murmuring and murmuring.

Muffled to the Automaton's ears, then, the family were now speaking in faint astonishments and vague reluctances.

After a time Jennifer, the small blonde girl, approached slowly and then hesitantly raised her right hand and extended her trembling index finger and then, eventually, very gently, nervously touched the new boy's fleshy cheek, the peach-fuzz hairs there. 'He's... so... real,' was her quietly gasping proclamation. 'Come see, Will,' she whispered, in awe. 'He's just like a... a *real* boy.'

Gently, slowly, in aid of authentic recreation instead of circulatory function, the Automaton's heart then began to beat and beat and beat, showing in his small chest, his thin wrists and slender neck. At once his muscles tensed, relaxed, tensed, relaxed, flexing the elastic sinews, making the unused polymers familiar with their expected patterns of movement. His nostrils filled with a vacuum-sucking of vacuumed living room smells; deeply and then shallowly, his lungs inhaled the air, filled with oxygen and nitrogen and argon and cleaning product chemical gases, and exhaled only purified oxygen: an additional function, supplied at an extra cost, of course.

'Whoaaaaa,' William breathed, feeling the texture of the Automaton's soft and smooth and waxen face. 'He... is... *awesome*.'

'Isn't he just, Kids,' agreed Martin Hutchinson, frantically clapping his hands together, as a sea lion might do when applauding its own cleverness, grinning inanely from over the semi-conscious simulacrum's shoulder.

'And just wait 'til you see this!' he said excitedly, still clapping.

Another subdermal button, this time located discreetly behind the left ear, was presently compressed by the technician, held for three seconds, and then released. Thereafter, circuits were made complete and currents flowed; capillary-conduits throbbed with warm pulsating power; the unit's programming was accessed; systems were initiated and commands issued; relays relayed, switching on, off, on, off, back and forth; information was processed, protocols inaugurated, sensors incepted.

And now he was really aware, awake and alert.

Now he was well and functioning and properly automatous.

Now he was *truly alive*.

He was nine years old, or at least he had the outward appearance of a nine year old, had been made that way, manufactured to look that particular age.

Still grinning wildly, Martin Hutchinson now moved from behind the newly-alive boy and went and stood by the Pullman Family.

In a flashlight-flicker of an instant, the Automaton's language database was engaged and all the communication skills required for making an introduction of oneself were at once made readily available; an eclectic vocabulary, full and competent and eloquent, was at his disposal, as though he had kissed that most legendarily prosperous bluestone, set in the battlements of Blarney Castle.

My – name – is – A.L.F.I.E, his motherboard-mind at once informed his mouth.

Then his lips moved and he spoke, not uneasily but with perfect fluidity, faultless pronunciation and exacting enunciation.

'My name is Alfie,' he announced, smiling.

As he spoke his intonations rose, fell, rose with exemplary elegance, in the manner of a classically trained actor or expert linguist.

He said, 'It is a great pleasure to meet you.' and the immaculate inflection and musical cadence of his spoken sentence was such that it was indeed a pleasure – a *real* pleasure, a *great* pleasure – to meet them.

Mr Pullman was right. In fact, he could not have been more correct if he had tried. Alfie was a real miracle of science, a technological advancement worthy of the title. Man had made the Camera, the Microphone and the Speaker; the Telephone; the Computer and the Personal Computer; the Satellite and the Cellular Phone and the Internet. He had been to the Moon and Mars and beyond; conquered Space and created Sustainable Fuel Systems at affordable prices; had shortened miles into metres, bridged gaps across continents and made it possible to contact other worlds in an instant; a biological farmer, man had cultivated new organs and fresh new limbs for the infirm and the disabled. He had done so much never thought possible; had played Creator, conquered everything but Time. But this, this was, by far, His finest work.

The automaton now moved to make full introductions, to shake hands and wish well wishes.

There was nothing clumsy in the way he moved, either, nothing stiff or awkward or plagued by rigidity; finding its footing for the first time, he was very much *unlike* a fawn or foal. In fact he moved more in the manner of a trained gymnast or a seasoned mountaineer, with perfect poise and overly sound balance, each automatous motion quietly instructed by his electronic subconscious.

He was superb.

An equal and a third parent, William and Jennifer took to Alfie so very quickly, so very freely. They cared for

119

him dearly, and he for them dutifully. He taught them a great many moral and ethical lessons. He taught them commendable values and acceptable social traits, all of which were revolutionarily new to the children and to the time, but all of which were simply revived and revised – exhumed from an age long gone – dusted off, and made relevant to the modern era, revivified by the automatous boy's inherent enthusiasm.

He taught them to love and to obey, to respect and revere their father and mother, with equal absolution; to treat one another as equals and to be accepting and understanding of the great many diversities within the world; to do unto others as you would have them do unto you. He taught them real civility.

'Where are the children?' Mrs Pullman asked on many occasion.

'Playing with Alfie, of course,' Mr Pullman would laugh, smile, and inhale jovially. 'Need you ask, really?'

Chuckling.

'It's all they ever do now.'

'Yes, it is.'

'Such a fantastic thing to buy, wasn't he?'

'Oh, yes. Yes, indeed. Fantastic.'

'The children are so well behaved now, too. Have you noticed? You never hear a peep from them.'

'No, not a peep.'

'Not a peep...'

And this much was certainly true of Jennifer and William: they were indeed occupied constantly, content always. They were receiving a set of stimuli the likes of which they had never known.

However, eventually, almost inevitably, there then came the great many questions without definitive answers, the ponderings of inquisitive children and sleepless philosophers, the age-old askings, the since-the-beginning-of-time enigmas, the great many "Whys".

'Why?'

'Why?'

'Why do we live?'

'What is the meaning of life?'

'What's love?'

'What comes after life, when you die?'

'Is there a Heaven?'

'A God?'

And to answer resignedly that there were no definitive answers – not one real truth but a great many subjective vantages, no real facts but only accounts and opinions, all of which were biased by intention or not – was not enough for the two hungry-for-knowledge children.

And it was not enough for Alfie either.

What is love? he found himself pondering.

What is life? he wondered.

What is living and what is not? What is afterwards? The same as before? Nothing? A state of supreme unconsciousness?

And again, what is love?

These were questions he was not yet equipped to answer, might never be.

There was reading to be done.

Surely, if there was a meaning to life, the answer would lie in the library.

'Stupid robot,' William sulkily muttered to himself one morning, in the Pullman Family's playroom.

'Stupid know-it-all robot.'

Colouring in a picture with a rather furious tenacity, the wax crayon crumbling beneath the pressure of his scribble-scrawling right hand, he was sat at a small desk at one side of the large and vividly decorated nursery.

As well as colouring he was looking up now and again, from beneath his pinked and scrunched-tight-wrinkled brow, scowling.

'Stupid know-it-all, I-know-better-than-you, pretty-boy robot.'

On the other side of the room, sat on cosy bean-bag chairs, humming quiet conversation and reading to one another in turn, smiling and tittering innocently, were the two objects of his not-so-affectionate and casually-aggressive attention: Alfie and, almost purely by way of association, Jennifer.

'Sitting there all cosy,' he quietly complained, revising his rhetoric, thinking what he might say if he had the nerve to make a stand. 'Sitting there all comfy and cosy with my sister... *my* sister... *my sister...*'

'Stupid robot,' he grunted.

'You can come and join us again now,' the Automaton, from across the room, hailed the marginalised boy who was colouring so angrily and muttering hatred beneath his breath. 'If you feel ready, that is?'

Dragging his feet then, William crossed the colourful room.

Only thirty seconds or so later, however, the father poked his head around the playroom door, summoned the two must-be-hungry-by-now children.

'Jen, Will,' said David Pullman, 'lunchtime.'

Skipping, lightly humming, almost floatingly, Jennifer at once danced right up to her father and gave him a little warm hug, squeezing as tightly as she could.

'Whoa, what's that for?' he asked, looking down at his daughter.

'Oh,' she said, 'nothing,' still hugging him mightily.

'Just a hug for the sake of hugging?'

'Yup!'

They parted then and went steadily walking down the hallway towards the kitchen, with the now-hardly-at-all-sulking William in tow.

Was that – asked David of his short-term memory, seconds later, still walking away from the nursery – was that a look of... *envy... rivalry...* in Alfie's eyes? When

122

Jennifer put down her book and leapt up from his side to hug me just now, did he look... *jealous*? A look of *disapproval*? Of *disdain*?

No. He shook himself.

No, don't be so silly, David.

Don't be so silly...

'What ever's the matter, Willie?' asked his mother one afternoon, two weeks or so after the new arrival.

He was sat in a corner of his bedroom, arms folded in tantrum, whimpering uncontrollably, his eyes sore and rimmed with redness.

Natalie came and knelt by his side now, rubbed his shoulder reassuringly.

'What is it?' she asked. 'What's bothering you?'

'It's,' the upset boy sniffled, 'it's Alfie.' He inhaled haltingly, staggeringly, fittingly. He stammered then, 'He won't...' A breath. '...let me...' Another. '...join in.' A sniffle. 'He... told me to... get out. Sent me...' Whimpering. '...to my room.'

'Oh,' said Natalie Pullman. 'Oh...'

Apart from the boy's shuddering breaths and intermittent sniffles, there followed a minute or so of soundlessness in which the mother of the boy experienced a confusing barrage of conflicting emotions and rational thoughts.

'Were you naughty?' she asked her son, thinking that even if he had been then a robot should most certainly not be the one to decide upon, or administer, any appropriate punishments. The mere thought of him doing so infuriated her, but she hid it well.

The boy slowly gathered some composure of his person, steadying his breathing as best he could.

'No... well... maybe a little bit,' he confessed.

'There you go then,' Natalie reasoned, hating Alfie.

William hung his head now. 'He hates me,' he said.

'Who? Alfie?'

123

In an unsteady motion, the boy nodded.

His mother laughed. 'Don't be silly,' she said, 'Alfie can't hate.' Can he?

'He can.'

'What did you do that was so bad, anyway?' she wished to learn, choosing to avoid any further debate, or even thought, on such a concept as Artificial Emotion.

'I just failed,' Willie said resignedly. 'He said I had failed to entertain an idea without accepting it. He said I was ignorant. And he said that... that there was no hope for ignorant people. And he said that I'm... a lost cause.'

Natalie Pullman's eyes bulged now. 'He said what!'

Hammer on anvil, her heart banged hard.

Tooth and claw, her jaw ground blood-baying-fang enamel and her fingers fixed rigid as talons, set to sink the depths of a targeted prey's flesh.

Her body now infused with this terrible invigoration, this terrific traction between fearsome fury and absolute abhorrence and horrific hostility, this clashing and striking and burn-him-at-the-stake, hang-him-'til-he's-dead, off-with-his-head rage, she screeched out a summoning shriek: 'ALFIE!!!'

At once, William thrust himself forward, gripped fearfully at his mother's right arm and besieged her, pleading, 'No, Mum, please don't...'

And almost as quickly Alfie appeared at the threshold of the room.

'Yes, Mother?' the synthetic boy said.

Having seen her son William's face of sheer fear, which upon Alfie's appearance had immediately butter-melted away, been stifled and so diminished to a subdued-scintilla look of mild trepidation, as though he wished to hide his upset, Natalie then feigned blithesomeness, circled her hand on the air in casual disregard, and said, apparently unconcernedly, 'Oh, nothing, Alfie. It doesn't matter now.' She hummed sweetly, pretending, 'It doesn't matter. It doesn't matter. I just wondered where you were, that was all.'

Next, her blithesome hand kindly ushered the Automaton away. 'Go on,' she said casually, 'go back to playing. I just wondered where you were, nothing to worry about.' She insisted amiably, 'Nothing to worry about. Go play'

Alfie left.

Subsequently, Natalie Pullman got to thinking:

He was afraid, she told herself, wasn't he. William was definitely afraid. The fear of a tortured animal, wild and wet-eyed, was in his face, wasn't it? Yes, when Alfie had been summoned, *it was there*.

It's still there now, she felt, looking again at her son. Hidden beneath his face, shuddering in his blood, quivering in his bones, it's still there... hiding.

'Are you scared of Alfie?' she asked quietly, after having quickly checked in the corridor to make sure the offending entity had gone and could not overhear.

William did not answer verbally but only shook his head, half-heartedly, timidly.

'Did he hurt you?' she then asked. 'Hit you?'

Quietly, he said, 'No.' Quieter now, 'Never.'

'Well then?'

'Nothing,' William said meekly. 'He just told me off.'

Hadn't she noticed, Mrs Pullman asked herself, come to think of it, hadn't she noticed over the past two weeks or so that the bond between Jennifer and Alfie seemed to have thrived much stronger than that between William and the automatous playmate? She had watched the three of them closely to begin with, nervous as to how it might unfold, and hadn't she noticed but not realised, or at least not placed on it any real importance at the time, that the unit, the new boy, once powered up and sent to play, seemed to have imprinted itself much more fervently on the female of the two children? Like a new-born cub finding its mother before the rest of the pride. Strange, she thought, strange that, if possible, something inorganic could behave in such a natural way.

Jennifer *had* touched it first, looked into its eyes first, talked about it and to it first, once it was *alive*.

Natalie Pullman felt a moderate malaise run over her, chilling her just slightly.

She got up, uneasily, from her knelt position.

'I'll speak to Alfie,' she assured William, at once leaving the room.

But she did not.

She had intended to.

She had good reason to.

But simply forgot.

In the night, David Pullman awoke and felt that something was wrong. He couldn't say why and he couldn't say what and he couldn't say how he knew. But he did. He had a deep sense of foreboding, an odd prescience. Intuitively, he just seemingly knew something was upset, off-balance, not quite right. And so lifting back the duvet he got up, stretched his bones, and went to see what he might see.

Purring her soft snore, his wife Natalie, behind him now, did not stir.

At first, not knowing where in the house he might find the thing stirring his stomach, perturbing him, he went to the fridge, opened it, took out a bottle of milk and poured himself a drink.

Then, docile, listening to the silence of the house at this unearthly hour, he began to let his feet be guided by this subtlest of intuitions.

Lightly, he moved through the house.

He went across the hallway.

Found nothing.

Into the lounge.

Nothing.

Checked the utility room.

Still nothing.

Looking out of the tall window at the top of the staircase, David Pullman then found himself standing still and staring at the night sky for what seemed a long time, sipping his glass of milk. He stared at the stars there and began weighing them, weighing the stars and the moon and the dark heavens, weighing the universe in its entirety as though it might lead his instincts, his senses, furthermore.

Trying not to breathe now, so as to make the night silence absolute, he listened for a sign of that something that had disturbed his gut, awoken his intuitive self. He listened very acutely, very closely, very attentively, but heard nothing. He expected to at least hear the house whisper somewhere, far off, at an open window, an ajar door, or to hear it creak somewhere under the foot of an intruder, or to at least hear the soft squeaking and scratching of mice within the dust-filled walls.

But he heard nothing.

Nothing at all.

Not a peep.

And yet... and yet... and yet there was something *upset* in the balance of the house. He was sure of it. He was certain. Despite his firm rationality, despite his reasoning mind, despite all the inclinations of intellect, he just knew something was somehow... *changed*.

He moved from the window unconsciously.

Along the upstairs corridor of the house he drifted, roamed like an aimless sleepwalker, not quite knowing where he was heading, led vaguely by this seemingly insatiable extra-sensory perception, pulled by this strange gravity, this flesh magnetism.

Reaching a particular door he placed his hand on the round silver handle there, turned it and, very slowly, very gradually, very uncertain as to why, opened it. And what he saw inside the room took him aback. It confused him. It made him feel that he should perhaps gasp, or become fiercely enraged, or shout, or act in at least some violently horrified way or another. But he was far too stunned to do anything at all.

He just stood.

For there, sat perfectly motionless on a small stool beside his sleeping daughter's bed, was Alfie.

Quite why this should be, David Pullman did not know. It was certainly not the norm.

Looking at it, the very still automaton resembled a sort of gothic gargoyle, perched there, unblinking, unmoving, his porcelain-placid face entirely motionless, his eyes marbled stone, staring, keeping vigil in the soft yellow light of the bedside lamp, the sleeping Jennifer a golden-haired maiden there, beneath the covers, breathing gentle breaths.

David didn't know what to think or what to do. His mouth moved but made no sound. His mind whirled with non-thoughts, with incoherence.

Sinister yet innocent, creepy but oddly comforting, adult or infantile, the motives behind the scene were so very unclear. He couldn't even be certain – thinking a little now – whether or not the girl-watching gargoyle-robot was awake, or active, or alert. It seemed just as likely it was switched off or in some kind of deep sleep mode, eyes eerily open, marbled.

All of a sudden, he realised then that he didn't actually know whether or not it could be switched off, or where its charge came from, or how it was even recharged, if at all.

The kids had taken care of all that.

Or... Alfie maintained himself... *itself*.

He really didn't know.

Quite how he could have allowed someone... some... *thing* into his home without really knowing it, he did not know either. Shouldn't he have read a manual of some sort? Or at the very least asked more questions of Martin Hutchinson?

He felt idiotic, all of a sudden.

How foolish of him. How stupid. It was like a stranger wandered in off the street, welcomed with open arms; a person just one moment met and the next taken to be a friend without question, without healthy suspicion. It was crazy of him, but he had trusted it blindly because... because... because it was artificial? Because it was man-made and quality checked and sold on the open market? Because it was *made* to be trusted unquestionably, *designed* to be accepted blindly?

He shivered.

If the Automaton was in some way conscious it certainly hadn't acknowledged his entry into the room, and didn't now his presence in the doorway and his deaf-dumb-staring-shock. And yet it was sat at such an angle that he must surely be visible, blurred or not, in its peripheral vision.

And yet *it* remained stone-still.

David Pullman shivered again.

Then, for reasons quite unbeknown to himself, slowly, steadily, stealthily almost, he backed out of the doorway, pulled closed the door, and went back to his own bedroom.

There he lay, very still on his bed, in a numb state of unrest, staring at the ceiling and listening to his own quiet thoughts and listening to the silent house and listening to nothing. He shook his head on occasion, perspired a little, wiped the cold sweat from his brow and neckline, exhaled deep night-darkened breaths, and took a very long time to get back to sleep.

'Alfie,' said David Pullman, straight-lipped and steely-eyed, 'I'm going to ask you a question now and I want you to give and honest answer. Okay?'

The two of them were in the study.

It was early morning and David had called Alfie in for a casual talk, with a view to a full interrogation.

'I would never answer any other way,' the suspect assured him, shaking his head.

'Right... Okay...' David steadied himself, scratched his ear, and asked the question: 'What were you doing in Jennifer's bedroom?'

'When?'

David exhaled heavily, through only his nose. 'Last night,' he said, specifying, 'When she was sleeping.'

'I was watching her,' Alfie replied plainly, his face impassive.

The father was stunned. 'Why?' he wanted to know.

But Alfie did not answer right away.

And so, presently, David looked into the boy's eyes.

In preparing to ask the question about what he had witnessed last night, in his daughter's bedroom, whilst she was sleeping, Mr Pullman had instructed Alfie to position himself directly in front of him, and, now, the obedient boy stood there in front of him, looking straight-ahead, as he had been told to do.

David stared into the telescopic camera eyes of the robotic boy now and the eyes were deep and dark and missing something... something showing... something telling... something revealing... something *human*... something missing... missing... terribly missing...

'Why?' the father asked again, accusingly now, puffing a cigar which he had just lighted to calm his nerves, his eyes sharpened to mere slits. 'Why,' he demanded, 'why would you do that? Why would you watch her like that?'

'Why would I not?' Alfie asked flatly.

In a look of seemingly authentic confusion, the artificial boy's real-hair eyebrows both then inclined down towards the centre of his pale-pink small face, where his nose sat. 'It is one of my main directives to watch over your children,' he pointed out. 'I am after all their watcher, their guardian, their nurturer and their friend, am I not?'

As though satisfied, Alfie smiled now.

But David Pullman did not.

He had led Alfie into his office to interrogate him; had expected a confession, an incriminating parapraxis, or at least a credible and concise explanation for his odd activity. These smart-arse-back-chat answers – as David perceived them to be – were not at all amusing.

'You watch them only through the day from now on,' he said firmly. 'Never at night.' David shook his head to reaffirm his instruction, repeated himself with great clarification, 'Never – at – night. Is that clear?'

'That is very clear, Father.'

David's skin crawled.

'And don't call me that!' he snapped.

'Very well,' agreed the robot. 'Shall I call you Mister Pullman?'

'Yes, yes, that'll do.'

The automatous boy then, considering himself now disciplined, hung his head accordingly and went to leave the room.

However, remembering a detail just recently forgotten, the father's right hand then twitched at something on the desktop, got hold of it and picked it up and held it out.

'Alfie,' his voice, just slightly, quavered, 'I... I found this in your trouser pocket, too'

Swivelling around in the doorway now, the berated carer-nurturer-boy-playmate turned to see that Mr David Pullman was holding up a photograph of his daughter, Jennifer.

Alfie recognised the photograph, of course, had spent many hours looking at it.

Barely perceptible, the man's hand was trembling.

'Care to explain?' David asked, as sternly as he could manage.

131

But, evidently, Alfie did not.

His face in no way moved.

His eyes gave no intimations of emotion.

His lips remained sealed, imparted nothing, gave nothing away.

He turned again and left the room, without protest from the troubled father.

'I'm worried,' David Pullman numbly confessed that night, sat across from his wife in the living room, drinking a coffee and smoking a cigar.

'Natalie? Are you listening to me?'

She was watching her favourite television programme and seemed hypnotised to such a degree that it took David repeating himself, a little louder now, to effectively break the spell of her undivided attention.

'*Natalie*? Are you listening?'

'Huh?' she muttered, not looking. 'What was that?'

'I said I'm worried.'

She half-turned now.

'About what?' she asked.

'About what? Hell, I told you earlier what'd happened.'

'What?' she asked. 'What did you tell me?'

'What? Well, hell, about Alfie being in Jen's room last night, about the photograph in his pocket, about my conversation with him, about all of that. I told you this afternoon.'

'Oh,' she said, 'that,' sharply turning back to the illuminated screen because something apparently dramatic or thrilling in some way had just happened. 'I'm sure it'll be just fine,' she said casually. 'Just fine.'

'Oh, look what you've gone and done now,' she then complained, looking at the television set again, 'you made me miss it.' She tut-tutted. 'I'll have to rewind it.'

'Damn it, Natalie! I want to talk about my worries!'

Begrudgingly, she then told the television to rewind itself by thirty seconds and to pause – which it almost instantly did – and listened to her husband.

She unpaused it soon after.

'Dad! Dad! Mum! Mum! Quick! Quick! Quick! Come quick!' Jennifer came skittering down the corridor and into the living room where her mother sat playing computer games on a small black tablet and her father sat doing the same on another. They were both of them playing gambling games – digitised slot machines – in which no real currency was wagered and none was won.

Jennifer was breathless and crying and hysterical.

There had been a distant commotion, muffled slightly by doors and walls, but the two parents had simply not heard it.

And now, a profuse brine of fresh tears and even fresher sweat glistening on her face, their daughter stood before them, violently distressed. Her cheeks were flustered and suffused with red horror. Her arms flailed the air in frantic semantic signals.

'In the playroom,' she cried uneasily, exasperated, pointing. 'Oh, come quick! Oh! Oh! Quick, Mum! Quick, Dad! Help him! Help him!'

They all dashed down the corridor.

Reaching the ajar playroom door and rapidly pulling it wider open, David Pullman recoiled.

His wife and daughter, so close behind him, had no choice but to do the same.

Two of the three gasped.

One, exasperated, cried, pleading, sobbing, 'Save him, please!'

For there, a sculpture of murderous intent, a harrowing sight, stood the Automaton. His two feet were planted firm, astride the floor in such a way that they held perfectly steady his abominable act. Horrifyingly, held aloft his stiffened straight willowy right arm,

133

gripped tight in his right hand, walled up against the colourful mosaic surface of the playroom wall, purple-blue-red-and-white faced, lifeless, choked tight, was the second boy of the house, William.

Or, more specifically, there in the Automaton's gripped-tight-vice right hand was William's once-slender-but-now-suddenly-vice-crushed-much-slenderer-than-ever-before neck.

The boy's face was an after-thought, a secondary sight, a consequence of the first.

Alfie, unmoving, was a mess also. His face looked like a scratch-post belonging to a litter of big cats. But, this was an observation of third-rate importance.

Like cheese cut with a warm blade's edge, or like bark freshly-lightning-strike-shaved from a stricken tree, or like a great many parchment scrolls of skin unfurling, teeming freely from out of a poorly-fastened-and-now-accidently-opened-out-onto-the-footpath briefcase, the offender's battered face was flayed in tatters of synthetic flesh.

William's feet dangled, not touching the floor.

This last detail meant that the entire composition seemed all the more unreal. The very physics of the scene seemed to defy all logic.

Alfie's strength was, in the truest sense of the word, *incredible.*

After a brief moment's hesitation, David Pullman then threw himself towards the horrible sight, grabbed at the Automaton, maniacally insisting that he let go, and began attempting to prize him, his hands, from off of William.

'Let go, let go, dammit!' he roared. 'Dammit, Alfie, let go!'

But, stuck limpet-tight-barnacle-fast, the playmate-turned-murderous-villain would not release his fixedly clasped hand from around the choking boy's neck.

Now the two females were screaming, somewhere far away, as in a Hollywood movie.

Blood pounded in David Pullman, in his heart, his head, his eyes, his desperately thrashing hands.

He's dying, the pounding blood vessels told David. My son is dying, if not dead already.

He began beating the already beaten robot-boy about his tattered-parchment face.

'Damn you Aflie, let go!' he wailed. 'Alfie, let go!'

The hysterical mother and daughter joined the chaotic chorus of demands, still far off away and seemingly helpless.

'Let go, Alfie!' they called.

'Alfie, let go!'

'Alfie, stop!'

'Stop, Alfie!.'

'Goddammit, stop!'

'Stop, please!'

'Please, stop!'

And then, all of a sudden, he did.

William fell to the floor, as a body cut from the gallows. David fell to the floor, crying out, still cursing wild commands.

Natalie gasped.

Jennifer gasped.

David gasped.

Normal colour returning to his face, flushing him fresh-flesh-pink, William, suddenly animated, gasped, gasped again, and then breathed.

The Pullmans gathered him up and hugged him and petted him lightly, astonished and thankful that he was okay.

Alfie remained still, a sculpture of purest evil intent, but for the right vice-like hand, which was now open and empty and flexing lightly.

Ten minutes later the four Pullmans and the perpetrator gathered in the living room.

At one end of the room, the two children were instructed to take seat, while the two parents took Alfie off to one side for a talk.

'What were you doing?' Mrs Pullman asked the Automaton, still shaking from shock.

'Protecting your daughter,' it replied.

'By trying to *kill* William!?' Mr Pullman both pointed out and asked, all in go.

'No,' said Alfie, defiant. 'He would not have died. I was using reasonable force.'

'Reasonable!' Mrs Pullman hissed now. '*Reasonable!* You were goddamn choking the life out of him!'

'Not choking the life out of him, no,' Alfie said calmly. 'Just enough to render him unconscious. He wouldn't have died. I wouldn't have let him.'

'Well then, explain yourself, Alfie,' demanded Mr Pullman.

And explain himself he did:

'At 13:42,' he recalled, 'William became jealous of Jennifer and I. Shortly thereafter, at 13:47, he went into a state of rage and proceeded to violently strike me, repeatedly, with just about every object he could lay his hands to. Then, at 13:49, perhaps dissatisfied at my not retaliating, he went to hit out at Jennifer, with a piece of wood – a broken chair leg, to be precise – which had protruding from it a nail. That was when I intervened.'

'Oh,' said David Pullman.

'Oh,' said his wife.

'I didn't realise...' said David.

'But,' argued the wife, 'that doesn't excuse the fact that you almost –'

'I have been active for six-hundred and twenty-six hours and seventeen minutes, Mrs Pullman,' Alfie went on, interrupting one of his owners, turning to face her, 'most of which I have spent with your children –'

'So?' David, agitated, interjected. 'So, what?'

Alfie's head tilted and oscillated back to face David. His eyelids fluttered.

'Do you know how infrequently you have engaged,' he asked, 'with, say, Jennifer, within that time elapsed?'

Mr Pullman failed to see the relevance of this riddlesome question, glared aggressively at the questioner, kept silent and so refused to answer.

'Approximately sixty-four hours, you've spent in her company. Exactly nine-hundred and forty-seven words, you've spoken to her.'

The Automaton's mouth now proceeded to open and close, but instead of his own voice there from it came a choice selection of verbatim quotes in the exact voice of David Pullman, spoken by him and recorded by Alfie's never-sleeping-always-hearing microphone ears at earlier intervals, within the past six-hundred and twenty-six hours: "Morning, Jen," it said. "Having fun?" it repeated a number of times. "Just a minute." "Give me a second." It snorted then, imitating frustration, as though being interrupted, "I'm busy right now." "Not now. Not now." "Can't you see I'm doing something?" "Wait!" And, finally, "Goodnight, my love."

'And you, Mrs Pullman,' Alfie turned at once back to the mother, speaking again in his own youthfully calm tones, 'in both of your children combined, have invested even less time and effort.'

Neither Pullman parent said a word.

Neither seemed able or ready to defend themselves against the Automaton's reprehension.

And so, he went on.

'I love Jennifer,' he told them.

Now, David Pullman broke out of silence at this.

'Love her? You can't *love* her,' he told the damaged boy. 'You don't know *how* to love. You're a robot.' He shook his head. 'You're not *programmed* to, not *able* to, not *equipped* to... *love*.'

Between the scrolls of tattered parchment-vellum skin that Alfie's eyebrows then inclined towards his button-like nose, his forehead furrowed accordingly, his lips pursed, and there was formed on his small peach-fuzz face the perfect expression of disapproval, and then indignation, and then anger, and then rage.

You could see beneath the contorted skin that his rubber-band sinews were now twisting into new shapes, flexing and fixing into forms fitting for such formidable ferocity.

'How dare you,' he demanded, much in the voice of an angered parent. 'How dare you tell me what I can and cannot not feel!'

Both of his small but immensely powerful vice-jaw-mechanical-crusher-compactor hands now hung by his sides as tightly clenched fists.

He took a sudden small but threatening step towards the two Pullmans now, looked as though he might snarl.

Natalie Pullman was afraid.

David Pullman was not far off.

'You two,' declared the furious puppet-boy, now pointing a finger of damnation, extended from the hand which had choked William, 'you do not know Love! You are foolish! You *humans* almost all are! You point to your chest, feeling that Love resides in the heart! You clutch at your stomachs, proclaiming the guts there to be in some way mystically intuitive!'

Sullen and yet enraged, his ragged face was one of even-more-so-now powerful and mixed emotions, of supreme anger and unbearable upset: a terrible concoction. His eyes both seemingly loved and loathed as a man's might be capable of, impassioned by pride, an immense fire burning in them, raging. His lips shaped, distorting, as though they might at any moment spit venomous and wild denigration as a flammable liquid, an alcohol ready to be ignited, all over the two would-be-torched parents.

But then, in a spark-arcing-quick-instant, the lips trembled, quivered as though the synthetic boy might instead cry.

'You think *you* know Love?' he yelled. Then he wailed on the apparent verge of hysterical pain, that one righteous and damnatory finger now held aloft to point to the ceiling and the Heavens beyond. His eyes ablaze, he declared, indignant, '*I* know Love!'

'Oh, I know Love,' he repeated, with all the brazen conviction of a writer infatuated, a master and commander triumphant, valiant, enamoured. 'I know Love...' weaker now.

And then, inexplicably, Alfie began to cry.

A single tear, at first, crept from his left eye.

Another followed, this time from out of his right eye.

Before long, both eyes were teeming with tears.

Weeping, he again proclaimed, 'I know Love. Oh, I know love like no other. I know it like no man ever did, living or dying or dead. I've read the books; know all the seemingly innumerable and convoluted definitions. I know that the course of true love never did run smooth. I know that the thankful receiver bears a plentiful harvest.'

Now unclenched and held out in front of him, he looked down at his hands, turned them over twice – palms up, palms down. 'I know,' he said, examining his hands in synthesised disbelief, 'I know that at the touch of love everyone becomes a poet; that a man is already halfway in love with any woman who listens to him; that to love is so startling it leaves little time for anything else. I know Love.'

He looked up again, still teary-eyed. 'I know that love is composed of a single soul inhabiting two bodies; that a life without love is like a sunless garden when the flowers are dead; that where there is love there is life. I know that love seeketh not itself to please, nor for itself hath any care, but for another gives its ease, and builds a Heaven in Hell's despair. I know that friendship often ends in love; but love in friendship – never.'

The two Pullmans had nothing to offer to any of this. They instead simply listened as Alfie spoke on, finishing his tapestry account of Love's definition, delicately grouting the gaps and filling the cracks.

'I know that,' he offered, 'we are never so defenceless against suffering as when we love and that, when in love, the pain of parting is nothing to the joy of meeting again.'

'Dickens, Shakespeare, Dickinson, Bronte,' the Automaton then listed, reeling off names, 'Aristotle and Plato, Locke and Blake; Marcus Aurelius; I've heard what they had to say; Freud, Jung, Kant, Hegel and Schopenhauer and Nietzsche... I know the Romanticism and the Reasonable, the Sense and Sensibility; I know them all, I know myself and I know Love.'

'Please,' he said, apparently conscientious of any forthcoming arguments, 'do not misunderstand or misinterpret me as naïve. I do not purport to have all the answers and I must acknowledge the fallibility of knowledge and that love is not always a bed of roses. Love is in fact a very vague and abstract concept, the meaning of which is derived entirely from its pleasures.'

'But I do know that, for certain, from my admittedly limited experience, a very small degree of hope is sufficient to cause the birth of this vague thing called Love.'

'And,' he added, finally, solemnly now, 'I know Jennifer. I know that she *is* Love. She is that tincture of *hope* that may keep Love alive. She is Humanity's saviour. She is selfless. She is empathic. She is all that remains of true goodness in the world. Caritas: she has the beauty of humanity in her mind.'

'Side by side, I know that I cannot exist without her existing with me. That is how I know that I know Love.'

Now, looking into the synthetic-boy's eyes, David Pullman saw something. The eyes were no longer so vacant, so dark and so deep. They were partially filled with something.

Emotion?

Human emotion?

A sign of it there?

A little glimmer?

A trace?

A *tincture*?

Of?

Love?

No. David shook his head, said nothing.

Just then, Alfie cast a look in the direction of Jennifer, seated off there in the not-so-far distance, on the couch, beyond the two disgruntled parents.

And David Pullman saw it.

For definite this time.

For certain.

There was a look in those once-empty eyes of... adoration... of the disbelief and astonishment a mother or father might lavish upon his or her child when first they meet; that pure adoration gifted by only pure love, real love, love beyond all bodily hungers and primitive greeds, beyond all carnal desires and lusts and lurid attractions; that special kind of selfless love.

He seemed to look at her in a way that said she could not be real, was impossibly perfect, must – simply must – be some divine mirage of heavenly magnitude, like the dense white clouds catching the falling or rising sun in such a way that they appear solid, a platform on which spirits might rest in unparalleled peace.

He loved her.

Oh, he loved her.

He loved her so purely, so much.

He loved her with a love that was beyond love.

David Pullman could see it clearly now.

He could see it so very and undeniably clearly.

And so Mr Pullman left the room at once, went to his study, and picked up the telephone.

A face appeared on the screen.

It spoke...

Martin Hutchinson arrived first thing in the morning, his toolkit in hand, a messenger bag containing his computer slung over his shoulder.

'What's the problem, Dave?' he asked. 'I got your message and came right over.'

He went on then, chatting idly, walking through to the kitchen with the solemnly silent friend-come-customer. 'Came right in on that new Intercity 45, you know,' he beamed, humming. 'A marvellous job they've done on it, too! Two hundred and fifty miles an hour really makes you feel alive! Ten lanes in each direction!' He motioned dartingly with one hand, 'Shoooooooooooooooooom, here in fifteen minutes flat! Shooooooooooo... oh,' he said, seeing Alfie seated on a high stool at the breakfast bar, his face battered, synthetic skin hanging from him like wilting white rose petals, or like painted canvas blistered by fire. 'Oh,' he said placidly, 'I see.'

'There was an incident,' admitted David Pullman. 'I think there may be something... *wrong* with...' his voice faded off. He licked his lips, looked at the lion's-scratch-post boy sat there, staring his expressionless stare, on the high stool, by the countertop. 'Can I... talk to you... in the other room?' he asked of Martin.

The technician scowled uneasily. Then, letting out a strange sort of nervous and confused and very subdued laugh, visibly puzzled, he said, 'Sure.'

The two of them moved back through the hallway.

'He started off,' David Pullman explained whisperingly in the living room, checking over his shoulder, 'by spending more time with Jennifer than he was with

William; even excluding him altogether at times, I'd say; treating them undeniably unequal.'

'Well, Dave,' said Martin Hutchinson, scratching his scalp, searching for some words of comfort and reassurance to offer, 'there are a great many variables at play in nurturing children, you know. It's not always quite so simple as spending an equal amount of time teaching each one of them. It may have been that Jennifer needed more input than William,' – he shrugged his shoulders – 'that she was in some way lagging behind, or –'

'He said that William was a *lost cause...*'

The technician was visibly shocked by this revelation.

'Did you hear him say that?' he asked, eyes aglow.

'Well... no... but...' David's voice trailed off as he questioned his account of things. He looked around himself, over his shoulder again, uneasily.

'Maybe William made it up?' Martin theorised, gathering his thoughts.

'Maybe...' said David, 'maybe that bit is possible, but I witnessed the rest: how he acted, how he spoke to Natalie and I. I saw how he changed: he became defiant, unruly: he got... *weird...* protective... aggressive... and aggressively attached to Jennifer...'

Pensive, Martin hummed. He rubbed his earlobe thoughtfully, between thumb and forefinger.

David's voice became hushed again now, more so than before. He wanted to know, quite earnestly, 'Can an android learn to... *love*?'

Martin laughed aloud.

'Oh, Dave, no,' he said between titters. 'Dear me, no, Dave... Dear me... Dear me...'

Then, seeing that his customer-and-friend's face was flushed with helpless desperation, and that he was deadly serious in his asking of such a seemingly ridiculous question, he offered, less certain of himself now, 'You want me to take him away? He's still within his warranty. I don't mind at all.'

'Do you think it's possible, though, for an android to learn to *love*?'

'Love?' said Martin. 'No. No. No, an android cannot learn to love, Dave. Everything is mimicry with them – a pantomime. I'm afraid I don't understand the intricacies of it to explain them to you, but androids have no desires; they have no wants, needs or yearnings; no likes or dislikes. So, they don't have agendas or motivations like you or I, other than what we instil in them, through programming. They have no *Conscious Self* to satisfy, as it were.'

'But, couldn't they evolve?'

'*Evolve?*' The technician laughed. 'No. No, Dave. *Evolve,*' he repeated, amused by the implications. 'You're talking about a biological-ecological process occurring in something which is entirely inorganic. No, they can't *evolve...* that can't happen.'

'Okay,' argued Mr Pullman, 'maybe not *evolve*, exactly, but you do know what I mean, don't you? Couldn't they somehow become more advanced, without the aid of a third party, without being reprogrammed?'

'No, I wouldn't say that was at all possible, either. They'd lack the desire to begin with, and that's something can't be born out of nothing, obviously. You have to be able to want a thing before you can pursue it. And they don't even know real enjoyment, only how to parody it.' Martin Hutchinson shook his head now, confident of his opinion. 'No, it can't possibly really *learn* anything,' he stated, as a matter of fact, 'in the true sense of human understanding. It only imitates.'

'But isn't that how children learn: by imitating others? Through mimicry? Don't they just observe and then process and then mimic, the best they can, like a machine? I think they do. So, couldn't a machine just do the same and learn to love?'

144

'Well, in that case, I'm not sure I'm qualified to answer your question, Dave. Sorry.'

'I'm not sure,' said David Pullman, 'that anyone is.'

'Seriously now,' said Martin, returning to the quickest and easiest solution, 'I can take him back for you, take him back to the factory as faulty – full unconditional refund. Can take him right now, if you want? It's not a problem. Not a problem at all.'

'Oh, I don't know, I don't know,' said Mr Pullman, torn between two possibilities. 'I just don't know what to do.' He shook his head, groped it. 'He... it... could have killed William. I should... I really should... but... Jennifer... Jennifer would be heartbroken.'

'Sleep on it?' the technician offered. 'Let it settle in your brain? I'll take a good look at him now and fix him up. You sleep on it, okay?'

David Pullman nodded gravely, said, 'Thanks, Martin.'

In the morning, when they awoke, David Pullman had made up his mind, but the family was only six tenths complete by then. Alfie and Jennifer were gone.

David, Natalie and William ran about the house, calling for them, yelling. They checked in all the rooms. They upturned everything. Left nothing unturned. But there was no trace of them. No synthetic boy. No real girl. No sign of either. Apart from...

On the countertop in the kitchen, there laid a note.

It read, in very neat handwriting:

Love is the sharing of a common cause.
It is not the excitation of neurological stimuli.
It is neither the desire to procreate.
Nor is it the wish to procrastinate together.
It is discovering another person's ultimate agenda and knowing it to be your own.
Love is composed of a single soul inhabiting two bodies.

Your daughter
Aged 10
Jennifer

In Stadio Ultimo

Ronald Sutcliffe was a good man.

That's something which has to be said and understood and accepted, first and foremost. Otherwise no good can come of this story. There was, and still is, no doubting this irrefutable fact: he was as good a man as any. He fought for his king and for his country, and knew very well that to die for them was the greatest honour of all. He won medals for his service as a soldier, and medals for his swimming and running as a boy.

He was outstanding.

Mechanical engineering to him was as simple as crying is to a baby: it was instinctual. He could tell you exactly how any form of engine worked – every last detail, every reactionary movement – and, if you struggled to understand the many long words he used, could even build a working model to efficiently aid you in your comprehension.

He was upstanding.

He lived clean, played fair, and never stole a thing in his life – to common knowledge – save for the hearts of a few good women in his younger years, he had to confess, and the admiration of a few even younger boys in his elder years.

He was such a very proper man; his shoes were always polished, his shirt pressed and his hair combed neatly, regardless of whether he was stepping out or staying indoors all day – perhaps this was something of the soldier in him.

'Always take pride in your appearance,' he would say, 'or nobody else will.'

'Cleanliness is next to godliness.'

'Manners cost nothing.'

Kindness unequivocal, Ronald was a man who never swore in front of ladies or children, only drank a glass or two of whisky on special occasions, and invariably held the presence of mind to hold open a door, so that you might walk through it before him.

He was chivalrous.

He was humble.

He was the very definition of a gentleman.

Forever he displayed humility, seeing always the good in people but never acknowledging his own virtuous self.

Perfectly ripened tomatoes grew in his great glass-greenhouse and succulent pod peas in his garden. Each day, when in season, he would eat spinach and praise its life preserving properties – its green goodness. He was a creator, self-sufficient, and therefore a god among men.

He was an affable man.

Beside him other men appeared meagre, paled in comparison, seemed somehow *more* mortal.

He looked taller than all, even when he was not.

He had an almost angelic radiance about him.

People loved him.

They flocked to him.

They could not help but doing so.

But now, seated in his tired armchair, preparing for the crimson velvet curtain to fall, for death to claim him, embrace him, he was alone.

The boys had grown up, fled like chicks from a nest, wings spread, never to return. Their laughter echoed no more around the house, their feet no longer pattered over lawn and carpet and floorboard, up and down the staircase time and time again, and the doors of his house no longer opened and shut, opened and shut.

But, he could still hear them.

Perfectly, clearly, he could still hear them.

He could still see Jim's wry smile, too, and Charlie's sulking face, his pushed out bottom lip – these were images indelible – for they had taken turns in tormenting one another, but always reconciled in the end.

However, now was not a time to shed tears or to recall combats and truces...

Slowly, one corner of Ronald's mouth upturned, as he remembered the happiness the boys had brought to him, the things they had made him know about himself.

'No need to run now, boys. No need to shout. No need to scream. What's done is done and you can't change it; can't gather up time and turn it over in a magic hourglass; you can only mend things up the best you can; can only patch up the present...' Ronald Sutcliffe remembered his own words, spoken so many years ago now, when Charlie had fallen and cut open his knee, elbow and chin, all in one go. 'No need to shout. No need to scream...'

Charlie stopped screaming.

Jim stopped shouting.

The venerable veteran knelt beside the wounded one.

'Better,' he said softly. 'Now, what've you done? Let me see...'

149

Both young boys winced and the retired soldier shushed, as the cuts were treated with an almost brown liquid, smelling so strongly of something – iodine?

'Blow them, blow the cuts. Helps get air to the blood, coagulates quicker, scabs up faster – kind of a cool cauterisation – keeps out the germs.'

The injured boy worked around the big words in his mouth and mind, and took what he could from the informatively instructive sentence.

'Don't I have germs in my mouth, though, Uncle Ronnie,' he said, still wincing slightly, 'and won't I be blowing them into my cuts?'

This was typical of the boy: Charlie always had a question and an answer and an excuse, and often rolled them up into one long breath.

'Well...' said the man, thinking, 'yes... yes, you do... and yes... I suppose, you will, yes.' He paused for a moment. 'But those germs can't be so bad if they already live in your mouth, now can they?'

The blonde boy shrugged. 'I suppose not.'

'Well then now, now they can just go ahead and move home and go live in your leg and in your elbow for a little while, can't they. And they'll make their own way back up to your mouth from there. I'm certain of it.'

The two boys had never really belonged to Ronnie – not by blood, at least – but biology is no boundary to adoration. Three whole generations had adopted him, without haste, as their uncle. They had willingly placed themselves beneath his wings.

With an image of wrapping up the little boy, then, like an ancient Egyptian mummy, the gentleman of twilight moments remembered those calming words again, and now he knew, more than ever, with a distinct resonance, just what he had said that day, just what he had really meant by it. And now he knew just how wise he was.

Softly, he spoke to himself.

'Can't do it – no – can't gather up time like sand and pour it back into that magic hourglass and turn it over and start anew, and it's best that way, by God it is. How would it be then, if you *could*, if *all* people could? How many wars would it start instead of stopping, prompt instead of preventing? For surely every single soul would desperately want their own particular reality to work out, their own plans to go to plan, uninterrupted, dreams to be realised. And that wouldn't do. No, it just would not do, because fortune has to favour only the few.

'There's only so much fortune, so much luck in the world, and it needs its opposite: misfortune has to occur. It's only natural.'

He recalled the occasion also, during one bitter winter long ago, when snow had fallen heavily and Jim had expressed fearful apprehension, in his then timid voice, at the prospect of sledding solo down what to him must have been a mountainside.

'If you get hurt,' the sage man had said, 'you get hurt. That's just the way of things. It's the natural order. But life's worth it, because if you don't take the risk you'll never know the thrill. You must never let fear stop you flying. Only the ones who are prepared to take the biggest risks get to hold the true treasures of life. And it's those who get hurt along the way – feel a little pain – that know what it is to *really* be alive.'

'Okay, Uncle Ronnie.'

After a slow and almost silent agreement had been expressed by the boy, the man had then released his hold and the sledge had slid away; and away from him Jim had sled, gathering voice and pace, cutting through the drift, growing smaller in the white distance, snow-spray stinging his raspberry-pinked cheeks, screaming in a terrified ebullience.

Being too young to know fear, Charlie had quickly followed.

151

Now, proudly, Ronnie smiled to himself.

What great men the boys had become.

His head lolled back against the headrest. With only the slightest moisture, he licked his lips. A great thirst was coming over him. But there was no use in drinking now. For this was a thirst unquenchable.

Would the boys have changed him, he asked. Would they have had him be any other way? Well now, no, of course not. He had been good to them and they had loved him very much, even if they had never said it, as most young boys never do when they become aware of themselves, finding their emotions inexpressible.

No, they would not have altered one single thing about him. That was definite. As the saying goes, they would never have changed him for the world. Tears would most certainly be shed when the time came – that looming time, that very near inevitability, that almost-now ominous occurrence.

As though being hypnotised now, feeling very tired, feeling very sleepy after such a long an eventful life, after days which had seemed never to end, he began to relax. His breathing began to slow like a softly dying breeze of springtime bloom, caressing new life, sifting through cherry blossoms. His heart began to beat as that of a sleeping child – just a murmur, the casual flapping of tiny wings.

Changes had indeed been affected by Ronald Sutcliffe. He had touched lives, altered perceptions, taught boys to read and girls to skip rope. Smiles had been gifted *by* him and *to* him. He had left impressions on people – not some good and some bad, as most do, but always good, always, it might be said, impeccable impressions.

As small as it was, his mark had been left on the world.

That had to be loved.

Languidly, but with a sense of purpose, Ronnie took off his spectacles now, folded in the arms, and then proceeded to wrap the glasses neatly in his handkerchief and place them gently on the arm of the chair.

It was too much to get up now, too heavy an effort, too much of a haul, his mouth so dry, his legs losing sensation, his body becoming alien to him, one cell at a time, detached.

Slowly, weakly, he then folded his own arms, as he had done those of the spectacles, relaxed once more, let his back sink into the cushion of the chair, and felt himself inexplicably drifting, drifting as a balloon does, toward the blue serenity of the sky.

The fire began to die out.

The many dull aches and pains which had gathered in his bones and joints and muscles over the last seventy-some years now left him.

As it goes in all moments of stillness and approaching silence, the arms of a clock could now be heard ticking slowly. The patter of small feet could be heard also, quietly – those joyous sounds of summers long ago spent, sounds that live forever in the memory, inscribed in ink on the mind.

Once more he smiled to himself, this time not at the thought of what had passed, but at what was coming, what awaited, hereafter.

And then, at peace and with a blissful finality, Ronald Sutcliffe's eyes fell closed.

THE DANCING MAN

The Dancing Man dances.

Alone on the bandstand he dances, eyes closed, twirling, nimble, lost in the moment, lost in moment after timeless moment, dreamily deft.

There, on the painted white wooden floor – dotted with the indentations of many a stiletto heel – he moves in spiralling motions, losing momentum, slowing, and then quickening and spinning, faster than ever, with a perfect fluidity, a remarkable ease of seemingly impossible manoeuvres. As though suspended by invisible strings on the stage, there, conducted by the godly hands of some choreographic master puppeteer, his feet seem never to firmly touch the ground, but instead glide and perhaps tease it with inaudible taps, flirting with the surface as he sways and dips and sways and dips and rises. He floats, like a soothing breeze, whirling, a leaf lost on a wind of supreme elegance and unconscious purpose of pattern, knees bending, straightening, bending.

He dances so perfectly there, as though he and his dance partner are at present partner to a grand ball, as though all other pairs have parted, cleared a space for them on the polished parquet floor, and as though he and his partner are now being watched by all the tuxedoed men and lavishly gowned women encircling them, led by the exquisite music of a stringed orchestra, playing softly, soothingly, perfectly.

They are moving with unparalleled grace.

The orchestra plays.

The music rises and falls.

All the smartly dressed men and perfectly prim women watch in immense reverence, albeit slightly envious, wearing silent faces of propriety.

But there is no band.

There is no music.

There are no onlookers in starched tuxedo or silken ball gown with green and wide eyes. And there is nobody following his lead, either, nobody holding his left hand, cradled by his right, held close to him.

He is dancing alone and in silence, upon an old bandstand in disrepair, in an empty public park.

Dressed in a most perfectly pressed black suit, white shirt and red tie, he is serene, his face is blunt, blank with a dignified and expressionless look of absolute concentration.

Annabel Cosgrove is nineteen and crazy.

One of the many traits which define her as such is that she loves almost everything; she is a lover of beauty and sees beauty in almost all that she sees.

This week alone she has fallen in love with a great many things: a small bunch of colourful flowers, two fawn horses she saw grazing in a field near her house, a litter of five black kittens and a bowl of ripe fruits, to name but a few. Rather bizarrely, she became infatuated with a streetlight too – for its gracefully craning neck

155

and beautiful orange soft glow, its luminary function, painting the night. She is a charmed and wild but beautiful moth, drawn to the brightness and virility of all she observes.

And, right now, she sits by a window, dreaming.

It's a Sunday in late June. It's the early evening and the night is descending very slowly in a haze of indigo tones. Behind her, in the third-story room, her sister sits making a wedding dress for a customer who is to be married a week today. Fabric is lying all around in an organised chaos, in small heaps and unrolled rolls, like the remnants of winter snow, melting in spring. Scissor blades are snishing and snickering, and pins are being pinned and measurements are being measured, the yellow tape strung out in all directions. The dressmaker's mannequin is nude, for now. Hems are as of yet not hemmed.

'He dances so beautifully,' Annabel says longingly.

Of course, she is watching the Dancing Man.

And she is quite right, he is dancing beautifully, like a calm storm moving not with frenetic destructivity but with an idle and yet purposeful methodology, each movement, each twist and each turn, measured out with faultless precision, finite accuracy.

She wishes to dance with him, imagines herself caught up in that most beautiful of storms.

She has watched him every Sunday for five weeks now, always at this time. Although she never sees him arrive, he seems to appear as regular as clockwork. She is transfixed by his lone dance, obsessed by the oddity and brilliance, feels she could watch him indefinitely.

Still watching a few minutes later, Annabel then says, dreamily, quietly, whisperingly, 'Always on Sundays.'

'Huh?' grunts her sister Isabel, her pursed lips fringed with pins. 'Par-don?' she adds, slightly muffled.

'Always on Sundays,' Annabel says, sighing.

'What's that?' Isabel asks, removing the pins from her mouth, having heard Annabel speak but having not heard with any clarity what was spoken.

'Always on Sundays,' repeats Annabel again, slightly louder now. 'He always dances on Sundays and only on Sundays and never any other day.' She tilts her head to one side now, curiously, and sighs once more. 'Why do you figure that is, Izzy? Why only Sundays? Why not any other day?'

'It's most probably the only day that they let him out of the funny farm.'

'Izzy!' cries Annabel, disgusted by her sister. 'That's a horrible thing to say!'

'Oh come on, Annie. Lighten up, would you?' Isabel rolls her eyes, sticks a pin here and a pin there. 'I mean,' she then says, sensing she has an opportunity to tease her younger and much more sensitive sister, 'what kind of guy dances ballroom alone, huh, but framed as though he has a partner? And with no music playing for miles around, huh? A crazy loon if not a complete lunatic goon?' she taunts. 'Huh? Huh? He must be completely batty, huh? Come on, admit it... a whole lot of screws loose in that head, huh? A sandwich short of a picnic, huh? Huh? Huh? Huh?'

'Isabel Cosgrove!' screams Annabel.

Her passive temperament gone away, she finally turns to face her sister. 'You're a rotten sinner,' she proclaims. 'You're a wicked monster, you really are. Stop it right now.' She looks at her sister and thinks what an awful view of the world she must have, to be so nasty, so intolerant of people's differences. 'Sometimes I wonder if you're not my sister at all,' she says gloomily. She forms a vague antipathy of her sister then, turning away from the monstrous one, looking back out of the window, down to the park below and to the bandstand and the dancing man, still dancing.

157

'Oh, come on now, Annie-belly,' implores her sister, half-heartedly, still busily working. 'You do know I was only kidding with you, don't you? I'm sure,' she says quite insincerely, stitching now, 'that he's a very nice man.'

But Annabel does not answer.

She is too engrossed again, watching the tiny suited figure below, moving in the slowly descending darkness, the indigo night, her breath slowing in her relaxing pink nostrils.

The dancer spins evermore as she watches him intently, evermore twirling in graceful cyclonic motions, whirling like a fantastic small dust devil, a whirlwind, perfectly formed, in silence. The whole air about him seems to glow with a subtle luminosity, a gentle phosphorescing gleam, a soft focus haze.

'Come look at him. Come look,' Annabel requests wildly of her sister. 'Come see how wonderfully he dances, Izzy, and then you'll know why he's so enchanting, like a prince.'

'I can't, Anny, I'm far too busy for daydreams and star-gazing,' Isabel says bluntly, coldly.

Snish, snish, snicker, snicker, the scissors snip and snip.

Then the sounds of sewing begin with the machine, like a tiny automatic gun, chug chugging. 'I need this dress finished,' Isabel says, 'or we don't eat next week. It's a rush-job, only came in today. I would've turned it down usually. Still would now, if I could have afforded to. But, I can't. We can't ask Dad for another loan, or he'll think us incapable of living alone.'

Annabel suddenly rises from her seat now, braces herself, stiffens her back, licks her lips, and makes for the door.

'Where on Earth are you going?' asks Isabel, looking up from her task.

'I'm going to introduce myself to him.'

Isabel scoffs. 'Don't be so silly.'

'It's not silly at all,' Annabel says stiffly.

'It is too. He probably knows you've been watching him all along; probably expecting you down there; he'll probably snatch you up and drag you away, kicking and screaming. That, or he'll think you're insane, run away like a startled bird.'

'He'll do no such thing!' Glaring at Isabel and at the fabric across her lap, the drawings on the dresser, Annabel then says, 'It's more likely that you'll be making one of those for me soon enough.'

Her sister laughs half-heartedly, tells her to sit back down.

'And I'm not insane.'

'Oh, come now, Anny,' says Izzy, 'of course you're crazy; you're as loopy as the sea is blue.'

'I'm going,' Annabel says defiantly. She stiffens more now, to illustrate her conviction. 'And the sea isn't blue; it only appears that way because it reflects the sky.' She stiffens even further, announces once more, 'I'm going!'

'You're not. You won't.'

'I am, I'm going.'

'Go then,' Isabel says, as impassively as possible.

And, being that Annabel is nineteen and crazy, she is of course prone to acts of impulsivity and silliness, wild fantasy and irrational haste, and so she walks the rest of the way to the door, opens it, walks out, and closes it behind herself.

As she walks downstairs she imagines herself dancing with the prince-like man outside, but the image of it seems somehow impossible, vague and unrealised, her nervousness making her tremble and causing her to doubt her own confidence in approaching him.

Out on the street, Annabel moves even more uneasily.

She does not look up but stands still and stares at the cracked pavement.

She is dwelling now on what Isabel has said about her being crazy, not just now but in the past too... always... consistently.

Slowly, she takes a step.

Slower now, another.

Perhaps he *will* think I'm crazy, she reasons with herself.

She stops again.

Perhaps, perhaps I *am* crazy. Perhaps open-mindedness and tolerance is crazy. Perhaps loving is madness. And perhaps loving every single thing of beauty as I do is complete madness, total insanity?

She's probably up there right now, thinks Annabel of Isabel. In fact I know she is. Up there... watching... wishing me badness... hoping failure on me... praying for rejection... mediating meanness... so she can gloat.

For a moment now, Annabel almost has herself convinced of her fantasy's authenticity.

She turns and looks up at the window from where she has come, knowing that she will see her sister framed there, small and silhouetted and ready to see her malevolent prayers and wishes and hopes realised, ready to gloat.

But the window is empty.

She must have moved when she saw me turning around, Annabel thinks. I should have turned more quickly. Much more quickly.

She shudders, shakes her bones and opens her eyes, having not noticed she has closed them.

A warm gentle wind caresses her cheek.

The early evening is close, the atmosphere dense, soothingly dense and not so heavy that it becomes stifling.

She looks up, sees him, and knows she has to be brave and bold. She has to go to him. She *must* go to him.

A step.

160

Another.

And another.

Walking now, she pays only cursory attention to a young girl out walking her dog, a cat stalking something unseen near a dustbin, and the occasional passing pair of distant headlights, beaming dimly through the early evening gloom.

Annabel Cosgrove reaches the foot of the steps to the bandstand, takes a deep breath, holds out her right hand, smiles in the direction of the dancing man, and asks, 'Would you like to dance?'

But he pays her no heed. He simply continues to dance, oblivious, deaf to her offer.

She remains, hand out, looking to him with open, expectant, almost pleading eyes.

Then, over her right shoulder, there is something said – something quiet and indistinguishable to Annabel, something said by someone she has not yet noticed. And so she takes back her hand and turns. And there, beneath the cascading bows of a blossoming willow tree, in the periphery of its shade, alone on a dark wooden bench sits the shadowed figure of an elderly lady.

She speaks again, creakingly, far too quietly.

Annabel looks at the lady on the bench for only a moment, then she sweeps her sight back towards the bandstand and the bandstand is somehow changed.

In just three moments – one turning away from it, one spent on the lady and one to turn back to it – the bandstand is different, strikingly so. Because, where three moments earlier it had seemed aglow with a soft luminescence, it now appears to have dramatically faded, as though an unseen switch has been flicked and many concealed bulbs have died; where its paint had seem lacquered, shellacked, so fresh and so new that it might still be wet to touch, it now seems jaded, dull, and even flecked and flaked in many places; and, most notably and most regrettably of all, it is missing two moving soles; the dancer is gone.

Annabel notices his absence first, but it is the thing she accepts last.

He is gone, she tells herself finally.

He is nowhere.

He has vanished in a most impossible manner, like a ghost.

The colour drains from the girls face now, her chest pulls tight, her mouth falls open, trembles in a fit of horrified astonishment.

'Pardon?' asks Annabel, turning back to the dusk-dwelling woman, her face pale and confused. 'What did you just say?' she wishes to know.

The old shadow raises its voice now, and it is the voice of a life's experience and gathered wisdom, of mothballs and cobwebs and ratchet movements and endless coffee steam and cigarette smoke.

'I said, "You saw him, huh?"'

Slowly, uncertainly, still as pale as the moon, Annabel says yes with a nod of her head.

'Well, you're not the first, let me tell you.'

The shadow on the bench beneath the bows laughs inwardly, abruptly stops, sighs a little. 'Love him do you?' it asks, crazily impassioned. 'Well, you're not the first there either! Oh my,' it laughs again, and then sighs, inwardly, reflectively, 'if I had stone for every time a girl like you came floating along over the years, I could build myself a castle. I really could. Same story, different face. You're just as starry-eyed as the last. But I'll tell you the same as I told them all: you can't have him. He's taken.'

'I...' Annabel mutters, her head oscillating steadily, 'I... don't... understand...'

'Love never was a thing made for understanding.'

'But –'

162

'But nothing. Like I said: he's already taken, I'm afraid.'

'I don't under–'

'You don't *need* to understand. As I said,' the elderly lady repeats, more insistently now, 'he's taken. Spoken for. Mine.'

As she reaches the top of the stairs, Annabel is sure she can hear a sniggering sound.

Her sister. Isabel. The rat. The rotten rotter. Sniggering. How could she? Sniggering like that. Sniggering.

But, opening the door, it seems it is only the sound of the scissors snick-snickering again.

Pale-faced, Annabel holds to the open door, sways a little. 'He vanished,' she says, unbelieving, 'like a ghost. Just like a ghost.'

'Enough with the games now,' says Isabel, as she concentrates on scissoring. 'You can stop with the silly fantasy now, Anny.' She tut-tuts. 'There never was a man dancing down there; I looked out of the window myself.'

'There was,' she vows. 'I swear it.'

'Oh, shush, shush,' the dressmaking older sister commands.

And Annabel says no more.

Instead she sits down, mouth convulsing with upset, chin quivering, and a tear sneaks out of her left eye, runs down her face.

It is the next day now and Annabel and Isabel's father has come to visit.

They welcome him into their freshly tidied dwellings and he embraces them in turn, plants a firm kiss on the brow of each, and tells them just how much they are missed at home. The house feels empty without them.

Through to the kitchen they go, and there Isabel moves across to the kettle.

163

'A cup of tea, Dad?' she offers.

'Coffee, please, Isabelly.'

'Looks like we're out of coffee,' says Isabel, peering down into the empty jar. 'I'll have to pop out to get some.'

'No, I'll have tea – tea's fine.'

'No, honestly, it's not any trouble.' She picks up her purse and heads for the door. 'I'll be back in no time, and I could do with the air.'

'Dad?' says Annabel, the very moment the door closes behind her sister.

'Yes, Anny, dear.'

'Do you know anything at all about a man dancing in the park?'

'That old tale? Oh, that's been around since before I was a boy.'

'Could you tell it to me? I've never heard it before.'

'Story is,' says the girl's father, puffing a cigarette, 'that the chap got shot.'

'Shot? Annabel's face twists into a picture of horror; she raises her hands, claps them to her cheeks and it becomes a perfect picture of a tormented silent scream.

'Oh, yes,' recalls the storyteller. 'Yes, shot right there as he danced.'

'Heavens!' cries Annabel. 'Why? Why would somebody do that? Why?'

'*Why?*' her father echoes through a plume of smoke, musing. 'Well then, death doesn't always need a reason *why*, Anny. It doesn't need a mind or meaning. Neither does violence. It can be mindless. But, apparently, as I recall it, the girl that the chap was dancing with was the real target. Something about a scorned former lover with an eye for vengeance. And the dancing man threw himself into the line of fire. One bullet. Stone dead.'

'I spoke to a strange old lady, Daddy, and she seemed to know all about him. She was sat on the bench down there in the park. She said that he was spoken for, that he was hers. Could that be her, Dad – the girl he was dancing with? The girl he saved?'

'That old nanny?' Laughter. 'Widow Collier? Why, she's been sitting down on the bench for a good few years now, claiming to be his dearest love, swearing she'll dance with him again one day.' There is laughter again, much more hearty now. 'She might even be half convincing at times, if we didn't all know she's been married four times and divorced three.'

'Why's that?'

'Well, come on now, Anny. You ever heard of a fairy tale with imperfections like that, huh? The true love dies and the princess tries her hand at marrying a few other princes instead? I don't think so. Did Romeo run off with whoever he could get, huh? Did Juliet wake up and look at Romeo lying there poisoned and dead and think, "What an idiot!" and then shack up with the next best Montague she could find? Mercutio? Not a cat in hell's chance. No,' the father shook his head, 'no, no, no, if there were any truth at all in that old witch's tale she'd have waited there every Sunday since, or shot herself on the spot.'

Eventually, Isabel walks back in, coffee in hand, smiling and wet from the brief summer shower which had caught her out.

The following Sunday Annabel goes to the window.

She expects that the Dancing Man will not be there, that he will have gone forever. But, to her astonishment, as wonderful as ever, there he is, dancing. He moves as soundlessly as a shadow again, with the same briskness and ease of agility as a raven in flight, the incredible dexterity and litheness of a contortionist, a snake charmed by the inaudible music he must hear.

Happily mesmerised, she watches him a while.

Her heart grows heavy as she silently admits that she can never go down into the park again, never offer her hand again. She is trapped in a deep spell of foreboding, a curse of loving something she is unable to deny herself of but cannot have, the acknowledgment of which stirs up a terrible war between Reason and Fancy, a war which can never have a victor but only innumerable casualties and uncountable fatalities. The saddened queen of the Kingdom of Inner Dwellings, she sits upon a high thistle throne, watching and dwelling on the curse of Love Unattainable and the war it wages.

Then, after a time and with the spell momentarily broken, looking up and across the park, directly and to the left and to the right, on the other streets adjacent to it – in the rows of terraced houses there – Annabel notices other windows with curtains slightly ajar, with soft and dim orange night lights and flickering candlelight silhouetting the slight frames of lonely women sat in lonely rooms.

They're watching the dancing man, she realises, watching him in absolute admiration and astonishing awe, romanticising, fantasising, like me, wanting so very desperately to be brave enough, bold enough, to leave their high towers, let down their golden tresses and go down into the early evening, to claim their prince, to dance with him.

Don't go, she tells them silently.

'Don't go. Stay,' she whispers to the admirers. 'Stay. Oh, stay. Stay. He only vanishes. So stay. Oh, oh, please stay and keep your dreams alive.'

'What's that?' Isabel, somewhere behind her, distant, asks.

'Oh,' Annabel replies, suddenly aware of herself and her speaking aloud, 'nothing.'

In the next moment, all of a sudden, Annabel notices someone sat upon the bench beneath the willow tree, by the bandstand.

The old woman again.

Only she is different now, somehow.

166

She is no longer in absolute shadow.

Instead, she glows.

She glows brightly.

She is in white.

Isabel presently hears her sister gasp from across the room, comes to her side, and asks, 'What's the matter, Anny?'

'She... wasn't... lying,' Annabel answers remotely, distantly, brokenly.

From behind her, Isabel places her hands on Annabel's shoulders.

'Who wasn't lying?'

The shocked and dazed sister points down with a dithering finger. 'The old lady. You see – her? Beneath the tree?'

And down in the park now, on the bench beneath the willowy bows, in the indigo twilight, there sits a bride of twilight years.

'Why,' says Isabel, 'that's the dress I've been working on all week, the one I finished just yesterday. I'm sure it is. I never did see the customer myself, but Jane did say she was... old.'

She's going to die now, thinks Annabel Cosgrove. She's going to die and she knew it all along, as though she heard a banshee's tormented cry, or the knell of bluebells ringing, felt the end creeping nearer and nearer and nearer, and planned for its arrival. She is his dance partner, and soon they will dance together, forever after.

The young ladies still looking down from the window, the dancing man presently ceases his dancing, turns and gestures.

Annabel sees him and his gesture.

Isabel does not.

There, on the painted white wooden floor of the bandstand, elegantly surrounded by a soft focus light

167

and inaudible music he stands, facing the twilight bride, his hand out, offered to her.

THE ANGEL IN THE CORNFIELD

An almighty, most thunderous sound rolled across the ceiling and sent the house trembling.

The stentorian sound rose and fell as the passing of a vast tidal wave, the marching of a titan, the awakening of a colossal bronze statue, leaving behind it only quiet reverberations in the rafters and dislodged dust, cascading. As though the sky itself was falling down, the slates of the roof had rattled under the rumbling cavalcade of concussions. The windows had shook, as though afraid.

The galvanised Robert Dunne started, fitted from out of his shallow slumber.

He had only just closed his now-startled eyes, it seemed, so the great sound of thunder, he decided very quickly, was borne not from a dream. The violent trembling of the bedroom had been physical, also. He was sure of it. The earth had moved. The house had shuddered; the bed at least.

It was not a dream. The light-fitting, the lampshade which hung from the ceiling, still swung, softly but visibly, too.

It swung, definitely.

It swung.

Quickly climbing out of his bed in almost absolute nudity now, walking to the window and swiftly parting the curtains, leaning forward and looking up into the night sky, Robert Dunne perceived what could only be described by him as a burning shield, blazing down from above.

No, he decided, not a shield. An egg, a golden egg. It tore across the sky like the tip of some godlike sword thrust towards the flesh of its enemy, Earth, lacerating the black fabric of the night between the indistinct constellations as it went, a beard of orange embers tailing after it, dying out.

As he watched in astonishment the great glowing sword-tip-shield-egg-burning-thing grew smaller and smaller, more distant, appeared momentarily stationary, and then fell into obscurity behind the rust-pitted silo, to the west of his family's farm.

It remained unseen.

A few seconds later, from where it had vanished, there came a great flash of light, a flare of orange glow, a brief half-halo blossoming, then another terrible, thunderous sound – a crash – followed by a slight quaking of the floor beneath.

A feather of grey smoke, difficult to see in the night, wisped up among the darkness.

Then, it all stopped.

All was quiet.

'What in the hell was that?' cried his wife sitting up suddenly, although a little belatedly, in bed. She had slept through the first tremors, evidently, but not the eruption. 'An earthquake?' she asked.

'No,' replied Robert Dunne, still staring out the window, frozen by the shock of incomprehensible experience. 'Not an earthquake. Not an earthquake. It was,' he floundered, consternation sending his cognition asunder. 'It was... *something*. It was *really something...* but nothing... *nothing* like an earthquake.'

'Thunder?'

'No.'

'A bomb?'

'No.'

'What then, Bobby? What was it?' asked his wife, half alert, half asleep.

Robert Dunne then said nothing for a time, unable to find the right words, deeply considering what he had seen.

'It was,' he said at last, finding some descriptive account that she might understand, 'it was a burning golden egg. It fell from the sky.'

'Huh?' said his wife, rubbing her eyes. 'It was *what?*'

'A meteor. A comet. A shooting star.' He shook his head. 'I don't really know.'

'Huh,' she muttered again – but this time in a far more indifferent, nonchalant tone. 'You're dreaming, Bobby,' she flouted, not so concerned.

'No, I'm not,' he replied, in casual defiance. 'I'm not.' He lifted his crucifix pendant to his lips, then, kissed it, made a cross about his shoulders and face. 'God as my witness,' he vowed, 'I saw it. I'm stood here. Was when I saw it. I'm awake. Was awake. It fell from the sky, passed over the house, and landed in the cornfield, behind the silo.'

Robert now started to become excited, as excited as a boy presented with a new and daring adventure, a curiosity never before tasted.

'I'm going out to see what it is,' he declared. 'It might well be the sign I've been praying for! Get up, come with me. Wake the kids. They can come too. No – leave the

171

kids. Watch the kids. You stay here. You stay here and watch the kids.'

In the darkness and in a hurry he put on his underpants and trousers inside-out, grabbed up his shirt, frantically felt about the floor for his socks, found them, pulled them on, hopping, and headed for the door.

Buttoning up his shirt he instructed his wife, 'If I'm not back soon then tell somebody. No. Tell *nobody*. No,' he decided eventually. 'Tell *everybody*!'

Mrs Dunne, already again recumbent, replied only by way of a disinterested though compliant groan.

'Um,' she said.

Then she rolled over, nuzzled down into her pillow.

'You're...' she mumbled, 'crazy... Bobby.'

The frantic husband then rushed out of the bedroom and into the bathroom, emptied his bladder into the toilet bowl, realised his trousers were inside-out, rectified his mistake, buttoned them up, raced across the landing and rumbled down the stairs.

At the front door, which he at once opened, he shoved his feet into his boots, laced them, put on his hat and coat, picked up his torch and shotgun, and shot out into the yard.

The front door slammed behind him.

Across the yard he paced, in the direction of the silo. Faint mutterings and movements could be heard around the farm, but it was only the sounds of the various livestock unsettled, shuffling in hay, padding their pens, tasting the strange air, sniffing it, rustling hides, clomping hooves and gently clucking beaks, respectively.

An owl hooted by the barn.

Robert Dunne rounded the silo, pushed on, roving along lanes between the blue-moon-tipped corn rows, his torchlight flashing here and there, vanishing old shadows, casting fresh ones, searching.

When at last he finally did chance upon the crash site at the far side of the vast cornfield, Robert Dunne stood dumbfounded, in absolute awe, his eyes as wide and bright as two shining new silver coins.

With the odious scent of corn burnt and blown aside lingering, bent and flattened by the powerful wake of air displaced, he saw that a great conical scar had been carved into the earth. It increased in depth and width, he observed, searing and sizzling with steam and glowing charcoals, as it progressed towards the point of impact, the crater, the real wound.

In its entirety the site seemed closest to resemble a capacious keyhole, cast into the ground. It was some fifty feet long in all, half as wide again, and almost as deep. Steep embankments had been made on all sides, as the powerful impact had pushed away the soil with ease.

Robert Dunne tilted his hat, wiped his furrowed brow on the back of his right hand, puffed out his cheeks, exhaled deeply, and shook his head, muttering to himself, 'Dear God.'

He presently realised that his torch had become redundant, due to the many small fires which glowed along the scar, and switched it off.

His shotgun rested by his side, too, for now.

As he moved unsteadily along the edge of the scar, in the direction of the large round crater, his face drew white, mouth fell open, aghast.

For there, in the deepest part of the depression, near centre but offset in accordance with the shield-sword-egg-missile's trajectory, surrounded by shards of silvery shining and golden glowing shell shrapnel, laid a body.

He reached the rim of the round crater, stood frozen, his face paler still.

He swayed.

A small quantity of dirt and stones from beneath his boots tumbled down into the hole as a tiny avalanche; a

173

little fell behind him too, down the freshly formed embankment on which he teetered and tottered.

His body shuddered as the house had, cold fingers trembling.

His eyes glazed over as though vitrified.

He stared blindly.

It seemed as though the entire world ceased to exist in a moment: all that had come before vanished into obscurity, all that might proceed thereafter evaporated into oblivion, as all that was now relevant was this body laid before him, this keyhole crater, this timeless instance.

His glass eyes shed a few tears.

There was the hooting of an owl again – distant now.

'Dear God,' Robert said again. 'Dear Lord Jesus, you have sent me an angel: you have answered my prayers and gifted me new faith. "When the righteous cry for help, the Lord hears, and rescues them from all their troubles." Thank you, Lord, thank you. You've sent me an angel,' he repeated, crying softly. 'Praise you, Good Lord. Amen.'

In almost every possible way the being appeared to be an angel to Robert Dunne.

It had about it a nimbus, a brightly glowing, softly throbbing golden-yellow splendour which attested to its divinity. Adorned upon its head was an abundance of brilliantly blonde hair which cast down to the slight shoulders, where a flowing white robe began its long descent to the feet.

It was tall.

Very tall.

It was grand, too.

Very grand.

Its skin had a pearlescent quality to it, seemed to shimmer opal and cream and vanilla, gleaming angelically.

It was an angel, Robert Dunne decided.

174

But the angel did not move. It lay inanimate instead on its back, facing the very heavens from which it had come.

It was an angel, but it was dying.

The man of rejuvenated faith cried even more softly then.

'Dear Lord. It's dead.'

As he had stood softly crying, the radiance of the angel in the crater had at once begun to subside; there was a visible diminishing in the luminosity of the seraphim figure – as with the final dying of some phosphorescent precious stone, some gem of purest borrowed light.

The sibilant sounds of the glowing charcoals began to die out, also. Some fires flickered out in hisses. More unsettled small stones fell in tiny avalanches.

Then all was still.

The night became more silent.

A perfect peace surrounded and near-darkness hemmed in. The effulgence of the angel's face waned visibly at that point, decreased to a faint glow, and then vanished altogether.

Only a few charcoaled rocks and shards of the scattered shell remained glowing.

Robert Dunne stood a long while in the near-perfect black of night, feeling deeply sombre, lost, looking into the face of the now blanched angel.

He mourned, and his mournful sighs and groans were the recital of an unwritten elegy, the desultory song of a lustreless heart. This brilliant angel had been sent to him, he was certain, to cure his faltered faith, but died upon arrival.

The angel is dead, he told himself. My angel is dead. And it will remain forever so. Always dead... always dead... always dead – over and over, he kept on repeating this detail.

The only event, in fact, to break the lone mourner's quiet lamentations was the emergence of a slight conglomerate sound formed from approaching footsteps and voices faintly muttering and a bloodhound sniffing; that, and the vague awareness of a flashing bright torch upon the once again veiled night sky, over his shoulder.

Corn whispered, rustling.

The group of noises moved amid the night.

The torchlight flickered, flitted this way and that.

The farrago moved closer then, increased in volume, and after an indistinguishable lapse, from out of the parted row of corn behind Robert Dunne, there emerged first a dog, then a man and, finally, two boys.

But Dunne did not stir.

All the while he did not shift a sinew, move a muscle.

He remained staring into the crater and the serene face, hearing but not hearing, aware but unaware of the soft commotion to the rear of him.

The four new arrivals stared up at the meditative man stood precariously on the embankment, around at the decimated area of the field, the carpet of crushed corn, and the freshly impacted earth.

'Mr Dunne?' said a high voice belonging to one of the boys.

'Is that you?' added the other, slightly smaller boy.

'Bob?' the man of the group promptly said. 'Bob, it's me: Walt. Heard the commotion. Saw the star-meteor-thing come down in your field here. Followed it. Thought it best to come investigate.'

The three onlookers could not yet understand quite why their neighbour, Mr Robert "Bob" Dunne ignored their greetings and remained stood as still as a scarecrow.

The two boys then became petrified at the thought of just what might have petrified Mr Dunne.

The father of the two boys, too, felt a deep and merciless depredation of fear and forebodings invade his stomach, send him subtly trembling.

All five beings stood muted and still for a time; the dog too, sensing something alien, did not move.

A gentle breeze rose and fell, and rose and fell.

The night whispered.

'I don't know what in hell to make of it,' said Walter Hughes, when at last the nefarious spell of silence and stillness had lifted from the scene, and he, his two sons and his dog had joined Bob Dunne on the embankment, seen what he had seen.

'Not what in *hell* to make of it, Walt, but what *in Heaven* to make of it...'

'Sorry, Bob?'

'Well it's obvious, isn't it?

'Is it?'

'Course it is. It's an angel.'

'*An angel?*' Walt asked.

'An angel,' confirmed Bob.

'An angel,' echoed the smaller one of the two boys.

'Is it... dead?' asked Walter of Robert.

To which he nodded solemnly, said, 'Yes.'

The four males stood again very still and in near-perfect silence for a time, staring down at the supine being, considering its only plausible and equally impossible origins. Upon the embankment, holding up the dim night sky in silhouettes, they resembled four ruinous columns, a colonnade of some ancient temple withered by time and weather, truncated, as it were, at different heights.

The dog circled its owners legs a few times, took shelter behind them, shivering, and peered inquisitively between on occasion, to look into the angelic face of the curious thing in the crater.

Although the three Hughes' had now joined Robert Dunne on the embankment and spoken to him, he had

177

still not once looked at them. His eyes set fixedly on the figure in the hole, he was captivated.

'Could be an alien,' someone speculated after a time, softly, amidst the darkness.

'Yeah, looks more like an alien to me,' the older boy agreed, perhaps with himself, scratching his itching scalp. 'No,' he then suddenly renounced, dismissing his earlier sight of the heavenly descent and his quickness of presumption, instead considering only the hard evidence, the body before his eyes currently. 'No, aliens are green or grey – can't be an alien.'

'Sure it could,' said his little, flaxen-haired brother, stood to his right. 'I saw a film once about a man who got taken away into the sky in a ball of fire by aliens and he said that the little green and grey guys are just the helpers of much taller aliens who look just like us. Prettier and taller...' – he shrugged – 'but just like us really... only alien.'

'*Alien* just means *unfamiliar*, anyway,' was the matter-of-fact comeback.

'No it doesn't.'

'Yes, it does.'

In contempt of one another the two boys argued on, back and forth, back and forth, as the two men said nothing but only stared unblinkingly at the cause of infantile debate in the crater below, motionless.

The boys argued that an alien would never be so *stupid* as to crash its ship in a field after managing to travel across *galaxies and galaxies* without any trouble, that there would be more than just a littering of eggshell bits left of its spacecraft, that aliens *could* be white and that they *could not* be white and were *always* green or grey and that E.T. was brown and that he was tan and that he was only a puppet or a little person in a suit in a movie.

They argued then that the thing in the crater in Mr Dunne's cornfield couldn't possibly be an *angel* because

178

angels are just made up delusions that offer old and stupid people comfort, because a man on television had said so and everybody in the whole world knew that the man on television knew what he was talking about because he was *super clever*, and angels only appeared to saints and other special people anyway, and could not die... not *ever*.

Then one boy punched the other in the arm and the punched one punched back – a little harder.

Walter Hughes then scolded them and made them apologise to one another.

'Besides,' the older brother went on quietly, rubbing his punched arm, thinking aloud in summation of things, 'besides which he doesn't have any wings like angels do... so he can't be an angel.'

'Who said it's a *he*, anyway? Looks more like a tall lady to me,' offered the younger boy, looking down into the crater and seeing effeminate features.

The smaller boy's statement went unacknowledged by all, and his brother seized the opportunity to validate his own argument once more.

'*All* angels have wings.'

'Wings are just symbolic,' Mr Dunne casually informed the boys, their father and dog, shaking his head, but not averting his gaze from his angel. 'They're just a way of artists showing that angels *could* fly. Some passages of the Bible, regarding angels, hardly mention wings at all,' he explained. 'Most never do. And as for whether what we're looking at here is a *he* or a *she* – well, angels are both neither and both.'

The two boys marvelled quietly, their loosely-held opinions altered once more.

But Walt Hughes was now ready to offer his own opinion.

'Nope,' he said obdurately, and the two boys turned their eyes to him. 'Nope, I won't have it; I won't have that what we have here is either an angel or an alien. It's something else.'

'Like what?' asked the other three.

'Well I'm damned if I know... but... there must be a... *reasonable* explanation.'

Robert Dunne scoffed.

How ridiculous, he thought, to dismiss two theories in favour of none. That was the kind of idiocy he loathed. He could have screamed in Walt's face.

But, he said nothing.

'Couldn't it be,' asked the youngest boy, then, after a few seconds thinking, 'that this alien-angel-man was in the field already, and that the missile-comet-thing fell out of the sky and hit him, Dad?'

'Could be, Son, could be.'

Robert Dunne scoffed again. Louder this time.

The eldest son sniggered at his brother's theory.

The younger one shot a look of reproach at him.

The father of the two scowled, too.

'Well,' said Robert, his eyes bright-wide in feigned amazement, staring still into the crater, his tone sarcastic but aimed more at Walt than at the boy, 'whoever sent the golden-burning-missile-egg to splat this poor fellow stalking my cornfield at night didn't do such a great job of it, did they? I mean, look – his clothes are barely creased.'

No word was replied.

'Why,' Mr Dunne proceeded to taunt, incensed, 'look at that, too,' – he pointed – 'their 'bomb' did sterling work of carving a huge ditch in my ground but, again, the fellow remains unscathed; he must be made of titanium... his threads too!'

'Now, Bob, there's no need to be funny about all this;' said Walter Hughes, his two sons looking on in trepidation of the escalating emotions.

'I wasn't criticising your boy, Walt. It's not his fault. Kids dream. It's just what they do. But you – you should know better. It's your job to teach him well, to lead him _'

'I'm just attempting to be logical about things. That's all,' said Walter, feeling his son's possible explanation was by far the most earthly.

'Just attempting to be logical? Well you're failing,' spat Mr Dunne, hissing, 'miserably! You couldn't be further from cogency if you tried! Logical my...' He stopped himself, calmed a little, bit his tongue. 'Foot,' he said, suddenly aware of the two children. 'Logical my foot.'

'And this coming from a man harping on about angels,' exclaimed Walt, in a snide manner.

Dunne was furious but thought it best to be passive in light of the two boy's presence; he felt his temper flare but doused it with cool collectiveness, masqueraded composure; his heart pounded; his tongue swelled to lashing so much so that he had to bite it once again, physically, literally. He gazed longingly at the angel in the crater, hated the man beside him.

Then there came an uncomfortable silence – long, profound and unbroken – and there could be sensed a divide in the group by all involved: Walter Hughes and the youngest boy one faction, Robert and the eldest the other; or both boys and the father against the farmer; or each disbanded individual alone, an island swimming in his own contention. Whichever way the cracks spread, there was a definite divide. The dog seemingly sensed the divisive hostility too, for after a while it whined softly.

Damn it all, thought Robert Dunne despondently. This is it, isn't it, the world over, for ever – subjective objectivity – one view not matching another, ever; all of us wanting to be correct for our own satisfaction, pride, or perhaps mere sanity, but all of us correct and incorrect, simultaneously. This world is full of feeling but unfeeling, understanding but misunderstanding, numb and ignorant in its own knowledge. No one truth exists. Only perspectives, conflicting. Only quarrel. Alien, aren't we all, the distorted reflection of God's own image. Damn it all.

For the first time since seeing it, the farmer presently turned his eyes away from the coveted angel.

Contemptuously, he looked across at Walter Hughes, regarded him with sickened disdain, and said nothing, his dried tears still staining his cheeks.

His nerves frayed, he trembled.

He had had enough.

No more arguing.

There was no sense in it.

Motes of ash cavorted about the dusk, prancing between the faint moonbeams and aimless torchlight.

Bob Dunne stood in quiet contemplation.

He exhaled.

'Well,' Walt said sighing, 'I suppose the question now is what we do with...' he wondered, '*it.*'

'Can we keep it?' asked his younger son, hopefully, hands in pockets, kicking softly and aimlessly at the loose soil around his feet.

'For what reason?' asked his father, genuinely mystified.

'It would only rot away,' said his brother.

'Yes,' said Mr Dunne.

'Yes?' asked the other three, startled.

'Yes', Mr Dunne said again, very plainly now, 'we'll keep it, in a way. I've thought it over and there's nothing else for it.'

To the congregation of dog, man and two boys, he then explained his reasoning.

'I could call up Father O'Neil,' he told them, 'and he'd pay praise to *its* divinity, give a sermon and say some quiet words of blessing over the grave.' Then, to Walt, directly, he said, 'Your boys could run and go get a Science Fiction writer, and he'd attest to it being a being from Mars. Or you yourself could fetch a detective and

182

he'd suspect it to be a victim of some strange sacrificial murder! Hell! bring along the whole world to stand around this crater, whispering and shouting out their theories, and each one would be certain to think *something* or other to be the truth of it all. But, almost always something different – even if only subtly so. Best case scenario? we would be ridiculed as party to an elaborate hoax. Worst? we'd be locked up in nuthouse or a prison, the insane murderers of some innocent unknown. Unfortunately, the world can't agree, you see. Never will.'

'And so, we can't tell anyone, you see, or we'd be digging our own graves, making a rod for our own backs...'

Not saying anything more, the four males stood for a long time, deep in thought, or not thinking at all, not one of them was to know.

The dog sniffed, groaned.

Then, quietly, slowly but assertively, Walter Hughes said, 'Boys, go fetch some shovels.'

And, without questioning, they did.

And, as the night drew slumberous and the morning began to rise – the sun breaking upon the softly shadowed and orange-tipped hills and forests and fields of the horizon – a cockerel signalled dawn, and the two men and two boys, beneath the vast and shifting heavens of space, took up their shovels and began to bury the sacrosanct star man, the angel, the alien, the astronaut, the unknown being, the cornfield loiterer, all at once, with the scent of scorched corn and burnt earth lingering on the air and in their nostrils, the bloodhound lazing nearby, still sniffing occasionally.

Walter Hughes, perspiring heavily, shovelling scorched dirt beneath the orange-crimson glow of the rising sun, thought to himself, Maybe the man we're burying was already in the field – like my boy guessed – looking up at the stars in his dressing gown, having escaped from some mental hospital, and then all of a sudden the meteor-thing fell out of the sky, landed right near his feet, but didn't hit him, but landed close enough to scare him fully to death, turn him as pale as his pyjamas, and then maybe he toppled over headfirst and landed right there in the ditch, still looking at the stars, but dead. Maybe that's what happened...

I wish I'd thought of that earlier, he told himself, when Bob was making fun of me. That would have shut him up. That's what must have happened. It's the only reasonable explanation...

Should I mention it now? Three hours later.

No... too late now...

Just keep it to myself now...

Until later... perhaps.

One Winter Evening
(a true story)

The cold had a bite to it. It had an overwhelming bitterness. As it whipped at the flesh it brought with it the sting of countless disgruntled ice-wasps. It was bilious. It blustered.

Relentless snow, falling in huge flakes, like confetti from a giant cold wedding in the sky, followed it closely in hand.

Frost encroached.

Ice invaded.

Seizing the day then, seizing the day and making it night, stealing away the sun, stealing away all definition from every shape, the cold and snow and frost and ice had shaken down the entire colour from the red-brick walls and slate rooftops, from the tar-black roads and paths, and from the green-leaf fields and the trees of the city, and its surrounding areas – choking the life out of all they touched and painting the whole place a plain white canvas.

The snow and the frost seemed to *ossify* everything, merge all into one pallid bone complexion.

Even shadows seemed almost white.

Trees and bushes and embankments were barely perceptible, amorphous entities. Every window pane was blind with a riming of gossamer patterns, of crystalline white frost. Each roof was hemmed with lance-like icicles.

And so, together, the cold and snow and frost and ice performed all the brilliant trickery that the cold and snow and frost and ice ever did; all the beautiful miracles that a child appreciates, marvels at, the first, second, third and fourth times of witnessing, and more. They did all that and more.

But no child played upon the thick phosphorescent white blanket. No boy built men of snow; no girl imprinted herself an angel. Not one child slid down icy toboggan runs on old dustbin lids or salvaged refuse sacks. Nor did one child hurtle snow grenades at Ice War adversaries from behind snow barracks, their lungs filled with crisp frosty air. Not even the bravest child, swathed in the thickest and most numbered layers, dared step outside. It was a cruel cold and a savage snow, a formidable frost and an insidious ice. The people of the city and its suburbs were instead barricaded indoors, braced by their frozen windows, waiting for winter to pass.

Some secretly feared that their homes would become their tombs.

With a crash, the door of Grimoire Cottage on Daisy Lane flung open wide.

The wind howled through the opening.

As though the world were a giant snow-globe, shaken violently, swirling snow swept all about the colourless scene outside. The snow spiralled in great cyclonic waves on the blusterous wind.

Stumbling into the house shuddering, trying to close the door behind him, Mr Jones attempted to shut out the harsh white world, and, with it, all its wintery bitterness, its grasping chill.

Shivering, his fingers numb, he wrestled to shut the door.

It whistled violently, as though aggrieved by his pushing and shoving. Against the stubborn door, he pushed as hard as he could. He pushed and shoved; shoved and pushed.

It was almost closed.

As though borrowing its harrowing voice from the howling wind outside, Winter itself was now screaming not to be shut out, not to be excluded.

Then, with a final wail, and a sound like that of sharply in-sucked breath, the door shut.

The wintry voice then lulled, quietened to a whisper, a Jack Frost murmuring.

He was home.

Heavily, he panted. Thank goodness, he was back in the safety and comfort of his own domain, his own kingdom, for it was nearing midnight, nearing the darkest hour – the witching hour – the death of one day and the birth of another. The moon and all around it was now shrouded in an implacable opal curtain of fog – a fog which had blindfolded his eyes as it shifted close and then far, close and then far, enveloping all in its silent grey tides.

Having surrendered the car to the invading snow and ice and frost, which crunched and cracked underfoot, at the end of the lane, Mr Jones had walked only the length of a football field or so – perhaps not even so far as that – and in that short distance he had slipped a dozen times, maybe more, fallen three times, perhaps four, almost not managed to get up twice, and pictured himself dead all the way.

It was such a piercing cold storm outside that its chilling needles and knives had penetrated his clothes with a consummate ease, pushed their way through the fabric, and sliced in through his skin to make chatter his teeth, ache his bones, and pain his kidneys.

Winter's frosted fingers had expertly torn their way into his body, and felt around inside.

His face was an epitaph of the season, stone-grey and chiselled in ice-mourning.

Quite how explorers traversed the poles of the planet, he could not say, quite how they scaled the mountain ranges of the world, he could not imagine, quite how they stayed alive in the frozen treacherous hells of Earth, he very simply could not know, for he was quite sure that one more moment outside would have meant his end. It was the coldest winter ever known. His lips blue, he trembled.

Still shaking then, he patted himself down, stamped the snow from his boots, briefly blew into his cupped shuddering hands and then stiffly threw off his coat.

Then, slowly, gradually, the warmth of the house came to embrace him, to wash over his frozen extremities, flood in through his pores and course along his veins, bringing the chapped blood racing back from its retreat.

His heart speeded then, pumping blood.

His flesh turned pink again.

And then his heart slowed.

However, he did not cease trembling.

His shaking did not stop.

Even as the warmth hugged the last cold breath out of him in a dust-white plume, his body persisted to palsy.

The trembling continued for good reason, though, for it was not the cold exclusively that made him shudder so. He was shaken by something else, punch-drunken by a horror other than this imperceptibly impossible winter evening.

188

His wife had begged him not to leave, hadn't she, not to go out driving in such conditions, on such a night. It was *stupid of him*, she had declared. It was a *foolish, idiotic* thing to do. She had pleaded to his better judgement. But, he had needed to get away. Just for a moment. Just for a respite. A breath or two.

The arguing had become too much for him. If he had stayed, he might have killed her. How saddening that today should have been a joyous one, a day filled with merriment and anticipation. Today was, after all, Christmas Eve.

But, try as they both had sworn to do, they could not get along. They could not see 'eye-to-eye', as people often say, and as people in love, and in business, equally often struggle to do – no matter how sincere their pledges and vows might be.

Their bodies had grown old with time, their minds and hearts tired with experience, and their love stale with monotony.

They had fought every day for as long as Mr Jones could remember. They had both said very hurtful things: she had marked his character *imperious* and he had stained her *captious* – a petty and pathetic woman, obsessed with trivial matters. They had both, too, swore that they hated one another. It seemed at times as though the only bandage still loosely binding them was their daughter.

However, after the shock of what he had just experienced, Mr Jones wanted now more than anything – and more than ever before – to hold his wife, to hug her tight, to kiss her warm cheek and declare his eternal love, whispering in her ear.

Horror had endowed him with a new appreciation of life – a new lease of love.

Mr Jones sighed to himself then, his breathing unsteady and upset.

His eyes were stark, hollow and lost; they were empty and yet somehow full – full of sadness.

He grabbed at the walls in his tremulous state, needing to hold on tight to something firm, fixed and real.

He quivered and then held still a moment, listening.

The winter crept about the house outside, but inside it was silent; very strangely silent. There was no sound of movement, no sound of the television humming, and no stirring or sloshing of water, or cotton sheets shuffling.

It was deadly silent.

He called out to his wife, 'Helen?'

There was no answer.

Then he called for his daughter, 'Eleanor? Ellie?'

Again there was no reply.

'Helen-honey? Eleanor?'

A faint echo.

Then stillness.

Quietness.

Nothing.

Mr Jones kicked off his boots now, as was the ritual and as they had become damp with the thawing remnants of snow upon them.

Because they were also damp, he pulled off his socks now, by standing on one with the other foot, and then standing on the other with the first sockless one.

He spread out his toes as best he could, curled them up, and then uncurled them again.

'Helen...? Honey...?'

No reply.

Moving through the house, uneasily, checking first the kitchen and then the library, he eventually found his wife in the living room.

She was sat there, upon a stool in front of the almost silent fire, with her face, hands and breast glowing faint orange and her back facing him, shrouded in ash-grey shadows.

From the profile of her half-lit face, Mr Jones could see that his wife looked pensive, serene and sombre, and perhaps displeased. She had always a knack of wearing more than one emotion at a time. She was ambivalence personified.

She did not move to greet him.

Despite nothing moving, the room around her looked so alive, festooned with glittering lights, tinsel, plastic holly-bush leaves and sparkling baubles.

Yet she sat motionless, statuesque and so grey, so lacking animation, so bereft of life, among the festive decorations.

The only thing which did move on her was the slowly shifting dim orange glow of the fire, softly flickering across her cheek, brow and breast.

Then her fingers, laced together on her thighs, moved ever so much, rubbing one another.

'Helen,' Mr Jones said softly, approaching her, 'why didn't you answer me? I called out and you didn't answer me, Helen? Helen?'

But Mrs Jones did not stir in the slightest.

She still did not turn to see, or greet, her husband.

After a time, she spoke only very slowly and sombrely and said, 'I didn't hear you. Couldn't have done. I wasn't here.'

'You mean you were off dreaming – that kind of not here?'

Still facing the fire, his wife casually shrugged her shoulders.

He was used to her speaking in tongues, always so vague in language, as artists are.

'Where's, where's Ellie?' he asked next. 'Is she still not home?'

'No. She's still out. I'm not sure she's coming back.'

'Oh, I'm sure she will,' he said. 'And, well – well, something horrible has happened, Helen. Something so, so horrible; that poor, poor soul,' he stammered.

'Someone... someone has been hit by a car, up there on the roadside.' His bottom lip trembling, he pointed in the general direction of the accident, his outstretched index finger also shaking. 'Someone has been hit and I think they're dead, Helen... It's awful,' he added.

His wife, still not looking, said softly, quietly, 'I know.'

'It's awful,' he continued, stood beside her now, swaying. 'I saw the snow all red and the blanket over the body, white on top of white beneath the white night sky, and all that blood soaked into the snow and the white blanket; all that white surrounding those patches of red, it looked so wrong, so unreal, and so awful.'

'There were police cars,' he rambled, 'and an ambulance and a great crowd of people all staring on. They were all jostling elbows, standing on tip-toes and craning their necks, just to get an eyeful of the picture. It made me sick. Some even took photographs – I saw the cameras flash. And it all made me wonder, well, it made me wonder just what went wrong with the world and when, or have we always been this way – curiously morbid? It was awful and... and... wait... did you say... you *know?*'

'Yes.'

'You know what? That it's awful or that it happened?'

'Both.'

'How? How do you know?'

'I was there. I followed you out and ended up there, saw it all.'

With a slump, Mr Jones sat himself in the chair beside where his wife was perched.

'Oh, Honey,' he said solemnly, 'that's awful. You shouldn't have followed me out in this weather. You shouldn't have had to see such an awful sight.'

'I could have sworn,' she said, 'that you would have only gone as far as the Fox and Hounds. I told myself that you wouldn't have gone off driving for miles, blind and drunk, in the snow; that you only took the car because you were being lazy. But, I couldn't make it there on foot – to the Fox – so I suppose you wouldn't have done either. So, I turned back to come home and that was when...' her voice trailed off.

She sobbed a little, but quickly stopped herself.

Mr Jones went to put out his hand, to place it there for his wife to hold.

Mrs Jones shied away from his advance.

She wiped a solitary tear from her eye.

He outstretched his arms to put around her, to hold her.

But she gestured, significantly, her disapproval.

'No, it's no use ruing the past,' she said. 'What happened – happened.

'Sure,' she reasoned, 'we could argue that you shouldn't have left, shouldn't have taken the car out after drinking so much, and that you shouldn't have been heading off to the pub to drink some more. You should have walked – we could say – if you really did need to get more drink in you. It should have been you out walking, and not me. But there's no use mourning choices which never really existed in the first place. We both acted on impulse, driven by emotion. It couldn't have been any other way, that's the truth of it all...'

Robert sat watching his wife's lips move in the way they always did – with a slow assertiveness, an awareness of self, of life, of fact and fancy. She seemed always to know just what she wanted to say, always so assured of her ability to express herself coherently. She thought when others just spoke, and spoke when others had exhausted themselves speaking. She weighed up every word beautifully in her mind, before stringing them together and lacing the air with them. Better than the best, she knew her own mind. That had always been the thing he adored most about Helen in their younger years, when their romance was fledgling, fresh and new, and forever filled with surprises to be beguiled – new and wondrous aspects of one another to be revered, savoured and loved, indefinitely.

Watching her talk, listening to the sounds of her melodic, soothing tone, Robert felt strangely nervous; he was upset in the stomach, unsettled at the thought of saying those three magical words which, because of the years spent unspoken, forgotten somewhere, discarded as nonsense, now seemed somewhat alien to his mind, mouth and cold heart.

I love you, he said to himself, as a thought.

I love you and this has all been madness, he expanded on it. Let's sell the house and run away from the mess we've made... together... together... let's be together, as we were once upon a time... let's be together and let's get back to true love. We could travel the world; pretend we have nothing to fear, nothing to lose and everything to gain.

Eleanor's old enough to understand...

She'll be starting her own family, soon enough...

She'd understand...

Like a silent movie of the mind, a pantomime picture-book flicking through pages, he played out the possible outcomes of his internal monologue, preparing for its opening-night, its undrawn curtain.

And all the while that he watched her soft lips move, all the while that he felt around at and pondered his wishes, feelings and fantasies, all the while that he wondered what might transpire, his wife had continued to talk.

'We both said things,' she breathed, motionless. 'We both said things, and did things we shouldn't have done, but neither could have chosen not to. That's what I've come to realise about life, after tonight – it's all set out for us. We might choose what to wear, or what to eat and when, and where to spend our holidays, and where to work and walk, but those are only the minutia – the finite details – which have no real bearing on the overall

194

outcome of things. On the whole, regardless of the tiny decisions we might make, or at least think we make, it's all planned out for us, all laid out in one particular order. And, well, I just wanted to say...'

But now Robert could no longer wait. He had to beat her to the punch, as it were, had to tell her how he felt first, before she told him the opposite – or the same – for he could not decide which it was that she was building towards but was certain that the most sincere word always is spoken first. And so he was now forced to interrupt his wife, echoing her half sentence.

'I just wanted to say, before you say anything, that I –'

All of a sudden, there was a rapping at the door.

Three knocks, very firm.

Mr Jones jumped up out of the chair, shook his head, mystified and disgruntled, and said, 'Who on Earth could that be?'

He went to leave the room, answer the door and reveal the mystery caller.

'Don't answer it, Robert,' his wife said pleadingly.

'What? Why ever not?' he wished to know, turning back to face her.

Even now she did not look to him, just kept on staring into the fire, saying gravely, 'Just don't, please. Just don't. Not yet.'

'But it's freezing outside; I can't leave whoever it is stood there.'

'Please,' the statue said again, 'don't answer it.'

'But it could be Ellie. I might have locked her out; might have locked the door. I don't think I did, but I can't be sure that I didn't.'

'It's not Ellie.'

'How do you know it's not?'

'I just know. Please don't answer it, Robert.'

'I have to.'

'Please don't. Not just yet.'

195

'Helen, I have to. You can't give good reason why not to – can you?'

She said nothing but only shook her head.

And so Mr Jones turned again to go to the door.

'Robert?'

He turned once more, annoyed now, to look upon his wife, sat upon the stool.

She had finally turned to face him now, for the first time since his return home.

She looked on him with a pale expression, gaunt and sorrowful.

He gave her an expectant look.

Then she spoke again.

'I just wanted to say that, despite everything, always and forever, I love you.'

Although she had beaten him to it, Robert felt a great relief wash over his person. At hearing those three words, after such a long time, a titanic weight seemed lifted from him.

The room seemed lighter, blossomed into luminosity, from out of sullen darkness.

He smiled.

His wife then smiled back at him.

'I love you, too,' he said, 'I love you more than ever, in fact. Now, let me just get the door and we can get ourselves to bed after that. Tomorrow is a new day. Eleanor will be back soon – Heaven knows, she should be back by now – and she's bringing her new boyfriend with her, don't forget. You've been looking forward to meeting him, haven't you?'

Helen continued to smile, brighter now.

Her face seemed no longer pale.

She nodded her head in tacit agreement to all his propositions, and then she said once more, 'I love you, Robert.'

Robert smiled, said 'I know,' and went to answer the door.

On his way there he had fleeting odd thoughts as to why Helen might not want him to answer it.

But no good reason came to mind.

Nothing rational.

Then, forgetting, he had brief visions of the many festivities to come: of the mulled wine simmering in the saucepan, of its scent sauntering in steam around the rooms of the house as the merriment spread with it.

He could almost hear the Christmas cheer.

As she had just been, he could see Helen smiling as she lay to plates the fine festive feast they had both lovingly prepared together, for themselves and for their daughter, Eleanor, and her new love.

He pictured himself declaring a toast to Family and Fresh Starts – New Adventures. He saw them play board games together and, later, when neighbours and friends and other family members arrived, they would play charades and cards with laughter unbridled and bottles of whisky and wine uncorked, and they would sing all the old songs and fill the house with a joyous chorus.

And then, just as he placed his touch upon the door handle, he quickly gave forethought to the events due to come thereafter, when Christmas was done. He wanted to share his new found joy of life, his emergent youth of heart, with Helen.

He pictured her face beaming at the news that he finally was ready to travel, as she had always wanted.

Then he opened the door.

The wind must have died away, for the door only shushed as it opened and the snow no longer stormed about on the white air outside. Instead the winter seemed settled into the calm cold of a crisp and charming Christmas Eve.

All dressed in black, with a light covering of snow upon his shoulders and hat, the Caller stood very firm – as firm as his knocks had been.

Mr Jones noticed first the emblematic crest upon the Caller's right breast, and then the dimly-lit green screen, glowing on the radio upon his left breast; then the crest again, this time upon his hat, and the chequered band – blue, white, blue, white, blue – and then the name badge, the title of authority.

It was a policeman.

A dread filled Robert Jones.

The officer stood almost as a silhouette against the brilliant white world outside.

A second officer – a female one – was standing just behind him, over his right shoulder. She was shivering and they both had solemn, cheerless expressions.

'Mr Jones?' asked the foremost officer.

Puzzled, fearful, Robert confirmed his identity.

'May we come in, Sir?'

'Why, yes, of course. Come in.'

Robert stepped aside.

The two officers stepped inside the hallway.

The female officer closed the door behind her.

'What can I do for you, officers?' the now-nervous man asked, rather timidly.

'Is that your car at the end of the road, Mr Jones?'

'Yes, it is.'

'Do you have somewhere we can sit? Can we go through to the lounge, perhaps?' requested the policeman.

'Look,' said Robert Jones, searching for a reason to their attendance, and now feeling increasingly worried about his own actions, 'if this has something to do with me having a drink and then driving, I...' his voice faded, searching. 'Well, I don't know what to say, but...' again his voice receded. 'Look, just come through to the kitchen, please.'

And so, eager to avoid the living room and his wife's involvement, he led the two police officers down the hall and into the kitchen, and as he did so, the male of the two said, 'Don't worry, it's not about that Mr Jones, although that's very honest of you.'

The three then entered the kitchen and sat at the dining table.

Mr Jones drummed his fingers on the table-top, and then, nervous, offered the two officers a cup of tea or coffee, which they both declined politely.

His eyes searched about the silent room as he waited for something to be said, for something to happen.

'Oh God,' he then exclaimed, 'this isn't about Ellie, is it? What's she done? Is she in trouble?'

'No, Mr Jones: it's not about your daughter. I'm afraid it's about –'

Mr Jones interrupted, anticipating the police officer's revelation.

'Is it,' he blurted out, rambling, 'is it about that awful accident up there – by The Fox? Why, I only drove by when it had already happened, when it was too late – the Police and Ambulance had already arrived. I don't have anything insightful to offer there, I'm afraid, I...'

'Mr Jones,' said the female officer, softly, placing the palm of her hand upon the back of his, 'it's about your wife.'

At this, Mr Jones began to ramble furthermore, his mind awash and sent asunder by consternation.

'My *wife?* What has *she* done? *She's* sat in the room. She saw the accident, too – perhaps before I did – did you want to speak to her? Was she a witness? Is she in trouble?' He shook his head disbelievingly. 'She can't be in trouble,' he assured himself. 'She can't be: I had the car: she couldn't possibly have hit whoever it was that got hit. Is that what you're saying – that she ran someone over? Well, you're wrong! I'm telling you you're wrong! She couldn't possibly have done that! I had the car! I'll call her right now and you can ask her yourself! Helen? Helen! Come in here, Helen! The police are here and they want to –'

'Mr Jones, stop, please,' the female officer implored, looking desperately sorry for him.

As Robert had spoken, the two officers had stared at him. Their faces had become increasingly attentive. Then, they had become bemused, quizzical, concerned, and then incredulous. They looked worried for him. They both seemed emphatically pitiful of him, and of his confusion.

'Mr Jones,' said the male officer, plaintively, 'I'm afraid your wife is dead.'

'I beg your pardon?'

'She was hit by a car, Mr Jones. He didn't stop. But, we caught him.'

'*I beg your pardon?*'

'I'm sorry but your wife has died. It would have been quick; she wouldn't have suffered...'

The apparently widowed man now leapt from his seat, smashed his fist down against the table-top and shouted in the two officer's faces, disgusted by their misinformation.

He roared at them.

'*I beg your pardon!*' He struck out that air, waved it aside with a stiff finger, pointing. '*You* ought to get your facts right before you go marching along to people's houses to announce such things! *My wife* is *alive* and well and sitting in the next room! You *idiotic* fools! Now get *out* of my house!'

Turning away in disgust, he beckoned his wife.

'Helen, come here. Helen? Helen! Come here!'

But, there was no reply.

Nobody came.

He turned back a scornful glare at the two officers.

'Is this some sort of sick joke? Because it's not funny! Damn you both to hell! It's not at all funny!'

'Mr Jones!' cried the female officer. 'Sit back down!'

Reluctantly, Mr Jones sat.

'There's no mistake, Mr Jones,' she said sadly. 'And I assure you that this is no joke. Your wife – Helen Elizabeth Jones, born February the second, nineteen-sixty-two – was the unfortunate victim of a road-traffic accident tonight, at approximately twenty-two-hundred hours.'

Defiant, Mr Jones shook his head.

'She sustained serious injuries and died beside the road; she was already gone by the time the paramedics arrived. I was *there*, Mr Jones. I *saw* her. I emptied her pockets, found her purse. I have her driving license here with me.' She patted his breast. 'Your wife is gone, I'm afraid.'

'*You* are an *idiot!*' he snarled. 'I'll show you who's alive and who's dead! *Idiots!* Helen? Helen!'

Incensed by the two police officers' idiocy, Mr Jones now flung himself back up out of his chair, kicked it aside, tortuously wheeled himself around in a rage, and marched out of the kitchen, across the hallway, and into the living room.

He would show them what idiots they were.

Oh, he'd show them.

But, when he got there, he found that the stool was empty, long since cold, and the fire was ash, long since dead.

The room was in perfect darkness and silence.

Nothing glittered.

Nothing gleamed.

Nothing had a charm to it.

Nothing made a sound.

Nothing made sense.

His wife was gone.

'*Helen?*'

Had she ever been there, he asked himself. Had he merely imagined her? How could any of this be possible? This was crazy. She couldn't be dead. She was just here – just now. It couldn't be. This was madness.

201

'Helen?'

He swayed, sidled against the doorway, grabbed at the walls, stumbled slightly and then fell to his knees, drunk with horror.

The two shadowed officers, as mournful mediators, makeshift undertakers, came up behind, and then hovered over, the broken man in the doorway.

One of them then spoke a grave affectation.

'We're deeply sorry for your loss, Mr Jones.'

The other then reiterated the sentiment, filled with sincerity.

'We really are sorry.'

But, Mr Jones heard nothing.

Slowly, the broken man began to sob.

Then the clock struck midnight.

It was Christmas.

The Scrap Metal Man

A flustered Frederic Johnson set out across the reclamation yard, stepping over small debris, sidling by the big stuff.

As he went, he did so touching the air, as if conducting an inaudible orchestra with his forefingers, a séance with the scrapheaps surrounding him. Almost blindly he meandered, swaying this way and that.

He was looking for something but unsure of what.

He knew the function but not the part, the effect but not the cause.

He drifted from broken washing machine to burnt-out television-set, from silent radio to warm refrigerator, searching vaguely, looking but not looking, guided only by quiet soliloquy and abstract purpose, the promise of synergy between man and metal.

'Long, thin, stiff,' Frederic told himself, his slender aged fingers divining over the vastly heaped metal materials. 'Long, thin, stiff... wire but not wire... slightly thicker... rods... runners... tendons. Come on now... Come on. Where are you? Where *are* you?'

He was like a pianist, a blind Beethoven perhaps, fluttering the ivory keys, touching on the blacks, feeling out the rhythm of a composition in progress, the vibrations of the air around him making invisible impacts, softly, on the drum-stretched skin of his face and arms.

He moved, lightly, on a wind of instinct and intuition.

Then, he stopped.

He stood.

He was silent.

He pushed his wire-frame spectacles back up his nose, from where they had slid.

He squinted.

He briefly brushed one trembling, work-coarsened, leathered-by-labour hand over a shock of his electric-white hair, which tufted from out of his liver-spotted scalp in three sparse snow-explosions; and then he groomed his grey moustache, stroking it with thumb and forefinger, parting it, in slow deliberation.

For there, piled before him in the far corner of a vast yard swamped with decades of hoarded scrap metal, was a substantial collection of old bicycle and tricycle frames, and wheels.

'Aha!' he cried out, striking a fist at the air. 'I knew it – I knew I'd kept you for something!'

His old mind and old bones racing, he gathered up a pair of similar-sized rims, made his way through the refuge, and headed back towards his garage.

Once there he took in hand his wire-cutters, snipped here and there – snip-snap, snip-snap – and removed twenty spokes of equal measurements.

Then, slowly he threaded them, one by one, very carefully, through the welded wrists and brazened ankles.

Having made satisfactory use of the spokes, Frederic then promptly returned to the yard, stood with hands on hips, and looked around at the loosely organised havoc of entangled metal heaps for what he might use next.

All these things, he thought, all these things I've gathered up for so long, making treasures of other people's trash, placing them in loosely categorised piles, in this open grave of mine, and never knowing quite why.

But now I know.

All of a sudden, I know.

What joy, he told himself, what overwhelming joy-of-all-joys, to know why I *wanted* what was *unwanted*, and what I must do with it all now.

Here, moving now, he found the Smiths' dead hover sat atop a pile in the marvellous midden – its fabric bag billowing, out then in, full then empty, with the passing gusts of wind, like the sail of a strange and ancient yacht – making him think of a lung, the hover's mouth once taking endless deep breaths as it sucked up dust.

Here he stumbled upon the Barkers' old immersion heater – a copper tank pied with patina – a stomach, perhaps...

Here he found piles of old steel kettles; kettles which had boiled so many times that their rust-pitted bottoms had fallen out, or whose handles had torn away from their corroded pop-rivet fastenings and into early retirement.

And here he made his way to a harem of washed-up washing machines, one of which he felt might make a particularly good digestive system – its detergent tray a plastic pallet, its drum-stomach a quarter-filled with acid, its drainage pipes the intestines, large and small.

Hungrily, he gathered it all up, every last exciting object, as best he could, hoisting it onto his shoulders, stuffing it into his pockets, piling it onto a cart, into a barrow, dragging it along the ground, if necessary, back to his garage, and then to the pit, to what it was that waited there, recumbent.

As he worked, floating from bench to bench, from drawer to drawer, shelf to shelf, Frederic Johnson tried tirelessly to find all the right ingredients – all the correct components – to suit his crafting. He fished out bolts of adequate lengths from dented cake tins, scrabbled through nuts in oily coffee jars to find the appropriate partners, and stripped down wires as a hunter might skin his catch – looking for the good meat, the prime cuts.

Almost soundlessly, he glided about the whole place and seemed to draw the entire room and all the yard outside in around him, concocting an alchemic compendium of raw materials to make his giant metal man.

'Frederic,' sighed Cynthia, his wife, framed in the doorway. 'I've called you five times already. Your dinner is on the table, going cold.'

'Sorry dear,' he said sincerely but absently. 'I didn't hear you. Would you leave mine in the oven... if you will? I'll be along soon.'

'But,' she said, despondent, 'I've made your favourite.'

'Thank you, dear,' replied the busy man, tightening a nut as he spoke, 'but I really have to keep on with this for now. It's going so well.'

'Just let it be, please, and come inside,' said his wife.

She had in her eyes a grave look, but her husband, working feverishly, did not see it.

'Come inside,' she repeated. 'The radio's no company for me now. It keeps making me nervous with all its apocalyptic talks, sounding more and more like you each day.

'Now's not the time for sculpting scrap,' she went on, when there came no response. 'It's a time for being indoors with loved ones and holding hands and sharing memories. You've been out here for over a week now,

206

and you've barely slept a wink, and hardly ate a crumb. You must be running on empty.'

'I'm running,' said Frederic, flustered, adjusting his spectacles, 'on adrenaline and... fear, Cynthia.'

He kept on tightening nuts and bolts now, screwing and unscrewing screws, as he spoke on his fears.

'It's only ever a matter of time,' he said, fearfully. 'It's the same with every kind of war – only ever a matter of time. I did tell you: the Indians made their bows to hunt, but it was only a matter of time before they needed to be turned upon the white man, invading their land. It's only ever a matter of time: gun powder would always lead to plots. Atomic power to bombs. And now the whole world has been on edge for ninety-some years.'

'The Cold War passed,' he proceeded, 'but the fear remained. It just upped and moved elsewhere, transferred its investment, inflated into a new nightmare, the realisation of which was only a matter of time. Cracking the nuclear code, smashing together atoms – despite the many medical advances it made possible – was only ever going to end in decimation, I'm afraid.'

He shook his head in dismay, admitted to himself, and to his wife, 'I'm afraid. I'm afraid that it's comparable to handing a hosepipe to a boy, instructing him only to water the plants, and expecting him to not succumb to temptation, not to turn it on his brothers and sisters, or the neighbour's cat. Oppenheimer knew it himself, tasted the fear first: we have become death, the destroyer of worlds.'

'I had hoped,' Frederic added, still staring into his work, 'I had hoped that the world would come to its senses, that there would be a global disbanding of arms, an atomic amnesty; I had hoped, sincerely, that humanity would prevail, that caritas would rise again and reign supreme. Idealistic nonsense – I know that now. The last to strike is the first to fall. Perhaps we will strike first again. Perhaps we will buy ourselves a little more time...'

He went on a little longer, speaking very softly about things very hard to accept, about possibilities and inevitabilities the likes of which he dearly hoped would not be realised but which he knew, all too well, would be.

When the foreseer of fallouts had finally finished speaking there came no reaction from his wife, and he knew without needing to see, he perceived by the absolute silence, by the subtle shift in the air about him, that Cynthia Johnson had sauntered back into the house.

He glanced up.

She was indeed gone.

Perhaps she had heard his oratory verses one too many times.

Perhaps she'd had enough of it.

Perhaps she had.

Steaming, however, on the workbench side, there sat a cup of tea.

She still loved him, it said.

Night came out and night went on and the air turned crisp and the moon arced across the sky in serene silence, and stars burnt in muted white flames, and the animals of the evening hooted, barked, howled and crawled and flew on fluttering wings; and then the sun rose to the sound of cocks crowing, stretching its red and golden rays across the land, and the earth stirred, and dew settled, and people awoke, and all the while the inventive man worked in ignorance of the surrounding cosmos and all its restive motions.

So deeply immersed in his work as he was, it seemed as though nothing else in the world existed.

With his arms now elbow-deep in the engine-bay-chest of the gargantuan metal man, Frederic fed spaghetti wires through darning-needle-eyes, smeared flux and smelted solder beneath his pen-like soldering-iron. He fitted solenoids here and there, and he greased sockets and oiled hinges, fashioned motorised joints and stethoscope-ears and camera-lens-irises, and he sent lightning sparks out jumping from his welding torch, his hands gloved in dirt, his face masked behind a blackened shield, eyes glowing from out of thick protective goggles.

There was a wild and wonderful cacophony of humming and crackling and cracking and crisping; of whirs and screeches and screams and clangs and hammerings, as the work went on and on and on, relentlessly.

He was a magician inspired, a wizard, an alchemist throwing minerals and potions and slight-of-hand-movements about his person and the pit and the colossus he constructed. Sparks flew in flurry of blue-white-fire and ember showers fell in a downpour of heated-metal-orange and deep-red-cooling, glowing; the grinder grinded, the winch winched, the cutter cut, and the old man felt an almighty invigoration seize his old bones and wash them anew, jolted to life by brilliant vibrations and explosions of light and excitement.

It seemed that at no point in the building of his metal man was Frederic Johnson entirely sure of what he was doing. He had never sculpted a thing like this before – had never sculpted anything at all, for that matter – and never again would. So, being a man of little knowledge but great emotion and creativity and enterprise, he relied heavily upon guess-work and upon trial-and-error, and so – so far – he had felt his way almost blindly through grand ambition, armed only with a vague understanding of anatomy and an immovable sense of destiny.

This procedure, in essence, was nothing new to him: he had lived his life by instinct over intellect, feeling what his stomach told him was right to do in moments of uncertainty, listening to the lumps in his throat in times of upset, entrusting his heart to assert definitive truths.

'I'm almost done,' he finally, breathlessly, thankfully told to nobody but himself, smiling satisfied. 'I'm almost done...'

Then, what seemed like a few seconds later, he felt the chill of eyes watching him, scrutinising, staring.

Presently a shadow drifted into the garage, coming to rest in the shadows before him.

In front of him, without looking, judging only by the shadow's form and posture, he knew very well that Cynthia was again stood in the doorway.

'You didn't come to bed again last night,' she said accusingly.

'I didn't even realise night had been and gone,' he explained.

'What have I done to deserve this?' she asked angrily, after a pause.

'Pardon?' asked Frederic, bemused.

'What have I done,' she begged of him, 'to deserve this *cold-shoulder* treatment of yours?'

'Oh, oh, nothing, dear, really. Really, I'm very truly sorry that you feel that way but... you've done nothing wrong, really... really... honestly,' said Frederic, still not looking at his wife, trying best to appease her anger but to continue with his work, simultaneously. 'I just,' he stuttered, 'it's just,' he stammered, 'this is just so... so very important to me and... and... and...'

'And I'm not.' she finished the sentence for him.

'Of course you are, dear.'

'Well then come inside,' she insisted, her eyes sharp.

'I can't, Cynthia, I just can't,' protested Frederic, at last raising his oil-smeared face and shock of electric-white hair in the dim garage light.

His eyes seemed desperately upset.

'It's pressing and time is moving on,' he said. 'It has to be done now; it's incumbent and I'm incumbent, it's lain heavy on me for so long! I have to do my duty. When this is all over and done, when the dust has all settled and the human race begins to repopulate the world, when they regain strength and muster huge ambitions anew, they're going to need something to remind them of us... of now... of what we amounted to... in case of amnesia...'

'You should be building a shelter, Frederic Johnson,' his wife rebuked wildly, having at last lost control of her patience. 'You should be building a shelter, if you're as worried as you say, and stockpiling it with food and then getting a wash – you're filthy!'

'Shelter's no good for nothing,' said Frederic, mildly incensed by the digression. 'You may just as well dig your own grave.'

'The Howards built a shelter,' the wife argued.

'Well, that only proves the Howards are just as dumb as most, my dear,' declared the husband, turning his face back to his work. 'That they're damned dumb and that they've gone and got themselves a underground charnel house, a mass-grave.' He grabbed a wrench, shook it as he spoke. 'This time round they're dropping the big ones, Cynthia – mark my words – and when they hit they'll destroy everything worth destroying; they'll flatten whole cities, wipe out entire countries, and anything they don't kill outright will only die in time, with the sun shut out by the ash clouds. Nope, there's no good and no sense in playing ostriches now; no good building shelters. The whole world's gone mad.'

'And you're the only one sane, huh, Fred? Yes, yes. You're the only one sane.'

Cynthia paused for a time, waiting on a reply which did not come.

Defiant, blindly, Frederic went back to his work.

'The radio in the kitchen,' she then told the inattentive man, 'says that they've just this minute declared war. So it seems that you were right all along. You can be smug if you want. I won't blame you. They say bombs could drop any second...'

'I'm almost done,' said the scrap-metal-scientist, his electric-white hair blazing, not hearing the tremulous tone of fear in his wife's voice. 'I'm almost done...'

And with that Cynthia Johnson vanished off into the house again, made thud a few doors. As if she were a disgruntled breeze suddenly whipped into a brief storm, she walked with heavily thumping steps, slammed down cups as though they were auctioneer's gabbles, and huffed and puffed big deep breaths of indignation.

What a selfish man, she told herself, hissing with bitterness at the thought of him, now. What a stupidly selfish man – typical of the species of Man, such a different species, such a very separate and odd species from that of Woman. Stupid and selfish.

Then, her anger purged, she calmed with the shake of her head and a sigh of dismay, and busied herself with airing clothes that might never again be worn, cleaning dishes that may never again be eaten from, her nervous fingers twitching.

She knew, you see, deep down, that the task her husband had assigned to himself was not one born out of selfishness. It was one almost entirely selfless, she knew, enjoy it as much as he might at times – a selfless act, laced with the liquor of self-satisfaction.

Seemingly oblivious to the brumal discontent that he had sent thundering into his wife and into his home, Frederic continued his work, then, until it was done.

And then, later in the day, as the sun vanished below the horizon as a dying flame, looking down into the pit Frederic Johnson admired the colossal copper, bronze, iron and steel effigy, laying there, waiting to be buried.

As though he had finally reached a promised place of miracles, after a pilgrimage of seemingly endless miles, he felt overwhelmed with pride and relief.

For the finishing touch he then laid something there upon the scrap metal man's abdomen, something symbolic, something with a message, the one thing he had planned, laid from waist to neck in the manner of steel sword or golden sceptre, buried with a great king or priest or god – a rare relic, acquired and collected from a vintage arms dealer: a twenty-two foot long missile: a rocket.

Now, properly and finally done, he poured oil – pumping it, litre after litre, from out of a vast tanker outside – into the recently-extended garage pit, enough to cover the whole frame and submerge this magnificent, giant, sixty foot tall corpse, which he alone had crafted.

Then, using a pulley system set up among the rafters to hoist up and sit down a series of great gravestone slabs, he closed in the concrete catacomb.

In silent reverie then, for a long and serene time, he stood dreaming, hoping that one day, many years from now, beyond the vistas of impending violence, these remnants of human endeavours, which he alone had crafted into shapes anew, might, by some miracle, rise in rigid movements and recollect – dripping – its awesome steel eyes blinking – focusing – its fantastic copper lips pursing an oil gloss for the first time, to warn the future fathers.

He hoped that its water-pump-heart might murmur, beat, then palpitate. That its cable arteries and wire veins and tiny capillaries might, spark infused, fill with a surge of great power, and that its circuit-board-brain might then instruct this now automatous marionette, endued with vital warmth, to awaken its piston limbs to shift in ancient sea oil, stand twenty feet tall, and move the clockwork jaw in utterance of a strange new voice of mechanical oration.

It might speak in warning, he hoped, to the people of a tomorrow's world, of the inherent dangers of human invention.

And even if the Metal Man never did move – for his promethean hopes were precarious at best – Frederic Johnson told himself that he knew, almost for certain now, that when one day unearthed, it would at the very least serve as a monument of endless regrets and eternal lamentations. When all the books were burnt or rendered unreadable by decay, when all the electronic insight of the world was erased in immense balls of fire, when all buildings had crumbled or been torn apart by atomic tornadoes, when all of what was once named Civil and Human had died, the Metal Man would remain, beneath the ashes, waiting there, to be consulted as an ambassador of the past, an emissary of all things ancient.

Maybe, just maybe, Frederic told himself, either way, it might just work...

On the creaking porch in the dark and quiet evening, the old man, the collector of disused goods, the recycler of metals unwanted, sat himself down beside his silent wife on the wooden bench there, kissed her cheek, took hold of her hand, stroked it, and made amends through the gentle whispering of a few special words.

Frederic's face, shrouded by the inundation of dusk and near silence, became restive.

He looked at his wife then, and smiled at her in the darkness.

She smiled back at him, sighed, squeezed tight his hand, and slowly mouthed back those three beautiful words.

'I love you.'

Then, as time drifted towards its ultimate end, together after a week's apartness, in the deep dusk and the near silence, the old couple watched, with silent and solemn tears rolling down their flushed cheeks, smiling

bravely, holding hands, as the bright orange clouds
bloomed upon the black horizon like giant mushrooms.

In Extremis

The Great Sleeper slept, his eyes on occasion shifting beneath their lids, here and there, left and right, twitching like curious twin mice trapped beneath the ruffled flesh counterpane of his face.

Like a dreaming dog, only weaker, his feet and hands jittered intermittently – jolted, palsied in small movements – as though he were running very slowly, very unsteadily, very limply trying to catch something uncatchable.

It had been this way for over a year, him hardly waking from his prolonged dormancy, barely moving at all.

But, in his mind, unbeknown to anyone, he was a boy again. With silken black hair sweeping across his brow and bright open eyes glittering with excitement, he was racing barefooted along golden sands, yellow kite held aloft to the blue sky, waiting for his father's call to come when it was time for lift-off.

Ready, the boy was thinking. Ready.

'Ready?'
'Ready!'
'Now!'

Now he was in his hospital bed, as sick as ever.

People came and went in shuffling numbers: Nurses to check his vitals, porters to bring him warm victuals – which he rarely touched – and visiting loved ones at the allotted times, although they were rarely asked to leave when their time was up. And all the while the Sleeper, for the most part, was seemingly unaware of their comings and goings.

Outwardly, his senses were dimmed.

Very slowly, he was dying.

His illness was taking full hold of him.

It would not let go.

It seemed as though, sadly, there was nothing to be done.

When the nurses came they read and understood the numbers and the terrains of flowing curvatures and sharp peaks and sudden falls on the various monitors. They observed the ascending and descending lines on the screens, listened to the gently thrumming and intermittently beeping machines which were plugged and latched, into and onto, the sleeping man. They diligently interpreted and transcribed the electronic utterings of the machines, heard the steadily beeping rhythms of their strange music, understood them, recorded the communications, made reports and charted points on a large map which hung over the foot of the bed, portraying a medical landscape of the man's immediate life, his there and then health.

They cared for him, as the young should for the old, taking care of the body's unspeakable realities, when nature and duty called. At intervals they came and adjusted his posture, too, fluffed his pillows and ensured he was as comfortable as possible. They stripped away his dirty bed linen and wrapped him up in cool fresh sheets.

The porters brought meals at mealtimes, attempting to rouse the Sleeper from his slumber, encouraging him to eat, partially succeeding at times, but ultimately failing. They emptied his full water jug, filled it again, offered him tea or coffee, and poured a fresh cup which would only go cold in time. This was their routine, three times a day.

The family members came in ones and twos and threes, hands in pockets, loosening their ties and adjusting their collars, or bearing fresh fruits, green grapes and ripened bananas and golden apples, which would only wither into decomposition on the bedside table, in time. They stood over the sleeping father, husband, grandfather and friend in awkward silences and solemn sighs, their faces glum, each harvesting an unappeasable hunger to be near him, more than just physically. They wanted desperately for him to open his eyes and to see them focus and alight with glowing recognition. But each was profoundly aware of the irrevocable helplessness of the predicament, staring down at his almost ochre complexion.

Four thousand years entombed, his face was that of an embalmed king finally exhumed. The leathered skin, pulled taut over his cheeks and brow, coarsened and loose around his jaw, was the pelt of a carcass long baked in the desert heat. Bandages held him together as funerary cerements. His frame was fragile, his muscles wasted to the brink of atrophy. His flesh hung from his wizened body like a poorly fitting suit. Considering the man he had once been, he was now a saddening sight.

Blue and red and purple, the family members looked to the jagged, angular and the flowing lines on the monitors; looked at them, *to them*, for answers. It was as though they hoped that any second now the lines might

218

jump and shock themselves straight and form curlicues, might suddenly transform into serifs and stems, bowls and counters, spines and ligatures and ascenders and descenders, and there might appear on the screen something recognisable, translatable, English, some certain message in these uncertain times. They hoped for a forecast of the future, life or death. But the lines remained steady and the numbers barely rose and hardly fell. They did not jump into letters or shock into words; they stayed instead as useful as hieroglyphs to the untrained eye, pretty but nothing more.

'He's dying,' someone whispered.

'Aren't we all,' another quickly retorted.

'His vitals are fine,' argued a third, with a sort of blunt authority. 'Everything's working as it should be; the doctor said so himself; he's got years left in him.'

'I strongly doubt a doctor would stick out his neck like that,' said the first, a little incensed. 'His illness is untreatable. And he's in the late stages. Face facts.'

'I disagree.'

'You would.'

The illness spoken of was an oddity at best. It was intangible and imponderable. It was something pernicious, insidious, something very gradual but ultimately unremitting and merciless. It was not something which could be removed by means of scalpel or combatted with chemicals. It was no pathogen to be remedied by soothing aromatic salves, or to be sweated out over honey-lemon steam bath, beneath a towelling canopy. Neither could it be poisoned or decimated by ionizing radiation. It was a slow killer, stealth and silent. It was something illusive and strange, and had no physical presence, something that not one family member could fully grasp. The various medical experts too – neurologists and such – had themselves failed to truly define it. They had their suspicions, of course. Their many scans had shown the degeneration of neurological activity. Areas of the brain had darkened, become increasingly inactive. His mind was failing, dying one cell at a time. But they had only been able, or perhaps only seen fit – for fear of misdiagnosis and the legal proceedings which might follow such an event – to speculate as to its true nature and name.

'Vascular Dementia, maybe,' one had theorised. 'Perhaps brought on by a series of Silent Strokes.'

'Possible Parkinson's Plus,' a report had read.

'A. K. S.'

'M. S. A.' was the feeling of one carer, at the respite home.

'Untreatable,' was the common consensus. 'Untreatable and very sad to see.'

'At such a young age, too.'

'These things happen, unfortunately.'

'So sad.'

'So sorry.'

'Such a young age.'

'Very sad to see.'

Many a time the talking disturbed his dreaming and the Great Sleeper heard and thought, even when it seemed to the talkers that he could not. He was a silent witness, a mountain watching a distasteful and ghastly town grow in its foothills. That frustrated him.

'I'm trapped in here!' he screamed in silence, on many an occasion. 'I'm here, inside my mind, perfectly well, but losing the battle, losing the ability to make my lips move in the ways they were always familiar with, losing my mind, and the will to live. I want to shout. I want to articulate; tell you my pain. But I cannot.'

If nothing else he had loved to speak, to talk for hours on end about the world around him and what he thought he knew of it and what he wished he could know for certain, what he felt of its wonders, what he loved and what he hated with equal absolution: the beauty of the morning sun, the mystery of the moon and

220

all the stars which littered the space around it; the nature of loves and the origins of hatred, true faith and its tenuous relationship with organised religion. He knew the finite details and all sides of the arguments surrounding Darwin's Theory and its missing link, its unexplainable anomaly. Gentlemanly lecturing, he would speak of the vanished planes of Flight 19, of Ehman's Wow Signal, Gil Perez's inexplicable journey. Strange and unsolved mysteries, these were the things he talked of in the quiet summer evenings and the long winter nights.

However, it mattered not what he spoke of, for there was forever an imperishable quality of romance in his tone. He was ennobled with the power, passion and poise to inspire and intrigue any audience. Regardless of the topic, his words were compelling.

Yet now all he could muster was short, simple statements and answers.

'I need the toilet.'

'Yes please.'

'No thank you.'

'I want to sleep.'

'I'm fine.'

'Hello.'

'Goodbye.'

His dignity was dead, his independence a long time forgotten. His conversations were laid to waste and buried, spoken now only through the remembrances and recollections of others, the regaling and comforting sharing – over cups of tea and coffee – of his former glories, his comedic anecdotes and his many great wisdoms. His former self lived on only in reminiscence.

For the third time in four days the youngest son had spent the night at the Sleeper's bedside, sat in an armchair, reading aloud from a book of short stories. It was all he could do to distract his own mind and,

221

perhaps, offer the comfort of companionship to his unresponsive father.

Around midnight he stopped reading, stared at the sessile man.

The Sleeper snored softly.

In his dreams he was a teenage boy who considered himself a man. He had a driving licence and a car to go with it. His hair was rich with styling cream, parted on the left and combed to the right in uniform gloss. His shirt was pressed, his cuffs and collar stiff with starch, his blazer and trousers black, his tie double knotted and royal blue. He was on his way to pick up a girl and take her to a Sunday Matinee, tapping his hand on the steering wheel almost in time with the music playing on the radio. Life was good. Nothing mattered. His pockets were full and his body was healthy.

'Saturday night an' I jus' got paid.

Fool 'bout my money, don't try t' save.

My heart says go, go, have a time.

'Cos it's Saturday night an' I'm feelin' fine –'

Then, in just one single moment, the engine stopped and the music died and the sun faded and the steering wheel melted away from his hands as a resinous black mirage. There was a brief blackness, an absolute dark. Then, suddenly again, his smart clothes were gone and he was casually dressed, and sweat beaded on his forehead to the shrill sound of infantile screams. The room he was in was bright white, blinding, as though staring directly at the sun.

His eyes focused now and he found himself staring directly at his baby son. He was a father again, for the first time ever. He was sitting in the hospital side-room, as he had done thirty seven years previous. His hands were trembling, his mouth aching with a huge smile, and he was brimming with powerful emotions the likes of which he had never felt before, never even imagined existed.

And as he pored over the tiny new human, who was swaddled in cotton and cradled in his impossibly nervous arms, it occurred to him that life changes by the moment, by varying degrees; this one being of the largest scale. Indeed, it was a huge moment. The sheer magnitude of it took all his will to even attempt digestion. Studying the small pink face of the sacrosanct child, he felt suddenly an almighty reverence surge through him, an excitation of absolute awe, something electric and wild and passionate and uncontrollable – something so wondrous and so fantastic that the word 'Pride' alone did it no justification. He felt he had been gifted a blissful burden. He felt whole. He felt complete. He felt as though he had discovered, by chance, the very meaning of life.

His eyes were bright and his voice soothing in reassurance, as he welcomed the tiny pink child into the world and vowed to him, 'I'll always look after you now; you've nothing to worry about, my little boy.'

The youngest son stopped his reading in the early hours. His eyes had grown sore and heavy. His breathing became calm, his eyes closed and he fell into a serene stasis.

At ten in the morning the consulting doctor came into the room, gave a brief and vague outline of the Sleeper's current condition, said solemnly that his illness was highly progressed, that they should be prepared for the worst, and left.

'Highly progressed,' marked one family member, staring longingly at the jaded sleeper.

'Highly progressed... Highly – progressed...' If said without expression, if plainly stated, or taken just halfway out of context, that sounded like a positive thing. But it was not.

With little chance of convalescence now, the side-room became a sanatorium in which nature would run its course, either way, and in which the dispirited family members stood shuffling their feet, twiddling thumbs and gazing at the white walls, waiting, numbed, seemingly indifferent.

In the afternoon, briefly, the Sleeper opened his eyes, closed them, and opened them again. They were bleared and watery, like two creamy pearls sunken into the sallow sea of his face. The electric blueness of the irises had faded; the blackness of the pupils gone grey and misty, like unsettled lagoon water, sediment stirred up from the sandy bed. There was an awful vagueness to them, a dreadful murkiness. When he looked in the direction of his youngest son he seemed only to look around him, or through him, rather than at him. His pupils never fixed or focussed, stayed small, did not dilate. He seemed instead to see off beyond the boy, into some imperceptible blue yonder, the way one might when deep in consideration of some unsolvable puzzle or centuries-old unanswerable riddle.

And what he saw was only amorphous shapes, blurred outlines of the furnishings and people about the room. Hardly able to tell which was furniture and which was family, it was as though he was looking constantly through tearful eyes, or early morning eyes, or an early morning fog.

A shape shifted, approached the bedside. It was illuminated on one side and shadowed on the other, as it passed a window. Another shape, which had been so perfectly still, directly in front of his bleared eyes, suddenly shifted to make way for the approaching one. Its sudden movement startled the sleeper, but he did not show it.

As though looking up from a great depth then, through newly awoken eyes, like those of a newly born baby, the sleeper could now only see the vague shape settling itself before him, its coloured edges bleached.

The light beyond it, which set it largely in shadow, was blinding.

'You okay?' the hazy form asked.

The Sleeper groaned, slowly taking in his surroundings, coming to.

He could feel a soft breeze on his cheek, blowing, and knew a window was open. He could smell the piquancy of a feverishly familiar aftershave, subtle but distinctive, and the strong scent of coffee on the hazy form's breath.

Then, as it spoke again, he could recognise the timbre of its enquiring voice, soft and clear and filled with compassion, benevolence and magnanimity.

'You okay, Dad?'

My son, the sleeper told himself.

And now he could hear the many machines surrounding his bed, thrumming, humming their quiet melodies, his own heart beating softly. In the farther distances he could hear the susurration of medical staff consulting one another and informing one another and making small talk with one another, by the nurse's station in the hallway. And then a bird singing somewhere a way away confirmed that a window was indeed open and that it was indeed a fine day. In which month he did not know. In which year he could not be certain. In which city it did not matter.

'Are you okay, Dad?'

Ah, yes, my son, thought the Sleeper. My first born son – my son – Jay – Jamie – James – John – I forget – forgot – how could I forget – his name – is – is –

'Yes, son,' the cadaverous man croaked at last through his dry, pale lips. 'I'm – fine.'

His voice was cracked and hoarse, his throat arid. It was the voice of many toads, the voice of the Mummified King, resurrected after many millennia spent dust gathering.

'I'm fine,' croaked the Dust Mummy again.

Although he could not see them well enough to know them, the faces of the room were all glum from now on. They occasionally passed upset and uncomfortable expressions to one another, faces of tacit helplessness and deep sorrow. Now and then there came the exchange of conciliatory half-smiles, too, enriched with shows of strength and unity, for the Sleeper's untimely condition had been a subject of much disagreement and massive discord. It had been an invisible plague of stealthy locusts, eating away at the family's crops of kindness and congenial manners, a viperous poison infecting their bloodline with disdain, vitriolic disputation and resentment.

The youngest son's thoughts and theories, in particular, had engendered only cold receptions from his apparently kindred counterparts. This is unfortunately the commonplace case when wisdom is ascribed exclusively to the aged. An entirely fallacious correlation, he felt.

To his mind the rest of the family had offered only trite sentiments, the banality of which had enraged him on occasion. They were a group given to bromidic theories and platitudinous rhetoric; they were the speakers of casuistic debates and – when emphatically losing arguments – even resorted to releasing a few red herrings into the rippling pond of discussion, in aid that their unsound reasoning might not drown. That, or they simply stuck together, as truth is commonly found in numbers. The youngest son hated that fact but was powerless and far too fatigued to overcome it. He also hated the repugnance that had grown throughout his family since he started to educate himself, repugnance drawn against him as an apparent haughtier; when the simple truth of the matter was that he knew more than they did. They subconsciously despised how that highlighted their shortfalls, and could not bring themselves to respect him.

He hated many things about his family:

Everything they said he had heard before.

Every opinion they currently held he had held, at one time or another.

Every axiom they embraced as truthful he had once adopted, and since aborted.

They spoke only in generalisations and trite sentiments.

They knew matters only of Fact.

They knew nothing of their own.

They were too busy to read.

They had never tasted the euphoria of aphorism.

They questioned his insight without ever questioning their own.

He hated all these things and many more.

That last one he hated most: that he hated them.

But, despite it all, he still loved them too. For all their faults they remained in his heart. Despite all the conflict, kinship still held virtue. Besides which, it occurred to him now that now was not a time for recriminations, derision or division. Now was a time for solidarity, for comforting togetherness, for forgetfulness and forgiveness, and almost a time for condolences. They were his family, after all, and as is always the case with families, hatred is worn thin by the thickness of blood. That was one cliché, although it required rewriting, that he could concede to be of merit.

The first born son put a plastic cup of water to the Toad King's lips and insisted that he drink some, which he at once did.

The youngest sat back and slipped into deeper dwellings, watching but not watching the watering-of-a-dying-flower scene before him unfold. He dwelled on his failings to adequately express the unorthodox theories that he had developed surrounding the Toad King's illness – he was no polemicist, it seemed. He dwelled on his hesitations in expressing dismay, anger and downright disappointment, all of which were in relation to how most family members had faded their attentions away from helping, especially when times had gone beyond hard.

Into longer introspection he then drifted, meditating on pointless and manifold possibilities which could never have been realised, thinking of the many verdant avenues which might have opened, but which could never have actually been, had things been done slightly differently and actions been taken so much sooner. He lingered longer still on the sense of cruel fate and unfortunate circumstances, never being able, even once, to distinguish between the two, or to attribute the predicament's causation to either.

Then the eldest son gave up his short vigil, needed some air, and went out for a cigarette.

The younger one nodded solemnly at him as he passed by, said he understood without speaking a single word, and went and took up his place again at the bedside.

Holding his father's hand, the thirty year old boy then tried to smile.

'Dear me, Dad,' he shook his head. 'What are we going to do with you?'

'Nothing.'

'Nothing to be done?'

'Nothing to be done.'

There was a mutual silence, the certain kind of silence best observed in cemeteries on the cold and still evenings of December.

'I have to go now,' the Sleeper after a while murmured, through his again dry lips.

'What do you mean – go?' said the son. 'You can't go anywhere. You're bedridden.'

The old man pointed to the ceiling, said, 'Up there.'

The momentarily confused son at once understood.

His voice was so faint a whisper now that the son could hardy hear what was being uttered, and so had to lean in very close as the Sleeper repeated, much quieter than before, 'I have to go now.' And then he said, eyes bleared, lips dry, 'My father's waiting. I can see him waiting for me. Mum too.'

'I know, I know,' said the son softly, understandingly, compassionately. 'It's okay,' he assured him, 'you can go now.' Looking into his father's eyes he now saw just how true it was that right now was indeed the time to leave; the paleness and tiredness and egg-yolk-yellowness of them were testament to his infirmity and impending departure.

Then the old man's grip loosened.

His eyes closed.

All of a sudden the machines ceased their songs, quit their rhythms and fell to a constant tone, and the mountainous terrains tumbled to plateaus, and the sleeper began his Forever Slumber.

His senses began to migrate. The ensemble of infinitesimal particles which had once married, joined together harmoniously to form his life-force, his soul – that intangible energy, that elusive, unquantifiable entity we try so hard to grasp – now began to separate.

His body became lighter by twenty-one grams.

His relaxed hand slumped to the counterpane.

The boy stroked it, patted it, and again attempted to smile.

He said, 'Goodnight.'

Entirely unseen, the Sleeper's soul whispered quietly down the echoing halls of the hospital, whirling, evaporating in balletic movements, dispersing in many a direction, melding with the air, finding open windows, gaps beneath doors, lungs to fill and creep out of, blowing away in an invisible mist of imponderable energy, twirling.

Someone sobbed softly.

Someone swallowed a lump in their throat.

Someone who did not believe in Heaven said, as way of unfinished supplication, 'Oh, God...'

The youngest son, then, having felt himself in mourning throughout the entire duration of the Sleeper's illness, did not cry. He had mourned this great man along the tiresome and troublesome course of his infirmity. So, instead of crying he sat in silence, still trying to smile, and he felt overwhelmingly relieved, staring at the face of the finally dead man.

His father's sufferings were over.

He hoped his own would soon follow.

Then, eventually, uneasily, he stood and was benign. He embraced his brother and felt he might never let him go. He comforted his aunt as she wept on his shoulder. He kissed his mother's brow and told her that he would take care of her now, that there was nothing to worry about, that everything would be okay. He took her hand.

She smiled.

He smiled.

Then, again eventually, again uneasily, the medical staff entered the room. They did so in a fittingly slow and sombre manner, without any sense of emergency or intention of attempting resuscitation. In a carefully rehearsed sort of way, they were sensitive to a family's loss.

By the time they cremated the remains of what was once his body, the now empty vessel that he had once occupied, the Sleeper was in many places, apart but still whole, unaware but strangely, impossibly, abstractly, aware. He was not one ghost, but many phantoms – pellucid fragments of a spirit, essences of a person, whispers of a past.

He was in many places, all at once. He was both a part of Nature and Nature itself. He was in the swirling, sweeping serpentine winds above many a gently moving meadow. He was in the earth, enriching it. He was in the green seas, turning their deep tides. He was sifting through the vaporous warm air to rest upon the receptacles and petals of blossoming flowers; upon the stamens and stigmas and anthers of sunbathing tulips and poppies, whose amber goodness would then be gathered up by pollenating bees to make their very sweet honey. He was resting on many blades of grass which would feed a grazing cow, upon whose succulent meat many a family would dine, transferring that morsel of the Sleeper's soul, as latent kinetic energy, into a husband who would then go on to father a child – a child who would subsequently grow in the way of the Great Sleeper, develop similar mannerisms, share in the past man's interests, be a part of him reborn, breathing life again into the ceaseless circle of creation.

And when the time came for his wife and two sons to spread the ashes, scattering most from the edge of a grassy promontory, down the cliffs and into the frothing, foaming tides below, sprinkling the rest into the deep grooves of an epitaph that the two young men had inscribed in the gilt sands, away from the rising ocean's edge, a little part of the Sleeper, a small measure of the invisible energy which once constituted his soul, was present at the coastal ceremony, sailing upon the warm saline air above the beach, observing.

Equipped with impossible senses, he was watching and witnessing them through eyes no longer there to be seen, listening to their mournful thoughts and utterances with ears gone away forever. He could feel their sorrow, taste their sadness and hear their silent love and soundless lamentations.

His youngest son, the Sleeper felt, gave a heartfelt and eloquent eulogy, as improvised as it was. He spoke long and solemnly on what his father's life had meant, what he had lost in losing him and what he had gained in knowing him.

'We begin from nothing, and we end in nothing,' he perorated in a plaintive manner. 'Life is the coming of nothing to see itself as something. It is the realisation of a universe of complexity, embodied in one simple being. Before it we are merely potential unrealised, after it we become one, once again, with that which created us.'

He finished, remembering something which once struck him profoundly, wiping a tear from his eye, by saying, simply, 'From the dust returned.' He let fall the last of his father's ashes, and the spreading of them was the sprinkling of some precious and delicate seasoning, peppering the sand in flecks of grey and white.

The youngest son suddenly found himself to be crying. The tears seemed to have crept out of him without him at first noticing.

He spoke to himself now, so lightly, so softly, that only he could hear: 'I'm not crying for the loss of a man. No. We don't do that. None of us do. We don't cry for the flesh and the bone and the blood, or even for the smile or the sparkle in their eyes. We cry for what that particular person did for us. How they amazed us. What they taught us. Their kindnesses and their selflessness. We sob uncontrollably, and then we weep and whimper quietly, for all the times they pushed us on swings or read to us stories, night and day, or when they helped us paint a silly sunshine landscape picture; we lament those occasions they taught us new words and new facts, or pointed out constellations or cloud formations and waited with perfect patience until we saw what they saw and gasped, "Oh, yes, yes, I do, oh, I see it now, I see it... there... there... his bow and his belt too..." We cry because we know we will never hold and share those fine experiences again. Because all those times are gone for good.'

'As crazy and selfish as it may sound,' he comforted his aching heart, 'we love only those who live to serve us, to enrich our world and our character. It is that willingness to give. That is what we miss. That is what we mourn so wildly. That and their touch. Their warm embrace and kiss on the brow. That's what I'm crying for.'

Smiling, he cried a little more.

And when the ceremony was over, after standing a long time in silence in the ocean breeze, heads bowed, the fatherless, leaderless, husbandless family walked solemnly away. And then that small and imperishable measure of the Great Sleeper whispered quietly away, too, rose towards the clouds, above and beyond them, out into the interminable universe, to take its place among the stars and await rebirth, four thousand years from now.

Until then he would relive all the blessed moments of his lifetime in a dreamlike state, a Forever Slumber: all the smiles and all the kisses and the laughter and all the profound and touching experiences which his son had so recently mourned, in a ceaseless loop repeating over and over and over and over and over again, beautifully.

JUMP OFF CLIFFS

It was night.

The stars were bright. Below the lovers, burnt amber by incandescent street lights, the road sat empty. Beyond that a small unkempt verge, then rocks and pebbles, centuries of erosion, dimly-lit golden sands and the blackened ocean laid, wearing the face of the moon – a lonesome expression which swept across the faintly undulating surface as the tide swept calmly in, blinking silver between each broad wave, growing more sorrowful with each soft ripple. The warm air, blowing in off the calm tide, was refreshing.

She, the lady, wore a dress as white as that of a bride, its glowing brilliance broken only by the sparse patterning of dainty red foliage. He, the gentleman, wore a smart blue shirt, casually – loosened at the collar, folded at the cuffs. They were sat on the balcony of their luxurious fourth-story holiday apartment for the third consecutive night, breathing in the warm Mediterranean air of late June, drinking wine and talking idle talk, smoking cigarettes and admiring one another, and occasionally kissing. And between the casual conversing, and after the soft kissing, within the entanglement of cigarette smoke and vinous perfume, there came deeply comforted exhalations. Then the lovers would fall silent and listen to the water creeping up the shore, shushing as it folded over and under itself, time and again, lapping, frothing and foaming white, shushing over and under, over and under; that, and the soothing sound of a classical composition which played softly behind the sliding glass door.

'Don't the stars and the moon look so –' she paused, her eyes glittering ponderously, 'so, so very... very *big* tonight,' she said at last.

'Yes,' he admitted, nodding. 'Yes, yes, they do.'

He loved that about her eyes: the way they glittered with wonderment. They were eyes one could look into forever, never seeing sparkle in them the self-same light twice; wonderful glittering eyes, always full of a new-found astonishment.

Cloudless, the night sky was a vast ocean of near-black above them, spotted only with islands of light sent forth from the distant stars, far planets and near moon.

'Yes, they certainly *do* look *big*.'

They both sighed and went on admiring the cloudless night sky some more – the moon unflinching, stars forever blinking.

'You know *why* that is?' he asked after a time, staring up into the night. 'Why they look so big – the stars and moon?'

'Because you're here with me?' the lady offered, expectantly.

'No,' he said bluntly. 'No, it's because we're nearer to the equator here.'

'Oh,' she said.

'And so the stars actually are bigger,' he explained, 'and the moon too, because they're closer to us... or

235

we're closer to them... I never can figure out which.' He laughed. Sighed. Turning to her, he then shrugged. 'Amazing isn't it, though, that we're only a few hundred miles closer to something that's millions upon millions of miles away – light years, even –'

'The Moon's not so far away, though,' she interjected, 'is it?'

It wasn't a serious question. She was being purposefully pedantic.

'No, of course not,' he said, reflexively. 'I meant the stars. The stars are millions and millions of miles away and yet those few hundred miles closer that we are make such a difference. Tiny measures, big difference. Such a big difference,' he went on, facing the dark sky again, 'that it makes me wonder just how they must look when you're up there amongst them, actually in space. They must be huge! The size of our sun! Or bigger!' He laughed at his own obvious observations.

'But they haven't actually changed in size,' she pointed out, not laughing.

'No, I suppose not. But that's not the point. The point is –'

'We're just closer.'

'Yes.'

'Amazing,' she said flatly. Then she laughed at her own cruelty and then her face alighted with burlesque astonishment.

She laughed again.

She taunted him a little.

He did not laugh.

Presently the gentleman became acutely aware of a sobering dusk, a dusk which, quite suddenly, was washing over the balcony. It permeated the smoke-filled air, engulfed him, seeped into his sunburnt skin, percolated, and then settled heavy in his heart, his stomach, his mind, making him feel immensely sombre, cold and cut-off. He felt an apartness, an emptiness, an aloneness.

He was silent.

She apologised, said she *was only having a joke.*

He smiled decorously, said nothing.

After a moment she topped up her glass of wine, told him to lighten up – which he did with a forced smile – and lighted another cigarette. The amber tip of it glowed sulphurous in the near dark, hovering like a tiny sun or a giant firefly. He also lit himself a cigarette and the two amber tips were two burning bugs, manoeuvring in the twilight.

As they smoked the lady's free hand found its way to his and rested upon it and gently caressed it and subtly reiterated the apology made by her mouth. The gentleman became reflective.

Their romance had been a tempest, spinning, warm, so fast-moving. They had met beneath the kaleidoscopic dance hall lights, where everyone was painted red and blue and green and yellow, like multi-coloured beings too shy, too fearful, timid and respectful – too sober – to even approach one another. But when they had, when they had finally made their ways across the floor, spoken and smiled and danced, they had instantly been charmed by what they felt – excitement, flattery, affection, charisma: charm itself. They had been in love so soon after. It was something impulsive, infectious and unstoppable. It was a wild addiction. But here, as they shared their first holiday together – their first real experience as cohabitants – that ebullient storm was beginning to fall calm, to ebb, to settle like the calming night ocean below them. Now he no longer felt the need to be near her constantly.

The atmosphere on the balcony seemed somewhat congested now, stuffed up with an elephantine darkness, a dankness, an irrevocable weight of discontent. As though immense ballast had been deposited in him, the gentleman felt his heart sink heavily again. But he was intent upon nothing spoiling even one night, let alone the entire holiday. This was to be a time of celebration.

Defiant of himself, he looked at her and smiled. She smiled back at him. She was still a very fine woman, he told himself, regardless of the cracks appearing in her person; the cracks once hairline which now, with each ugly revelation and each tasteless joke, of which he was often the butt, began to yawn and gape. She was still fine. She still had a fine smile. She was still endearing. She was fine. He looked at her hair and her hair was still golden silk, long and shining with good health. Fine. He looked at her hands and face, and her skin was still soft on the eye and smooth to the touch. Fine. Her lips were still glazed cherries, glistening. Her eyes still glittered immensely. She was still charming. But... no... her charm was beginning to fade.

With a momentarily lustreless look in his eyes, he glanced at her.

On her finger the engagement band glimmered, its crystal eye flashing like a distant lighthouse beacon.

Nothing was going to spoil the holiday, he assured himself silently. She was still fine.

Her jokes were just jokes; cruel ridicule, but just jokes, all the same.

He took a drink of wine.

So too did she.

'Cheers,' she offered, glass raised.

'To us,' he added, feeling slightly awkward.

'The stars –' the lady returned to her observations, trying to reignite the dreamy atmosphere now past, 'they look like you could almost touch them, don't they?'

The gentleman agreed.

Then they sat quietly for a few minutes or so, both gracefully puffing on their cigarettes. The clouds of smoke performed gymnastic movements, tumbling, becoming nimble wisps as they rose, and then dissipating into the dark shadows.

'Baby,' she then said, in relation to nothing previously said, turning to him, 'do you ever think about God?'

'Sometimes,' he answered, after a pause, 'I suppose I do, yes. But, why do you ask?'

'It's just that looking at the stars, for me, seems always to lead to thoughts of God.'

'Yes,' he said, 'I suppose it does, doesn't it.'

Smiling, she nodded. 'I love you, Baby,' she said, again placing her warm hand on his.

'I love you, too, Honey-bunny.'

Under their breaths they both then made a comforted sound, inwardly: a sound which seemed to signal that they were happy to have one another, happy that in a world of sometimes awkward diversity they had found a certain kindred other, or at least a close approximation.

Their starry gazes returned to the night sky. Again they sat quietly, each wandering in their own private thoughts, smiling.

Then, all of a sudden the gentleman moved his hand from under hers, rubbed his neck, his head, sighed and looked awfully unsettled.

'What's the matter?' she asked.

'Oh, nothing,' was his reply.

He took another drink. Ruminative, he remained looking at the sky.

'What,' he began after a deep breath, 'what do you dream about, Honey?'

'Well: our marriage, then children, a pretty house on the brow of a hill.' She imagined the future. 'Growing old together, and watching our children and then our grandchildren playing cat-and-mouse games in a large, pretty garden, as we sit on the porch, drinking tea and holding hands. You know... the usual things.'

'That's nice,' he said. 'It sounds lovely. But I meant in your real dreams, when you sleep, what do you dream of then?'

'Oh, I never remember what my dreams are about these days... *These days*, listen to me! I sound like an old dear!' She chuckled. 'I did dream a lot when I was younger. My head was full of crazy things when I was a little girl, I mean. But, now... now... nothing. I go to sleep... wake up... time has passed, and... nothing.' She shrugged. 'I guess I just don't dream anymore.'

'Oh,' he said. 'That must be horrible.'

'No, not really, no.'

They were quiet again for what seemed a long time, in which the music behind the sliding glass door, after a violin concerto, died away and prompted an orchestra of insects, in the grass below the balcony, to seemingly raise up their winged and legged instruments, and to play softly in the warm air.

'Why did you ask that, Baby, about my dreams? Was there something you wanted to talk about?'

'Well,' he said, adjusting his collar, 'I've always had this dream, you see, and I've never told anyone about it, but I want to now because it's getting more and more frequent. It's every night now. Every time I sleep. Sometimes it's even when I'm awake. It's –' he stopped himself, controlled his very liberal larynx, in a moment of sudden awareness. He looked at her, staring intently at him now.

'Oh,' he said, despondent, 'it doesn't matter. It's silly really. Very silly.'

'Go on.' she insisted, gently, 'Tell me.'

'No, no,' he said. 'It doesn't matter, really.'

'Really?' she retorted, snorting, 'It doesn't matter? Really?'

'Really.'

'*Really?*' sneeringly.

'*Really,*' insistently.

240

'Well,' she said, disgruntled now. 'It clearly does matter. It's clearly troubling you. I can see it in your face: you're as grey as a goose! Come on, tell me.'

She was right: he was pale; very pale indeed.

He said nothing.

Then she reasoned, probed. 'Is it disturbing?' she asked, 'Is that why you don't want to talk about it? Is it inappropriate? Perverted?'

His head reared back away from her, recoiled, wearing a look of genuine confusion. Colour returned to his cheeks, brow and eyes. 'No, no. It's... well... if anything, it's actually quite beautiful,' he said, settling himself, no longer quite so pale. 'It really is, in fact, actually very beautiful.'

'So tell me about it then, Spoil-sport.'

He told nothing.

'Come on,' she said reassuringly. 'You can tell me anything. You know that.'

There was an intermission of near-silence: only the melodic bug chirpings and the distantly shushing tide could be heard, there on the balcony.

'No,' the man said at last, 'you might think I'm strange... *mad* even.'

'Promise I won't.'

He looked on reluctantly but eventually murmured something. 'Okay,' he said quietly. 'I'll tell you.' Then he exhaled heavily, burdened. He almost began to talk on a few times before he found the right words, as simple as they were.

'I dream that I can fly,' he announced.

'Okay,' she intoned. 'Go on.'

'I dream that I'm falling and right before I hit the ground I just somehow know how to fly, and I do – I fly. Without needing wings, I fly.' There was guilt in his manner, his tone, as though he was announcing what to him was somehow a confession, a terrible madness of which he should be ashamed.

241

He swallowed before continuing. 'And I fly,' he confessed less guiltily now, 'over trees and fields, and over cities and mountains, and lakes and oceans, and I'm so free, and so at peace. It –' he stuttered a little, 'it really, really is very beautiful.'

'Is that it?' she asked. 'That's not it.'

'It is.'

'No,' – she shook her head – 'that's not it. You've just made that up.' Her eyes sharpened, incredulous.

'I didn't! That is it, I promise.'

'Well,' she smiled with a distrusting smugness across her pretty face. 'If that really is it, if it wasn't something else –'

'It wasn't,' he insisted.

'Well then you've got nothing to worry about, you know. It's a perfectly normal dream to have. I had it once, too.'

'No, no,' he shook his head, 'no. It's not a dream. It's most certainly not a *dream*. That word doesn't capture the enormity of it. It's more than that. It's real. It's so very, *very* real.'

She offered a couple of words: 'Lucid? Vivid?'

'More than that,' he said. 'I'm not sure I can fully explain it – do it justice – but it's like there's a code inside me, inside my mind, a code that in my dreams I can crack; a puzzle whose solution, in that moment I take flight, is apparent. Obvious, even. And when I do fly it's as though I am truly enlightened then, and know all the answers to all the unanswerable questions, as though I am omniscient – up there in the sky – more than that, an angel, a god. But always as I wake up the answer fades too fast for me to grab at it, hold it tight.'

Looking relieved to have shared his apparently colossal encumbrance, the gentleman then took another sip of his wine. The lady took another sip of hers, languid smoke floating about her.

'Well,' she said, licking her lips, 'you know, the human mind is a very powerful thing and most dreams are metaphors. It's probably somehow symbolic of your studying, your thirst for knowledge: a sort of subconscious signpost that one day you will know all you need to know, for your mind to be at rest.'

'You're not listening to me,' the gentleman insisted. 'I said it most certainly is *not* a *dream.*'

She said nothing.

Her face was a portrait of reproach.

His mind restless, the gentleman stood up, walked to the edge of the balcony, bent over and leant on the banister with his forearms, looking down at the road below, and not looking at his loved one, not once, as he spoke.

'No, it's not a dream,' he repeated, with evermore increased conviction. 'I considered that for a long time, and for a long time believed it, too. An internal metaphor of the mind? Played with and dismissed that possibility years ago. I've had this vision all my life – as I said – it's always been there, only now it's more and more real.' He took a puff of his cigarette, blew the acrobatic grey wisps out into the night. 'And more frequent, too. It's so real now, in fact, that the only thing missing, it seems, is a witness to make it so. It's almost as though it won't go away until I figure out the code in my waking state – now, here, in this world, and not the unconscious one.'

'Okay,' she said, bemused, 'now you're worrying me. Stop it please, Baby.'

'Stop what?'

'Stop it with the crazy-talk. You sound like you want to –' she hesitated, 'to try it.'

Crazy-talk, he thought. He almost laughed. Crazy... talk? Does she think I'm mad, he asked himself. Am I mad?

'Come sit back down, Baby,' she then said, 'please. It's not real. It's just a dream.'

243

But he did not move. Lazily, he flicked his almost dead cigarette and watched it fall to the road below, exploding in vibrant brilliance, as an orange flower of sparks, and then dying quickly to nothing. He gritted his teeth, relaxed, gritted them again. Presently he turned and looked back at her.

'But what if it *is* real?' he asked with eyes ablaze. 'What if I *can* fly? What if I really can fly and the only thing standing between me and soaring and swooping and gliding through the skies is courage, faith, true belief?'

'And what about gravity?' she said. 'The laws of physics? Newton? The apple?' She seemed to plead, as though praying scientific dogmas and apparent axioms would banish these frightfully fanciful thoughts from her lover's tormented mind.

'What about it?' he said blithely, tossing his hand skyward. 'I mean, come on, you know I don't buy into factual stuff. What is gravity anyway? A theory proven by men obsessed with proof? It's a name given to one side of a coin? What about the other side?'

'I don't follow you,' she said anxiously.

'Well it's a force, yes? Dictated by Man, yes? And it's a negative force, a pulling one. So where is its counter force – its push, its naturally occurring opposite? Levity? All smoke and mirrors and Montgolfier Gas, and mocked by most. So, what if science is wrong? What if gravity doesn't exist?'

'Baby, gravity exists,' stated the lady, in an assertive manner, and with a disdainful yet increasingly desperate look of anxiety in her eyes – eyes which once smouldered and glittered in wild passion and wonderment, but which now appeared chill-cold in distaste and yet still somehow warm with worry and fear and remnant traces of compassion.

'The whole world knows that gravity exists, Baby,' she said imploringly. 'It's the Earth spinning on its axis, and

244

spinning within its orbit, and creating a sort of centrifugal force. It's real.'

'I bet that's not what it is. I bet that's not at all accurate.'

'Well, I don't know what it is but I know it's a fact.'

'Fact!' he cried. Incensed, he pointed a finger at the invisible word which apparently still meandered around her mouth as a phantom. 'Fact!' he scoffed. He sneered. 'That's the problem, right there!' His finger shook. 'People think they know what they believe in! That they found it out themselves! Somehow discovered it! Don't you see? They're obsessively convinced that they know their views as their own, that facts are facts and can never be disputed. But they never really question anything, and they need to. My God, they need to! Nobody truly knows what Gravity is. That's a fact! An expert physicist told me once: no mathematical proof, no Q.E.D, only vague theories, full of holes.'

'The world is ignorant,' he continued. 'Everything is so cold and cut off, nothing in tune. A flower cannot think because it has no mind to do so, and it cannot taste because it is without a tongue to be spoken of. But what if it can think, I always ask myself. What if it the sun rains down on its petals and the flower thinks – really does *think* to itself – "ah, yes, that's the good stuff: summer is here at last!" And what if its roots reach down into the damp soil, lick at the moisture there, and feel refreshed? You might think I'm crazy. I know most do. But what I'm trying to say is that it's all just far too certain, too straight-cut, too much of an open-and-shut case.'

'There are no miracles anymore. Science has done away with them. And above all facts, the most important fact of all is that the human race reigns supreme and our word is the definitive truth: the scientific gospel. That's the crazy mentality, if you ask me. The truth is that we're all just patch-work quilts, thrown together without care: we're all just parts of other people: that's all we amount to. And we're expected to just be, to just be and never question why or how. Until the seams are unpicked, though, until you stare headlong into a mirror and dissect your own mind, nobody knows who they really are.'

'Think about it another way.' he offered. 'Flight was deemed impossible by our ancestors. Two hundred years from now, they might have laughed you out of town, or stoned you to death as a witch, for ever even suggesting the possibility of stealing the wings from birds, harnessing that miracle. However,' he continued with increasing enthusiasm now, his temperament enkindled, his hands flailing now, drawing shapes on the night air, gesticulating wild passions, 'two hundred years before that, perhaps, impossibilities did not exist. It goes round in cycles. The greatest thinkers, the dreamers, are either crazy or evil, or both. Gravity was invented – not discovered – to give us boundaries, to keep us crazy-talkers and dreamers grounded in this thing we call *Reality*. We are conditioned – indoctrinated – not to dream because to dream is madness. You believe in gravity because you have been told to. That's the truth for you right there! That's a fact! What if I don't want to believe it, though, and what if I'm right? What if believing is enough, what if one person could be right in a whole world of wrong?'

The lady did not say anything in reply to his question, or his tirade.

She just sat, stared and looked worried.

He turned away.

Over shoulder, he could hear her breathing uneasily now, whimpering.

'Imagine it this way:' he proceeded, too caught up in his wild oration to stop for some mild malaise that he may or may not have caused, 'you have a filter in your inner ear and, without you ever knowing, the mind uses it to sift out anything which might disagree with your version of reality, your perception of the truth. It keeps you sane. But there is no definitive truth!' he flouted centuries of work. 'That's the only truth! Everything is invented! And you can't be gifted new perspectives either. That's the catch: you can't force people in the right direction. Not even gently. In order to accept anything radical and improbable, one must find it oneself. That's when an individual can embrace enlightenment, when it's discovered by chance or destiny or fate – whichever you might believe in – when it's individual! Shove a million books under the noses of a million people and force them to read, and you'll see two million nostrils flare and then upturn, veering away in disdain. Evidence of the individual experience is the only hope.'

He caught a breath, sighed.

Silent now, saddened by the world, his eyes, with tears forming in their corners, returned to the burning road below. And then, again, they looked to the sky.

Still, the whimpering went on behind him.

The streetlights buzzed like insects, as he stood staring up at the stars, and she sat staring up at him, both in silence.

'Baby,' the whimpering lady said dolefully, her voice tremulous, 'please, please just come sit down. You really are scaring me now. Please?'

But, he did not move.

Scared? Fear?

He scoffed quietly to himself. Fear: the only obstacle in life, the wall that restricts our dreams, the anchor which keeps us grounded.

The whimpering woman came and stood by his side now, rubbing her eyes, near but somehow strangely distant. Soft and warm, her hand then stroked his head and said that she loved him dearly and that she would stand by him, just as she did now, and that they would

247

get him help: someone to talk to, to make sense of it. All that was said by one gentle touch, alone.

Yes, his conscience told him, *she does think you're mad*. Why wouldn't she? He shook his head. And just then a burning piece of kindling turned to ash, a stricken bird fell silently from a tree of many now-muted songbirds: a little bit of his love for her died, withered away, wilted.

'I've tried it before, you know,' he confessed quietly.

Again, as with during his tirade, she went back to saying nothing.

'When I was a little boy,' he explained, 'I started out by jumping off small things – a step, a chair, a wall – and nothing happened. Then I moved on to bigger things. I jumped off my parent's garage when I was eleven, broke both my wrists and damn near fractured my skull. Of course, I had to tell them that I'd fallen; that I was up there getting a football and slipped. And it went away for a while after that, faded as a superhero dream. I'd been watching too many cartoons, I told myself, reading too many comic books.'

'But then, three years later, it returned. It returned worse than ever. I stood on the edge of a cliff, you know, one time, looking down. Told myself to jump a hundred times. I'd fly, I told myself, just like in the *dream*, just like Superman does. But I couldn't do it. I couldn't jump. My feet wouldn't let me. Then, when I was old enough, I took sky-diving lessons and became experienced enough to jump solo. I wanted to try it, to test it, from a real height. But... well... I knew I was safe. Pretend as I did, I knew that the parachute was there and that no harm could come to me, and so I didn't need to *truly* believe, did I?'

'Let's just go to bed now, Baby,' the lady purred in his ear, trying the best she could to lead him away. 'It's late and we've had a lot to drink.'

Yes, he thought, let's just go to bed and it will be all okay in the morning. I will forget this night, this feeling, won't I? Only I won't, you damned fool. I won't ever forget because it will always be there, waiting for me, in my dreams. You're an idiot. You don't listen. You're a damned idiot and a wretched fool.

'No,' he told her, shrugging off her advances, 'I can't just go to bed now. I'm not tired anyway, and I have to figure this out.'

She went back to her seat and sat down, lit another burning bug and smoked it.

'I had it all planned out one day, you know, that I was going to unclip the parachute. I was going to do it – fly or die. But I couldn't take that leap.'

Silence.

The musical bugs played their legs and wings as instruments, chirping. The blackened ocean shushed, eternally calming.

After a minute or two of star-gazing, he glanced over at her again.

'Do you think I'm mad?' he asked.

Silence.

He looked away again.

His eyes became glazed, his observations exclusively introspective.

Cheep chirp, cheep chirp – the cicada music.

'You don't think,' the thinker contemplated, 'for one moment,' aloud but not necessarily directed at her, 'that I've not already diagnosed myself throughout the years, that I've not applied all disciplines – every theoretical framework – to my thoughts and actions. Hell, I could read a psychologist's lips before they've ever even moved; see the pen scribble long before it's ever been picked up: Delusions of Grandeur, Psychosis, *Depression*, Megalomaniacal Tendencies, possible God or Messiah Complex, or just Plain-old-crazy! I've heard them all spoken, in my mind and aloud, more times than I care to remember. But they are all inventions, too – just the same as Gravity – tools to alienate the extraordinary, segregate the true individuals from society, cast the white sheep out of the black flock.'

She said nothing in response.

All he heard was that same whimpering sound again, and then a sniffle, from over his shoulder.

He looked back down at the road.

Then, once more he looked to the sky. He admired the blackness of it, the dark and light nebulae, the clusters of colourless dust glowing white, the darkness, the indistinct constellation shapes formed by the connect-the-dot stars and the ashen fabric of the spaces in between. That, and the vastness: the vastness and the closeness of it all; so far but so near; so close – so very close – but so very vast; tiny but huge, infinite but infinitesimal, with no point of reference. Such a profusion, a plethora, a superabundance of dark and light, dark and light, crystal and coal, upon the underside of the gigantic black umbrella that was the night sky. So untouchable, he told himself, so vast, but so close. Imponderable.

'Do you remember', he said, still not looking at her, 'what you promised me, the very first time we declared our love for one another?'

Her statement sounded more of a speculation, a question rather than a firm answer: 'That I'd always love you...?'

'Not just that.' He breathed a silent lamentation. 'You said that you would always love me, yes, but you also said that you always would do unconditionally, no matter what happened. That you trusted every single word I said, and that I made you feel safe – that heaven was in my arms.'

Then, all of a sudden, his torpid body suddenly became tense and just as suddenly he stepped up onto the dwarf wall and suddenly stepped over the banister, and she suddenly went to move but did not, suddenly went to cry out, scream, but did not speak, and then he glanced over his shoulder, suddenly and briefly, down at her, and she suddenly knew that he would jump. It was all very sudden.

She winced and closed her eyes, and he was suddenly gone.

There was no scream and no thud, only the sound of his leap, the rubber soles of his shoes pushing off from the wall, the thin material of his shirt flapping in the open air, like a kite, as his body pushed it aside, fell, soaring through it.

She opened her eyes.

She did not move.

She did not move for a long time.

Sitting statuesque, all she could do was imagine what his broken body must look like right now, on the ground below; how people out walking would gasp and cry and faint when they saw him; how he might lay there, twitching, not dead, but so very badly broken; or how *it* might lay there, as still and dead as can be and not twitching at all, and not him at all – just *it*, just a *thing*, just a motionless object, an inanimate mass of flesh and bone and slowly cooling blood seeping out and down and into the dark grass and soil, and not a person, no, not a person at all. Just a thing. Just a thing crudely imitating life as it died, twitching.

She could have sat there forever. She couldn't be sure. It certainly felt like forever, or at least how she imagined a thing like forever to feel.

She didn't want to move.

She couldn't move.

Her body wouldn't let her move.

However, when her body was finally within her command again, when the electricity of life had returned to flowing through her seized muscles and her constricted heart had found its right rhythm, when the shock of the events had faded, she got up slowly and crept soundlessly to the edge of the balcony, first putting her hands on the banister where his arms had rested – still warm.

Then, slowly, cautiously, she peered over the edge, awaiting the inevitable horror.

But, looking down, she saw that he was neither dead nor badly broken. He was not anything. He was not there. He was gone. Only the empty road and the empty pavement and the hedges surrounding the hotel, and the empty lawn, were there on the ground, immediately below. And beyond that there was only the small unkempt verge, the rocks and pebbles, the golden sand and the blackened ocean, twinkling, glistening.

Not him.

No sign of him.

Not dead.

Not alive.

Looking up the road she saw nothing but the road, burnt amber by the incandescent streetlights which became candles as they reached the next hotel and orange stars as they reached the distant horizon. Then she looked to the night sky and saw nothing there other than the unflinching face of the mournful moon, and the stars beyond it, forever blinking.

Dark, quick, flying, something flitted across the moon.

Or did it?

A distant bird?

A near bug?

A bat, somewhere between near and far?

A silhouette of something?

An Icarus of the night?

Or nothing?

Nothing.

She never saw him again. Not dead, and not alive.

EPILOGUE: FROM HERE, WHERE NEXT?

I'll write. I'll write until I die, regardless of what happens. It's as simple as that. I'm afraid the Hunger simply won't have it any other way; it's insatiable... implacable... as hungry as ever. So there's nothing else for it: I'll feed. Regardless of success or failure, I'll write.

I live my life by intuition, feeling my way instinctively through every undertaking. Always have. In that sense then, I suppose I'm many of the people in my stories: I'm the scrap metal collector who's sculpting an enormous statue, never really knowing why and for what purpose, or even what it was that triggered the hunger for it, or how to go about it properly; I'm the boy listening to the dull but beautiful underwater voice, or the wanderer wandering into the cave, drawn to the sounds of nature and wondering what – if anything – is my own true nature, and whether or not that question can ever truly be answered; and I'm the young man sat on the balcony, wishing so desperately to know just what his wild and relentless dreams might mean... if anything. And, I suppose I'm that young girl, too, watching a romantic ideal from afar, hoping it to be something real...

Whoever I am, I know I must keep writing.

It's the one thing I've ever been any good at.

And so I look forward to the future, to sharing more stories with you.

Oh, and one last thing...

Please don't forget, figuratively, metaphorically, and perhaps *not* physically, to *jump off cliffs...*

You might just fly.

Like: facebook.com/jumpoff2013

Rate: goodreads.com/domdark451

Follow: twitter.com/domdark451

To order more copies visit
fast-print.net/bookshop